T0028927

HIDDEN VICTIMS

A NICHELLE CLARKE CRIME THRILLER

LYNDEE WALKER

SEVERN RIVER
PUBLISHING

HIDDEN VICTIMS

Severn River Publishing
www.SevernRiverBooks.com

This is a work of fiction. Names, characters, businesses, places, events and incidents are either the products of the author's imagination or used in a fictitious manner. Any resemblance to actual persons, living or dead, or actual events is purely coincidental.

ISBN: 978-1-64875-518-7 (Paperback)

ALSO BY LYNDEE WALKER

The Nichelle Clarke Series

Front Page Fatality

Buried Leads

Small Town Spin

Devil in the Deadline

Cover Shot

Lethal Lifestyles

Deadly Politics

Hidden Victims

Dangerous Intent

The Faith McClellan Series

Fear No Truth

Leave No Stone

No Sin Unpunished

Nowhere to Hide

No Love Lost

Tell No Lies

To find out more about LynDee Walker and her books, visit

severnriverbooks.com/authors/lyndee-walker

For Sarah Dabney Reardon, whose love of local history and magical deal-hunting abilities inspire Nichelle's stories almost as much as her kind heart and unfailing friendship inspire me.

1

Nothing is quite as exciting to a writer as a blank page. A new story, a new start—a fresh, unblemished expanse of endless possibility.

Except when it's a newspaper page with no ads on it. That's more of a terrifying abyss, where the only possibility I can see is unemployment.

"We're running thirty-two pages when we only have enough ads to justify twenty because I believe in you all and the work you're doing." Evan Connally pointed to the cost balance graph he'd projected onto the white-painted brick wall over Parker's desk.

I waggled a pen between two fingers as he spoke. I'd already gotten the stink eye from the advertising director for bouncing my blue Manolo boot heel on the scarred wooden floor of the downtown loft *RVA Week* now called home.

The part he wasn't saying was that we were sticking at thirty-two because anything less than that is just sad.

My eyes drifted to the windows lining the top half of the wall to Connally's right, where the sky was the kind of pillowy gray that whispered of snow, but the weather folks said it was just going to rain. Suited my mood. I'd never fully understood what my mother meant when she'd said "my nerves are shot" until these last few months. Between my twisted-up, inside-out personal life and this pressure cooker of a job, I had run out of nerves to frazzle.

The pretty blue bars on Connally's graph started above his dotted "acceptability" line. In October. November's bar was shorter, barely peeking over the dots. December's dropped below it, and January-to-date's was edging into downright stubby territory.

Connally surveyed the room, his eyes stopping on Sylvia Weston, the ad director. He had cleared the decks when he bought the newspaper, hiring Sylvia away from Channel Four and swiping those of us on the editorial side from the *Richmond Telegraph* to form what he'd spent October calling his "dream team." By December, he'd dropped the "dream" part, and a week into the new year, I feared we were barreling toward nightmare territory.

When Connally didn't speak for three beats, Sylvia chimed in. "The cash graph only tells part of the story here," she said. "You can't discuss declining ad sales without looking at circulation."

"That's true," Connally said. "And mathematically, even though we have a population explosion in our biggest circulation areas, circulation has steadily declined since long before any of us were ever here. That's the immediate problem at hand."

"Join the club," Grant Parker said.

"I'm sorry?" Connally's arms folded across his chest as he addressed our sports editor.

"Every paper in the country is facing this problem. It's why they're dropping like proverbial flies." Parker blew right past Connally's defensive body language and edgy tone. "Younger people are moving into cities, and younger people get their news online. But they grew up in an age where we all gave our work away online before it started to kill our business, so they don't want to pay for the content."

"The hole in that theory here is that our content is free, and it's free everywhere—this paper has always been one-hundred-percent advertiser supported." Connally's voice was sharp and dismissive. His not-so-veiled disdain for Parker made me want to dislike him—but whatever his beef with my friend, Evan Connally was a smart guy who was trying to do something good for the city in resurrecting and restaffing this paper. Maybe he'd been less than truthful about his "hands off" approach, but—well, it was his money we were losing.

Sylvia opened a file folder. "I can't sell ads to business owners who get no return because nobody reads the paper. The biggest week we've had since the new staff came on was Nichelle's cover story about all the hullabaloo around President Denham's speech—our rack circulation doubled that week, and online clicks were up nearly two hundred percent. We had forty pages the next week, and we earned them."

"Exactly," Connally said. "So in order for Sylvia to do her job more effectively, ladies and gentlemen, it's the news department's job to give her an audience for her advertisers to reach."

He made that sound way easier than it was to do from the front lines of a constant battle for that audience's attention. But one thing I'd learned about Evan Connally in nearly four months working for him: the harder something seemed, the more determined he was to do it, and do it well. At forty-two, Connally was a tech world billionaire, a Harvard alum who'd made his first million in photosurveillance technology before he was twenty-five, then sold his company at thirty-five to join the *Forbes* list and follow his interests whichever direction the wind blew. His current gust was old-fashioned, fact-driven reporting. Bob thought he sort of fancied himself a savior for a dying species. I was all for a journalism Jesus, and I liked working at the weekly.

"Nichelle." I stopped moving my pen and sat up straighter when he said my name. "What do you have for next week?"

"I have a preview of the legislative session and a hit list of bills already filed and ready for metro, and then the PD's new program targeting the traffickers and drug dealers in the western southside corridor for the cover. I have a ride-along with an officer at the second precinct set for today."

"Shelby Taylor had three pieces last week alone on overdoses in the motels along that corridor," Connally said, tapping his laser pointer on a stack of copies of the *Telegraph* he'd dropped on Parker's desk.

"I have those, sir." I tried to keep my jaw loose so the words didn't slide out between my teeth. Did he really think there was a universe in which I couldn't beat Shelby to a crime story? "I also have an exclusive interview with the detective who worked two of the scenes."

"But is that enough?"

"Enough what?" I swallowed hard. Bob scooted his chair closer to mine and cleared his throat.

I put a hand on Bob's wrist. I got this, chief. Connally liked to ask hard questions. I respected that, and I had certainly dealt with scarier characters in my career. "I'm going to need you to clarify your question."

Connally reached for the newspaper on top of his stack, today's *Telegraph*. "People already know there's a problem with drugs and prostitution in that part of town. I like your ambition for going deeper into the story and getting the roots of the issue and what the PD is planning to do to fix it." The hard line of his mouth softened. "I really do. I wouldn't have pushed so hard to have you here if I didn't think you were the best in the city at getting the big story. But the larger question for us, for our new strategy, is going to have to be 'why the hell are *RVA Week* readers going to care?' And it's going to have to be that every time, with every story." He turned to Parker. "Every column." And Bob. "Every cover and review. That's how we're going to bring these bars back above the line. That's how we're going to not only keep this place alive, but make it thrive. By changing the way we think about the news. Which is where Jordan is going to come in."

Parker's elbow bumped mine and I shifted toward Bob in my chair. He jabbed it at me again, but I didn't dare take my eyes from Connally.

Who the hell was Jordan? I was good at my job. So was Parker. So was Bob. But was Connally right? Were we losing money because we were trying to be good at the wrong things?

"So you're saying you don't want me to cover the same things Shelby is, because if people have seen it already, they're not going to pick our paper up to read it," I said.

Connally touched his index finger to the end of his nose. "See? That right there is why I hired you. You have an uncanny ability to boil pontification down to the actual point. Yes. That's exactly what I'm saying. Since when does Nichelle Clarke follow other people to a big story?"

Ouch. I flinched, and Parker's hand closed around my forearm. I didn't have to turn my head to see the glare he shot Connally. But maybe the new boss was right. I wasn't trying to follow anyone anywhere, exactly, but a newsweekly has a different timeline than a daily. I didn't have the luxury of getting stories before everyone else could anymore, because if we put copy on the web to be more timely, we cannibalize our rack circulation and hurt advertising. So I'd been focused on using our extra time—and space—to get more out of each story.

"I'm not sure you're being fair, Evan." A deep, smoother-than-hot-honey voice came from behind me, and I spun my chair around.

Oh.

Tall, dark, and striking strolled from the direction of the elevator in a tailored navy pinstripe suit, a mint green tie in a perfect Windsor knot at his neck. I fidgeted—the straight nose, thick dark hair, and well-cut wardrobe called up thoughts I was trying with everything in me to hold at bay so I could work instead of tumbling back into the doldrums I'd gotten so comfortable wallowing in over the holidays.

The new guy's dark eyes stayed on me all the way across the room, almost like he was looking into my thoughts.

"Nichelle isn't following anyone to any of her stories," new guy said, circling the collection of chairs and joining Connolly at the front of the room. "She's still on top of the pulse of police work and courtroom drama, but your publishing frequency is holding her back a bit."

He finished with a warm smile my way.

Ignoring the butterflies flapping in my midsection, I returned it. "If y'all have a way around that, I am all ears."

"Jordan Pierce, meet the heart of *RVA Week*." Connolly waved an arm our way. "Pierce here is the very best media consultant money can buy. I trust him to help us refine our new strategies and right this ship."

"I'm glad to be here, and I look forward to working with everyone." New guy kept his eyes on me for the last three words before he turned back to Connolly. "Evan, don't let me interrupt you."

Connolly rested one Armani-clad hip on the edge of Parker's desk. "I spent the holidays going back through the last two years of this paper, putting issues next to P&L statements, keeping a calendar of how the page count dwindled from nearly a hundred with a staff of twenty to what we took over at: seven people barely putting out thirty-two pages a week and sometimes not having the cash on hand to justify that. Increasing use of stringers was part of the problem: people who don't work here full time aren't as invested, so what looked like a good short-term cash-saving solution to the previous owners just exacerbated the issue."

"So I need to hire more reporters while we're losing money?" Bob asked.

"Not yet. The reporters you have need to work smarter, not harder."

Parker snorted. He's not a fan of corporate-speak. I seesawed the pen between my fingers some more.

"So what was it?" I asked.

"What was what?"

"The thing that did this place in? You said you looked at two years of stuff, watching it dwindle down from a thriving paper to almost nothing. What caused the circulation and revenue to drop off?"

"The same thing that caused those two things to go up at the *Telegraph* in the same time period." Connally raised his silver laser pointer. "You."

Bob nodded for the first time since Connally started talking.

"I'm sorry?" I stopped moving my pen.

Pierce stepped forward. "*RVA Week* used to be the place people came for the dirt that needed digging out around here. The staff built a niche in the city as the sort of rebel journalists who would write about the things city officials didn't want to see in the newspaper."

Oh.

"Then a baseball player and two cops died in an explosion down on the river, and you beat them to the story," Pierce went on. "And you kept beating them to the big stories after that, culminating in your first cover here, on President Denham's visit."

I wriggled in my seat. That was a decent piece. Of mostly fiction. I didn't like thinking about it, and had busted my ass in the months since to make up for it. But it seemed the job I was doing at the latter was rather lacking. And now this guy was saying it was because I wasn't myself, essentially.

Truer words never spoken, but I hadn't realized it was coming through in my work.

"Nichelle has had other stories here that the city would frown on," Parker said. "That gas leak that curtailed the president's speech wasn't the only thing she's written that didn't make them look great."

Pierce nodded. "That's true. Kind of. The other thing is, though, Nichelle might be getting deeper into some of the crime stories, but as Evan said, she's not coming up with anything new. And writing about the state-house and the schools and the planning and zoning department isn't cutting it because she doesn't have the inroads she needs in those places to produce the sorts of stories people expect from her. Having her name here helped for a few weeks." He pointed to the October bar on the graph. "But it didn't last. The people who followed her here did so looking for something they didn't get."

I opened my mouth, my ass coming up off the chair.

Connally held up one hand. "Nobody is saying your stories weren't good. I enjoyed them, myself, and I read five newspapers every day."

Pierce gestured to him. "But standing here now, can you tell me what a single one, besides the thing about the president, was about?"

Connolly shook his head.

Pierce looked back at me. "There's our obstacle in a nutshell. Your big exposés at the *Telegraph* had a sort of intangible magic: they were the thing people had to read, because everyone in their office and on social media was talking about it and they simply couldn't feel left out. Hell, the last six months you were at the *Telegraph*, they put a few of your stories—and your stories alone—behind a zero-freebie paywall, and they actually made money off it."

I knew all that.

What I didn't know was how to fix what was broken here.

"What about Parker's column?" I blurted. I wasn't trying to throw him under the Evan Connally Express, I just wanted to breathe for a second. The weight of everyone's eyes on me was cutting off my air supply. "It's syndicated. It kept the *Telegraph* going for a long time before I started working investigative pieces. And it was still a big moneymaker for them even with my stuff. So how come that didn't transfer when he did?"

"That's a great question, and one I'm still pondering myself, given expenses." Connally's eyes landed on Parker. "My best guess right now is that it has to do with his core audience and the fact that we don't offer home delivery, but I could be wrong there. I don't have enough data to know how to address that for certain yet."

Parker met Connally's gaze head-on, not blinking at the not-so-veiled threat to his job. "The RAU men's basketball team is looking to make a run at March Madness with a first-year coach and a lot of young players. That might pull some eyes online this week."

"I did pretty well picking up online ads from places around campus when I pitched that story to businesses," Sylvia said. "I've been trying to work with news where I can, and use upcoming pockets of interest to generate extra revenue as long as I'm not giving away anything big."

Pierce nodded approval. "We're going to get there, folks, and we're going to do it quickly. You have an impressive body of work, Miss Clarke, Mr. Parker. It's my job to widen that and keep Evan's graphs happy at the same time."

Connally clapped his hands together with a *thwack* that echoed in the cavernous, high-ceilinged loft. "This is why I put this team together. You're going to do great things, I can feel it. We just have to figure out how to get our paper back in the front of people's minds. Jordan will be here every day this week to brainstorm and help out. He'll keep me in the loop." He shut off the projector and began gathering his things.

Pierce rocked up on the balls of his shiny-wingtip-encased feet. "Thanks for your time, everyone. Let's go save a newspaper, shall we?"

Bob touched my arm, jerking his head toward his office.

I watched Connally walk toward the elevator, head bent in conversation with Pierce, and got up to follow my editor. I knew what he was going to say, because he'd been dancing around it since before Thanksgiving. He just loved me too much to come right out with it—I needed to get my mojo back. Nobody was more irritated than I was that I couldn't seem to find it, but I was flat ass out of time for wallowing.

Pierce patted Connally's shoulder before he turned back, putting out a hand for Bob to shake. "It's an honor to work with you, Mr. Jeffers." The words rang with an almost-reverent awe.

"Glad to have you aboard, Pierce." Bob gestured to the door. "It's usually open if you need me."

Pierce's eyes shifted back to me. "Evan tells me you have an appointment that's expected to last all afternoon."

"I'm going on a ride-along to the southside motel with the overdose problem," I said.

"The *Telegraph* already covered that."

"I'm not Shelby Taylor." I didn't mean for it to sound snippy, but I couldn't swear that it didn't.

Pierce raised both hands. "I come in peace. Just wondering if that's the best use of your time. I may go to hell for saying it out loud, but the opioid story has been done. It is horrifying and sad, but the fact is that people are numb to it. Nobody cares anymore." He brought his hands down and put them in his pockets as he spoke. "I just think maybe there's a better story out there."

"Nichelle has proven herself a decent judge of what's worth her time, Mr. Pierce." Bob put a hand on my elbow. "If you need me today, I'll be available in just a few minutes." He steered me into his office and shut the door in Pierce's face.

I gripped my pen until it dug into my fingers. Pierce wanted to hit the ground running. Shelby had the overdoses already. So I needed something else. Something—or someone—people would care about.

I had six days to find it. And thanks to Jordan Pierce's recap of my work at the *Telegraph*, I had the perfect place to start looking.

2

"I know what you're going to say." I kept my voice low, because even with the door shut, the three-foot gap between the tall, cubicle-like walls and the ceiling left our conversation vulnerable to prying ears.

Bob crossed one ankle over the opposite knee and leaned back in his chair. "I don't think you do, no."

"I shouldn't have tossed Parker to the well-dressed corporate lions, and I need to get my shit together."

"Sometimes it's hard, being right all the time." He shook his head. "That's the biggest part of the problem with you, kiddo. Always has been. You take everything on yourself. Look, you're good at what you do. Really good. I'm damned proud to work with you. But you can't save this paper by yourself any more than Shelby and Les can kill the *Telegraph* alone. Connally is a smart businessman, and he was right about a lot of things out there, but I know all you heard was 'we're all counting on Nichelle,' and you don't need that shit right now."

"I love that you want to protect me," I began, and Bob snorted.

"You spent the last two and a half years watching my ass, kiddo," he said. "I'm nowhere near caught up."

"Here's the thing: I think maybe Connally is right. I mean, I know he's right. I've been working stories like I'm still writing for a daily, and even though I'm getting more than they do, the more isn't moving papers. I didn't think about this before, but I see it now. I need to work smarter than them. And I think I know how, at least for this week." My eyes went to the door. "But Parker's not going to like it."

"Why?"

"I was going through the last three months of drug arrests at the Hideaway Motel yesterday, and I found something." I tapped my heel on the aged wood floor. "Charlie has been too busy with her series on those school board members in Henrico to see it, and Shelby doesn't know enough to. And I was going to let it go because the family has been through enough, honestly. But maybe I was thinking about it the wrong way, too."

"What?" Bob leaned forward.

"Katie DeLuca. She was picked up down there in October. Her mugshot doesn't even look like the girl Parker carried away from the river the night Nate died."

"Jesus."

"When Pierce specifically mentioned that accident, it got me thinking. Like he said, I've been reporting more in-depth on the stuff that goes on around here, but people don't really seem to care about understanding more. They've been looking at Shelby's pieces all week, and what do they do? They pity the faceless addicts caught up in the mess on southside and wad up the paper for recycling. But what if we put a face on it?"

"Nate DeLuca was a local hero," Bob said.

"Exactly. Not more information. The information that makes people care." I thumped my palm down on the arm of the orange velour chair. "Something that brings a routine crime story—a story Mr. Hotshot media consultant there says people have grown numb to—home."

He started to nod. "You'll have to be careful. Sensitive. People around here take their baseball seriously."

I stood. "I got this, chief."

"It's not all on you, kiddo."

"I appreciate that," I said. "But I'm beginning to think right now, what I need is a mission. This one will do."

"Do me a favor?" Bob asked.

"Anything."

"Watch yourself out there. Drug dealers aren't fond of cops, and you make a decent hostage."

"I have to wear a vest. It's part of the deal at the second. But thanks." I checked my watch. "I should head out if I want time to get suited up, though."

I was shivering in my car when my phone buzzed. I snatched it out of my bag and clicked the screen to life.

Aaron White, my favorite detective and the RPD's designated public information officer. *You have a ride-along in the 2nd today?*

I do.

Gray dots appeared immediately. *You will wear the vest.*

Of course.

More dots. *I have the stats you asked me for ready. Come by when you get done?*

My forehead wrinkled. He could email the stats. Which meant he wanted to see me for some other reason. Tips from Aaron usually led to the kinds of stories that would make Connally's P&L graph happier.

Sure thing. Send.

I started the car and steered from our chic brown brick loft building in Church Hill past stately row houses adorned with the wrought iron so popular in Richmond after the Civil War, around the fountain in Byrd Park, dormant for the coldest months of the year, and south. The road got rougher and more pothole-riddled under my tires, the buildings flashing by shorter, longer, in more disrepair. The sidewalks, usually dotted with people looking for work, for a score, or for some help, were eerily empty on the chilly gray day. Probably meant the shelters were allowing folks to stay in during the day because of the weather. But did it also mean this outing was about to be a giant waste of time thanks to mother nature?

I surveyed the parking lot at the second and pulled my coat tight around myself as I double-timed it to the door. The wind was colder than when I left the office. Pulling the door open, I glanced up at the clouds. Didn't look like rain to me.

Inside the vestibule, I pulled my press credentials from my bag and placed them in a carrier I pushed through a hole in the wall for inspection. A buzzer sounded and I pulled the next glass door and walked through a metal detector. Security was tighter here than downtown. I wasn't sure if it made me feel safer or not.

"Nice to see you again, Miss Clarke." The desk officer handed my bag back and waved me deeper into the station. "I liked your story on the school thing."

Nice to know somebody read it.

"Always good to see you, Jim." I hitched the bag over my shoulder. "I have a ride-along with an Officer...Brody? No. Brooch?" I fumbled for my phone.

"Brooks. He's a good kid." Jim reached for the phone on his desk. "I'll call him up."

I smiled a thank-you and turned to the gallery of officer photos lining the wall above the worn avocado-green plastic chairs in what served as a waiting area. At the far end, a large man was curled up across three seats, a threadbare blanket dotted with holes tucked tight around him.

"It's too cold out there," Jim explained. "Shelters are full, and he did three tours in Vietnam."

"You're a good man, Officer."

"Doing my best. Brooks isn't in at the moment, but expected back any time now."

"I'll hang out." I dug my phone out of my bag and touched the email icon. Three new messages. None of them the one I wanted. I checked it obsessively, not even really knowing what I was looking for. A dark web untraceable address? A random burner-style gmail? Surely Joey missed me, too, didn't he?

At the top of my screen was a new name I did recognize: Jordan Pierce.

I touched the screen.

Miss Clarke,

It was a pleasure to meet you. I hope we didn't make you uncomfortable—truly, I'm a big fan of your work, and I've told Evan that you're his most valuable asset at RVA Week. Now he's tasked me with figuring out how to leverage you to make the paper profitable. I've had a great chat with Mr. Jeffers, and would like to try a better foot with you. Do you have time for coffee or drinks, perhaps, so we can discuss possible strategies in a more private, relaxed environment? I look forward to talking with you.

Best,
  Jordan Pierce

Huh.

I tapped one fingernail on the side of my phone. It's impossible to read tone in an email, but for some reason my brain insisted on conjuring up a semi-sardonic one for him. I couldn't put a finger on why, but he struck me as the kind of person who didn't take anything too seriously and charmed his way through life.

Given that Connally brought him in to save the paper and I'd had months to see how smart that guy was, I couldn't assume anything based on a five-minute presentation and an email.

Coffee for the win.

Mr. Pierce,
  No reporter ever refuses a good cup of coffee. My afternoon is getting crowded, but may still be a bit up in the air. I will let you know when I'm free. Thank you for the note.

Cheers,
  Nichelle Clarke

I hit send as the door in the corner buzzed open. A young, uniformed officer with a fresh crew-cut and dimples so deep he didn't have to smile for them to show extended his right hand. "Miss Clarke. It's a pleasure to meet you."

I shook his offered hand, following him back into the office maze when he motioned me through the door before he let it fall shut.

"I'm going to need to grab you a vest," he said. "You signed all the release forms already, right?"

"I did. I appreciate you letting me tag along." I'd asked Aaron for an in Shelby couldn't get, and he'd passed me to the captain at the second, an old-school cop who abhorred corruption in any form and was at least as excited to talk to me as I was to him. He'd called to tell me this patrolman was the guy in the thick of the new drug crisis before he sent me case files from the last three months to review. "Is the captain in today?"

"He's at a meeting downtown, but he might be back by the time I'm off this evening." He opened a closet and handed me a heavy black Kevlar vest.

I put my bag on the floor and wriggled into it, pulling the straps tight but allowing room to breathe. Brooks finished securing his own and eyed my handiwork. "I think we're good to go."

Buckled into the front seat of his black-and-white patrol car, I opened my notebook and clicked out a pen. "How long have you been with the RPD, Officer?"

"Twenty-three months," he replied. "So just about long enough to start counting it in years. Like a new baby, but I'm getting my feet under me." His voice was deep and smooth, his round face congenial and open. I liked him already.

"What made you want to be a police officer?"

"My dad was a cop. So was my granddad, and my favorite aunt. So I guess you could say it's in my blood. I like helping people."

I jotted that down. "I understand you have a pretty dangerous assignment out here."

"Nah. The TV wants people to think it's worse than it is." He slid his eyes my way. "No offense."

"I don't work in TV." I winked. "But would you care to elaborate on that?"

"These folks are just everyday people who fell into a shitty circumstance." He turned onto Hull Street and pointed my way. "All you have to do is read the paper, any paper, or watch the news to know this shit is a problem everywhere. It's just that the folks out here lack the resources to fight their problem privately. The people I see on this beat are doing the best they can with where they are. The dealers are why we need the vests, but they're not what gets me into this car every morning." He clicked on his turn signal and changed lanes. "I didn't go to the academy to be Dirty Harry, ma'am. The people out here, they need help. So I do my best."

I scribbled so fast my hand cramped, not missing a word. In ninety seconds, new guy had delivered one of the most moving speeches on community policing I'd ever heard. I saw a pull quote in his future. And I ought to send that captain some flowers.

"Didn't mean to talk your ear off," he said after a minute of silence broken only by my pen scratching across the paper.

"Please, talk away," I said. "I'm kind of a professional listener."

I looked up about a block from the motel that had the most traffic and the most arrests according to the files I'd been reading. Brooks instead turned into the lot at a Dollar Tree. I followed him to the door, which he held open. He grabbed a small cart and headed for the food aisle.

He filled it quickly with tuna and chicken lunch kits, crackers, cookies, pudding cups, and pop-top cans of vegetables. I stayed on his heels, not saying a word. When he'd paid and loaded thirty dollars' worth of groceries into the backseat of the squad car, he settled behind the wheel and met my gaze. I smiled. "This isn't what I expected when I left my office," I said.

"The food banks couldn't feed a family of mice after the holidays. This means I don't have to arrest someone for holding up the Taco Bell on the corner because they're starving."

"And they tell you things because you're feeding them."

"You're a smart lady. But I feed the ones who don't have anything incriminating to share, too. Here, this job isn't about catching the bad guys. It's about taking care of the community. And that's what a lot of people, even people I work with, don't understand."

Boom.

There was a whole other angle, right there. I scribbled every word of that before I spoke again. "Why is that?"

He drove toward the Hideaway, not speaking until we were in the far corner of the lot, facing a peeling stucco building that had probably been beige before the paint was mostly obscured by a greenish-brown layer of grime nobody cared enough to wash away.

"Most of the guys I work with, they came to the PD from the military. Maybe from college with criminal psych degrees or forensic science degrees," he said. "You know what I majored in?"

"Regular psychology? Pre-med?"

His dimples really were something at full power. "Social work. Because I wanted to work in places like this. My dad always said good cops were needed most in the worst parts of town, and that's where they don't get them because the nice neighborhoods and the suburbs are more comfortable and less dangerous."

"I've been around my share of cops in the last decade. Your dad was right."

"Right. So what these precincts get are the problem cases, the rookies, and the guys who want to come out here and be John Wayne where nobody is going to notice or care."

My pen stopped moving. "Are you sure you want to say that on the record?" Not a question I asked...well, ever, but Brooks had managed to join my list of favorite cops in less than an hour, and the more he talked, the more I liked him. There were people who wouldn't appreciate that observation, but it was pretty true, as generalizations go, and it was a hell of a great quote.

"Should I not?" He tried to shrug under the bulky vest. "I guess I might piss people off. And I'm not saying I don't work with some great guys, I do. We're lucky, really, to have so many good cops in this city. I mean, since you got the really shit ones fired." There went the dimples again. "But just in general, everywhere, not specific to Richmond, the areas with the highest crime rates get the cops with the reputation for being the biggest hard asses. As you've probably already figured out, that is not me."

I looked up from my notes. "So if you're not out here looking to bust the dealers, then why do you do this? What's your mission, Officer? Assuming the captain won't fire you if I print it."

He took his foot off the brake and idled across the lot, parking in front of the center row of rooms at the U-shaped building. "My mission is to help the community, one addict at a time. And to keep the dealers in check so nobody dies in the meantime. How long have you worked here now? If I bust them today, by day after tomorrow, there'll be another to take their place. The war on drugs has been fought ass-backwards for forty years. You don't cure a community of a drug problem by arresting a dealer—there are always more dealers to step up and fill the supply void. They're a symptom. It's the addiction that's the big ugly disease. Cure that, and the dealers move on when there's nothing to feed on anymore."

Holy Manolos. I curled my lips between my teeth and bit down on an excited smile. I wasn't just going to write a story about how Katie DeLuca had ended up here after her husband died so tragically. I was writing a story about the cop who was singlehandedly trying to save her and everyone like her.

Stories that stay with people, that they talk about around the coffee machine. Connally said that's what we needed if we wanted to stay in business. I wasn't sure I'd ever had one—at least not one that didn't feature a corpse prominently—that fit the bill better than this.

I shivered—whether from the actual cold creeping into the parked car or the adrenaline spike of excitement I'd missed for way too long now, I couldn't say for sure.

"So how do we take a step toward that today?" I asked.

He nodded to a warped plywood door with red paint flaking off in several places, 128 stenciled in black numbers at eye level. "Tuck there likes pudding cups. He also usually knows if there's going to be trouble on a given day."

"Do you think I'll make him nervous?" I asked.

"The wind shifting makes Tuck nervous. But we get along. No cameras, though."

He pulled the pudding cups from one of the grocery bags and kicked his door open. I met him at the front of the patrol car and let him lead the way to the motel room. Three sharp raps on the thin wood rattled the frame.

We waited. Thirty seconds stretched to ninety. My eyes slid to Brooks.

He knocked again. "Tuck? I know I'm late, but I brought your favorite. And a new friend, too."

Still nothing.

"He was expecting you?" I asked.

"I saw him yesterday." Brooks's brow wrinkled as he knocked a third time.

The door and walls were newsprint-thin. Not so much as a fly buzzed inside Tuck's room.

Brooks's hand went to the doorknob. Dropped back to his side as he glanced at me.

"Go on," I said. "Something feels off to me here."

He tried the knob. Locked.

"Maybe he's just not here?" I asked.

Brooks shook his head, leaning to peer in a plate glass window that had probably last been cleaned when Clinton was in the White House. I leaned, too, shading my eyes against the glare with my notebook. Between the grime and the drawn curtains, we might as well be trying to see through the stucco.

"Tuck!" Brooks's voice was higher, more urgent. He put a shoulder into the sorry excuse for a door. It didn't put up much of a fight, creaking inward to let yellow-orange light spill onto the rotting wood under our feet.

"Tuck, I'm coming inside. It's Griff."

I followed, my eyes scanning a wall completely obscured by giant, pieced-together maps and detailed diagrams. In the front corner, a square card table held a dated laptop, plugged into an inkjet printer next to a stack of plain white envelopes with stamps already in place. A dresser sat against the longest wall, crowned with an old-school TV and a droopy, three-quarters brown Christmas tree sporting a handful of faded lights and three blue glass balls. I turned.

In the back corner, on the other side of a sagging bed, a bare foot protruded from behind the open bathroom door.

3

Brooks crossed the musty, dim room in three strides and whipped the door back.

I swallowed hard. Dead folks don't get more palatable with repeated exposure. I haven't ever puked—and I don't get as close as I once did—but it's never an easy thing to see.

"I'm sorry, Officer Brooks," I said, keeping my feet where they were, since judging by the blood and brain matter splattered across the dingy, once-white wall behind the dead guy I assumed was Tuck, this had just become a homicide scene.

Brooks's eyes were closed when he turned his head back to me. "Dammit."

Looked like this story was going to have its own corpse after all. A fresh murder scene was a rarity even in my craziest days. A million questions fought to be the first out of my mouth, but the look on Brooks's face made me swallow every one. I could ask who might've wanted Tuck dead and why and what the hell the maps were for later. The utter lack of dimples in Brooks's sagging face said Tuck had become more friend than informant.

He squatted, careful to avoid the blood pooled on the carpet, and used two fingers to close Tuck's eyes with a gentle touch.

I pulled out my cell phone and clicked on the flashlight, shining it on the map wall, squinting at the tiny print without touching anything.

Virginia, in blown-up topographical detail, a web of black lines of varying thickness marking roads major and minor. A fatter black mark ran from the northwest corner across the Blue Ridge and the Valley, all the way to the coast near Sandbridge, red and gold foil star stickers spotted along it at uneven intervals.

On the narrower wall over the makeshift desk hung paper with lists of numbers under headings, the rows marked with what looked like surnames —or maybe street names—in no discernible pattern. LaGrace, Fontaine, Jameson, Vallis. I scribbled them down. The printer had a single piece of paper in the output tray, but I couldn't see what it said without moving, and moving might accidentally compromise the scene more than barging into the room already had.

I might not have the first damned clue what was going on here, but I did know the makings of a big story when I saw them. Murder always moves papers, and I could put my readers inside this one in a way nobody else in town would be able to. Brooks, his relationship with the victim, and this look I was watching twist his earnest face—people would care about that. And if we could find and help Katie, too? It would be the most powerful thing I'd written in months.

Hopefully I still remembered how to make it pack a punch.

"RPD 2671 requesting forensics and homicide to the Hideaway Motel, 38647 Hull Street Road, deceased male, GSW to the head in room 128," Brooks said into his shoulder radio.

He let go of the button and sighed. "He's cold. Whoever did this is long gone. I'm sorry. I had no idea I was bringing you into"—he waved one hand —"this. They're going to want to question you, but you're free to go after that if you want. I can reschedule you for another day."

Was he kidding? "I'm good to stay," I said. "I'm still not blasé about the dead people, exactly, but they're an occasional part of this job, I'm afraid. I really am sorry for your loss."

He crouched again, examining the carpet around Tuck's body. "He wasn't dragged or shoved over here. Someone just flat walked in and shot him."

I twisted my torso back toward the doorway, noting the splintered wood of the frame opposite the deadbolt. It still protruded from the side of the flimsy door. "Someone he let in. Who locked the door from outside when they left."

Brooks stood, carefully retracing his steps across the carpet to the door and putting one finger on a paper cup on the edge of the desk. "He kept the room key right here. Everything always in its place with Tuck." He looked up, the dimples peeking out of the corners of a small smile. "How did you get that so fast?"

"Not my first rodeo."

"Of course. I just meant—that's the sort of stuff detectives usually pick up right away. That's all." He shook his head. "Damn. Tuck was a good man. These are the shitty parts of what I do."

I didn't dare actually ask the question hanging heavy in the air, because I knew he was already asking himself: had his visits cost this man his life? Most of the cops I knew stayed in touch with informants via text or phone, or meetings in weird places people didn't follow them. People who give information on crime to the police tend to skew pretty far to the paranoid side.

"He didn't like to leave the room," Brooks said, almost like he could read my mind. "And he didn't like the phone." He gestured to the night table, where a beige handset was coiled, unplugged and off the hook. Next to it, a lamp cast a sickly yellow glow over Tuck's bare foot.

So coming here was the only way to talk to him. Check. And most drug dealers work the streets between dark and the wee hours, so they're not exactly morning people. I could buy that Brooks thought he was playing it as safe as he could.

"How did he know things if he didn't ever go outside?"

Brooks aimed a finger at the window over the desk. "He watched. Tuck has—had—an uncanny eye for detail. Better than any cop I've ever worked with. Smarter than most of us, too. He had a PhD in science, but he really knew people. Body language, behavior patterns. He never told me something was going to happen that didn't end up going down almost like he predicted. If I believed in psychics, I'd sure as hell think he was one."

"How did he end up here, then? Was he an addict?"

"It's complicated. He was trying to get clean. Again." He bent to retrieve the pudding cups. "That's why the pudding. The methadone fucks up your taste buds, and it made Tuck's stomach sick a lot, too. He used to be a teacher. Environmental science, over at RAU. He was in a car accident that probably should have killed him about fifteen years ago."

Oh, hell. "When a lot of doctors passed out Oxy like M&Ms." I'd been reading about the origins of the deadliest drug epidemic in American history for more than a week. The drug company that invented OxyContin spent most of a decade marketing it as less addictive than other narcotics, and quick conversion to approved generics flooded the country with billions of pills before anyone figured out the company line was a big, fat, deadly lie. They'd been fined millions by the government when it all came out, but by then thousands of people were already dead and many times more were addicts who moved on to heroin when the pills didn't do it or they couldn't get them anymore. Tuck's story was depressingly common.

"Bingo. But he was a functioning addict. He still went to work every day, was a good neighbor, never strayed into street drugs."

"That's unusual for someone who uses opioids for years."

"He got really good at making the rounds to clinics complaining of different injuries. Before the DEA started tracking pill sales, nobody thought twice about writing a guy like him a script. When he saw the same doctor one too many times and someone started asking the questions that stopped his supply, he swiped a prescription pad and forged a dozen before a pharmacist spotted the fake signature. He did a year and change at Cold Springs."

"That's long enough to detox," I said.

"But he lost his job. His home. He didn't have a reason to try to stay clean, and he came out of prison into an environment where he was surrounded by temptation constantly and a quick high sounded preferable to facing the mess his life had become. He wound up here trying to help a former student he'd seen when he was scoring in the parking lot. She stayed in this room. Tuck moved in during the summer. He said this place was easier on his disability checks than the overpriced shithole apartment he'd found after he got out of prison."

Not many places will rent to people with a record, especially one involving using.

"He was good at reading people, but he kept his distance from most of them. I met him in September and it took me until almost Christmas to get him to trust me enough to let me into the room."

Yet he'd let in whoever shot him. I backtracked through Brooks's comments.

"He was staying here with a woman?"

Brooks shook his head. "Not like that. I mean, I never got that impression. He was sort of a stand-in dad, I think. Protective of her. They seemed to have a lot in common. Both of them trying to save the planet, but couldn't figure out how to save themselves."

I tipped my head toward the maps.

"Save the planet? That what this is about?"

"The map is a trail he wanted to hike, I think." He rocked up on the balls of his feet, toying with the pudding cups. "I asked him once and he got quiet. Said he needed help but I couldn't help him and I was better off not knowing. I figured he couldn't bring himself to go outside for long enough to go hiking, or maybe he just wasn't able anymore after his accident. But he talked sometimes about trips he used to take, and how beautiful the Blue Ridge was to travel. Sometimes it was hard to tell if he was talking about a trip he had taken, or one he wanted to." He gestured to the computer. "He wrote letters by the dozens to politicians, lobbying long distance for wind farms and safer crops. Sometimes she would take them downtown or go try to see people about whatever they were stirred up over."

I pulled the notebook back out of my pocket and jotted that down before I looked back at the wall. Sirens filtered from the distance, drawing closer. Brooks nudged the door open with his foot and stepped outside, waving for me to follow. I raised my phone and fired off a few shots of the map wall. A dream that big left unrealized in the wake of tragedy and murder would make gut-wrenching art if the story went the way I thought it might.

A white Ford Crown Vic rolled to a stop. Chris Landers unfolded his lanky frame from the driver's seat, his eyes on me and his mouth set in a tight line.

I hadn't seen Landers since before the holidays. And I knew better than to believe the scowl. He didn't mind me as much as he liked everyone to think.

"If it isn't my favorite homicide detective," I said, stepping forward with my right hand out to shake his. "You working alone today?"

"Resource allocation has been a very hot topic at the department lately." Landers shook my hand before he focused on Brooks. "Patrolman, what have you got here?"

"Tucker Armstrong, probably mid-fifties, occupant of this room for the past few months, single GSW to the skull." Brooks gestured to the door.

A forensics van stopped behind Landers, two officers pulling toolboxes out of the back and heading for the motel room when Landers pointed. They stopped to pull blue paper booties over their shoes at the door, dropping a box on the deck before they snapped gloves on and disappeared inside.

"One shot, you said?" Landers pulled out a notebook and pen.

"From what I saw," Brooks said.

Landers stepped around us and balanced on alternating feet to pull booties on over his brown tasseled loafers. He picked up a pair of gloves, jerking his head in the direction of the room. "Care to show me what you found?"

Brooks stepped forward. I put one foot toward the door and then pulled it back. Landers might not mind me being around, but there's a difference between tolerance and invitation into a working crime scene.

"Come on, Clarke." Landers held out booties and gloves. "You notice things. And you've seen it anyway."

I pulled on the gear and followed them back inside. The room was drafty and cold, barely comfortable with my coat on, but I also probably owed the thin walls for the lack of dead guy stench. I stopped on the door side of the bed. Landers and Brooks rounded it, the forensics officers dusting the door and frame for fingerprints.

"This was broken when you arrived?" Landers asked.

"No, sir. I forced it when he didn't answer the door. It was unusual behavior for him."

Landers's brow furrowed. "You had reason to believe this man was in danger?"

"Not any more danger than anyone else here, really," Brooks said. "He talks to me, but the local dealers already know I know who they are. Miss Clarke and I figure he let whoever it was into the room. The room key wasn't where he usually kept it, either, and the door was locked when we arrived. Tuck was big on having things in order."

The more I thought about that, the less I liked this whole thing. The guy was meticulous about his belongings, and paranoid enough to avoid leaving this teeny little room. So why would he have opened the door for someone he didn't know? I scribbled a note.

Landers crouched in front of Tuck. "That's a clean shot. Even spatter."

"He was executed," Brooks said.

"Right." Landers glanced back at the door. "This is the furthest corner of the room. So he probably backed up over here as the perp advanced on him."

I pointed to the bathroom door. "Why didn't he go in there?"

Landers didn't even look annoyed that I'd spoken. "Could be any one of a hundred reasons, but why do you ask?"

"I mean, if he was running from someone who was threatening him, why wouldn't he go into the other room? There's a door. I'm guessing it has a lock. Why not make the guy fire more than one shot? Give someone a chance to call the cops? It just doesn't make much sense to me that he stopped there."

"People do things when they're on the wrong end of a gun that they wouldn't do if they had time to think without gallons of adrenaline flooding their system," Landers said. "I see your point, but there's no way to know for sure why he stopped here."

"Speaking of the shot, did you question any of the neighbors yet?" Landers looked at Brooks.

"No, sir, I called it in and waited for you to arrive and secure the scene," Brooks said. It was weird for someone to repeatedly call Landers "sir." He was still the new guy in homicide to me.

He nodded to Brooks. "Do you know the other regulars here?" What he meant was "will these people talk to you in uniform or should I go knocking on doors?"

"Most of them, yes, sir." Brooks crossed to the door. "I'll see who heard what."

I turned sideways to let him pass and swiveled my head between him and Landers. "Who am I shadowing?"

"Hang out." Landers's voice was tight. Brooks disappeared, the medical examiner's navy van rolling up outside as he opened the door. Landers eyed the forensics crew. "Could you two brief the ME and tell them we haven't gotten photos yet?"

He wanted to talk to me alone.

They stepped outside and Landers gestured to Tuck. "This is three."

"Four. There were three overdoses in the last two weeks."

He shook his head. "Clean shot, no forced entry, no weapon on site. This is the third one in a week."

"I...what?" I usually only checked the week's police reports on Fridays these days, but two shootings within days of each other is the kind of thing reporters live for. So why wasn't anyone covering it? "Drug related? And while I still don't expect much of Shelby, why the hell isn't Charlie working this?"

"Taylor doesn't have your eye for patterns, and Lewis has been buried in some school board dustup for weeks now." The corners of Landers's lips tipped up just the barest bit. "A turf war leaving bodies scattered about isn't the sort of information we're going to volunteer if nobody's asking."

Except...I hadn't asked.

So why was he telling me? With Landers, there was only one possible answer.

Because he thought I could help.

Which meant my time for wallowing was officially up.

Three victims in, we couldn't assume Tuck would be the last. And I might have the inside track, but if I really wanted to impress Evan Connolly, beating Charlie and Shelby to a big headline was the fastest route.

Tick tock.

4

"Everything we know so far points to a drug turf war," Landers said. "But the fewer people who know about this until we know for sure what's going on, the better. Which benefits you these days as much as it does me."

Point taken.

"Why would a dealer looking for territory kill this guy? Brooks said he's trying to recover and he almost never goes outside."

Landers ran one hand through his burnished brown curls. "I don't know. I was kind of hoping you'd run across something about this place that would help me figure that out. You've been researching it, right? For one of your big cover pieces?"

"How did you know that?"

"White told me."

Ah. Probably why Aaron had texted and summoned me to head-quarters.

I shrugged. "This particular place is sort of the epicenter for all the bad things these days. As long as people pay in advance and don't mind the shitty accommodations, nobody asks too many questions. About half the clientele is transient, and the rest live here as long as they have the cash, like Tuck."

"Were you able to find out much about the owner?"

"I didn't really look. My focus was on what this is doing to the community, the people it's hurting, and the resources it's using. At least until I walked into this." My eyes went to the splatter on the wall. This might not be the story I thought I was coming here to write, but it was more inside my wheelhouse than anything I'd come across since my first byline at *RVA Week*. The tiny hairs on my arms popped to attention, my whole body tingling with a feeling that I was supposed to be at the Hideaway today. Like the universe had a plan all along.

Nine years at the *Telegraph's* crime desk had made me an expert on a couple of unlikely things, the southside Richmond drug scene being one of them. I knew how it had always worked, and if the rules hadn't changed with the product, it sounded like that was about to come in handy.

Street drugs are distributed in most American cities almost like a pyramid scheme—wherever a turf is hot, the kids actually selling stuff are like the new recruits with their sales starter kit and dreams of six-figure-a-month payouts. They hustle up new business and assume all the risk of getting busted. The real villains that Brooks had referred to earlier, the ones who are nothing but whispers and smoke and mirrors, are insulated behind walls of laundered cash and loyal henchmen. Taking one down requires months of coordinated effort on the part of local and federal law enforcement, and, like Brooks said, another will just filter in to fill the gap in a matter of weeks.

"It might make sense for an antsy kid who was afraid of going to jail to have done this, or maybe a supplier who thought Tuck was helping someone else into his ground." I wasn't really talking to Landers, but he nodded along anyway.

I scanned the room slowly, my eyes settling on the door we'd had to bust in. "My money's on a teenager. Brooks said it took him months to get this guy to trust him enough to let him in here. But he was a teacher. So a kid would hit his soft spot."

Landers jotted a note.

"Overdoses aren't the only fatal outcome with this drug, I guess," I said. "Though the numbers from that alone are staggering. Do you know how many Americans died last year?"

"Twelve thousand, give or take a few," Landers said. "I do my reading, too. Let's parse the origins of the epidemic later, when I've managed to put a lid on this symptom. You asked why, and really, it's nothing more than a simple, old-fashioned land dispute. Except instead of farmers after water for their crops, it's dealers after the hard-core junkies. And they're out of territory, so they're going to fight over this one."

"What do you mean they're out of territory? I talked to a pediatrician in Chesterfield last week who told me one of their blue-ribbon high schools has the worst opiate problem in the county. Wouldn't rich kids with too much time and money and too little supervision be a dealer's nirvana? Why fight it out here?"

"It's a class issue. The kind of people selling here aren't the kind of people who can walk into a school like that and blend in. The problem the doctor told you about is a real one, but it's a local one. Most of the dealing going on down there is kids swiping meds and using the internet to learn how to cut and package them to sell. The suburbs stick with their own." He moved to the door and motioned for me to follow. Outside, he pointed to a Chesterfield squad car sitting about a block down in the parking lot of a McDonald's. "That's a permanent post, not a cop stopping for coffee. The county line is just this side of that parking lot. They keep an officer stationed there around the clock, warning the city drug goons to stay on their side of the line." His lips tipped up the barest bit into a grim half-smile. "These guys are running out of ground."

I clicked my pen out and scribbled, my eyes on the squad car.

Territory disputes aren't uncommon in the world drug dealers move in. But three shootings in a week is enough to piss off the police—and that's something the average dealer usually tries to avoid.

"Were the other victims both men?"

Landers shook his head. "A man and a woman."

"Anybody with a record?"

"Both of them, both with intent to distribute. Plus, the woman had a weapons conviction for an unregistered handgun."

"Found together or separate?"

"You really do have a good handle on this. They were alone."

I glanced around. "Same motel?"

"No." He pressed his lips into a tight line.

"But—then why are you so convinced they're related?" A week wasn't long enough to have ballistics back unless he was blackmailing someone at the lab. Same for DNA and anything else I could think of that would definitively link crime scenes. But Landers wasn't the conspiracy theory type. Every "i" dotted was more a life motto than a cliché for him.

"I can't tell you that. I know that's a bullshit answer and I'm sorry, but I can't."

Then why tell me anything? I managed to avoid saying it out loud. He had to have a reason, even if I couldn't quite decipher it.

He roved a slow eye over the officers in the room, taking inventory of the scene. "You're with Brooks for the day, right?"

I nodded. So did Landers. "You have a good head for this stuff."

Not-so-subtle code for "figure it out for yourself." Landers didn't like reporters. The "people who won't talk to him will talk to me" didn't really hold water this time, because those same people seemed plenty willing to talk to Brooks.

I scanned the room slowly, watching the forensics team paying particular attention to the grungy carpet, a photographer getting Tuck, the blood spatters, and the map wall from every angle. Landers was the only officer here, but he was still being cryptic and tight-lipped—I was used to that from him, but what if, for once, it had nothing to do with me?

What if Landers wanted me to ask questions and pass him information because he didn't trust my new patrolman friend?

Brooks said he didn't get a single lead from his sources inside the motel.

"Nobody saw or heard anything," he said. "I talked to the clerk at the desk and three other people who stay here on the regular, and everyone says it's been quiet all night."

"Or they're not getting into the middle of it by saying they heard something." Landers leaned against the hood of his Crown Vic. "That's not helpful because we don't know if they're lying."

Brooks's face said he wanted to argue, but he stayed quiet.

Two assistant coroners wheeled a gurney out of the room behind us,

Tuck's still form barely outlined through the heavy rubber body bag. Landers watched them load it into the back of the big blue van before he walked over. I scooted closer, trying to avoid being obvious about it. Brooks snickered and waved one hand in a *go-ahead* gesture, taking two steps sideways so I could follow him.

"Just the one wound?" Landers asked.

"Yep. In just to the front of the right temple and out just behind the left," the stockier coroner said. "Explosive exit."

"He was sitting when he was shot," Landers said. "From the spatter I saw."

"I agree," the coroner said. "No apparent downward trajectory, though."

Landers nodded and waved them on before he went back into Tucker's room.

I pulled my coat tighter, barely noticing the constriction and extra weight of the vest anymore. "Never a dull day on the job, huh?" I asked Brooks.

His eyes didn't leave the coroner's van until it was out of sight. "I could do without the ones like this. I know my people. I didn't ask anyone I thought would give me a line of shit. Nobody heard anything."

"Is it possible for someone to silence a weapon that much?" The words dripped with more genuine curiosity than any I'd uttered in months.

"Like I said, this place isn't usually bumping when the sun is up. If people were sleeping, sure they could." He pointed to a long window in the front corner of the building, an easy football field from where we were standing. "The office is all the way over there."

"But that means there wasn't a struggle or a scream." I appraised the walls, no sturdier than the flimsy wood door. "That surely would've woken someone."

My thoughts raced, puzzle pieces forming in my head. Landers sounded surprised that Tuck was sitting when he was shot. But the ME said there was no downward trajectory, which meant the shooter knelt in front of Tuck to fire. Yet Tuck didn't scream, if Brooks's sources were right...

The pieces were there, but they didn't fit together. I was missing the ones that linked them.

"Tuck was afraid of something," Brooks muttered. He kicked a pebble and watched it skitter across the cracked asphalt. "He's been weird the past few days, talking crazy even for him, and yesterday it was like he was trying to get rid of me. I thought he was using again. I brought the pudding hoping I could get him to go back on the methadone if I was right."

I stepped closer, laying a hand on his arm. "He could have asked for help if something was wrong," I said. "You don't have a crystal ball."

"I could have asked." He shook his head.

I stayed quiet. Nothing I said was going to faze him right now. We had the rest of the day for me to work in my thoughts. I had a lot of them.

"Clarke?"

I spun, dropping my hand back to my side, when Landers called from behind me.

He was in the doorway of Tuck's room, his broad shoulders blotting out the orange-yellow light.

I stepped back onto the decking when he just stood there, eyes flashing like they did when I annoyed him. "Okay, I was way out here and I was just talking to Brooks. How did that manage to tick you off?"

"Were you telling Brooks that you knew this guy?" Landers's words could have sliced through stone.

My brow wrinkled. "I would have if I did."

Landers held up a piece of printer paper in one gloved hand. "Seems one of the last things he did before he died was write you a letter."

5

Dear Miss Clarke,

We share a mutual friend and I have long been an admirer of your work. I have a story I think will interest you, and I'm becoming convinced you're the only person who might be able to stop this disaster before it's too late. Please. I need to speak with you as soon as you receive this. Meet me at the McDonald's near the Hideaway Motel on East Hull Street Road on January 9 at 10 a.m. I'm having trouble getting information into the hands of the people who can use it to effect change. I believe you're the answer to my problem. I promise, this story will be worth your time.

Sincerely,
  Tucker Armstrong, Esq., Ph.D.
  Richmond, VA

I read the words for a third time, tipping my head to the side and holding the paper out so Brooks could see over my shoulder.

"I'd never heard of this guy until we pulled up here this morning," I said, my eyes still on the paper.

"Brooks? Did you know about this?" Landers barked.

I glanced at him. His jaw was tight. Why was he so worked up about this? It was weird, sure, but it seemed like it ought to bother me more than it did him, and I didn't know enough about what was going on to be more than intrigued and a little confused.

Landers was too damned high strung for his job sometimes. He needed an office cubicle somewhere that didn't push his blood pressure into the danger zone thirty times a day.

"No, sir, I didn't."

"You didn't tell him you were bringing Clarke here today?"

"No, sir."

"Who is this mutual friend he's talking about then?"

I raised a hand when Brooks's eyes narrowed. "Detective, if the guy knew I was coming here today, why would he write me a letter asking me to meet him Thursday?"

Landers shifted his weight onto his back foot, uncrossing his arms. "Valid point. But then what the hell is this about? Brooks?"

"How the hell should I know? The guy was good at watching people, observing problems before anyone else saw them. But he was guarded about what he told me. He would get quiet sometimes and tell me I was better off not knowing things. He never asked me about talking to a reporter."

I touched the letters on the bottom of the page. "Brooks, I thought you said he was a teacher."

"He was. That's what he said, anyway. At RAU."

"Or maybe at RAU Law?" I shook the paper. "According to this signature, he was an attorney."

Landers plucked the letter from my leather-wrapped fingers, looked at the bottom, and slid it into an evidence sleeve. I put one hand on his arm and pulled out my phone. "Can I get a photo of that?"

He held it out so I could snap one, Brooks moving in to look over my shoulder at the paper.

"Anything you find out that could pertain to this case, I better know about it before anyone else does," Landers said.

"Of course." I raised an eyebrow at Brooks. "He would've lost his law license when he went to prison. Maybe he just didn't like to think about it."

"Could be."

I pointed to the stacks of file boxes. "Could a legal case have something to do with all this?"

Landers shook his head. "It would take more than some maps and a letter to make me think this was anything other than what it looks like. Especially given the circumstances." He was trying to hit on the similar murders without saying so in front of Brooks.

Interesting.

"So. What now?" I clapped my hands together.

"Hopefully no more corpses." Brooks checked his watch. "It's time to run the alleys."

"Hopefully?" I glanced around. Alleys in this part of town might not be guaranteed dead-people-free. I didn't have the luxury of being squeamish, but one a day was enough.

His dimples reappeared as he jerked his head toward the car. "Come on. I'll tell you what I know about Tuck."

"Quick study on the way to a lady's heart there, aren't you?" I pulled the passenger door open.

"Just trying to get your mind off the scene," he said. "Most people aren't used to seeing something like that in the middle of a Tuesday morning."

"I'm not most people, but I do appreciate the concern."

He pulled out of the parking lot at the Hideaway and hung a right almost immediately, into an alley between the motel and a thrift store. Walls stretched high just outside the windows on both sides of the car, the space hardly big enough for the cruiser to pass, never mind allow him to open a door to get out.

"Aren't we going to run over anyone who happens to be back here?" I shrank back into my seat. Claustrophobia hasn't ever been a challenge for me, but running cars into brick walls is another matter.

"This isn't the final destination." The front bumper peeked out of the narrow space into filtered, fractured gray-green sunlight as Brooks turned expertly from the narrow alley into a wider one behind the buildings. "Welcome to Rutopia."

My breath caught. "I'm not sure that's the word I'd choose." The space between the ass-ends of the buildings and the ten-foot chain-link and vinyl fence was barely wider than the car. We were surrounded by overflowing garbage bins and a couple of dumpsters. And tarps.

Attached to various abutments from the fence to the dumpsters, there had to be thirty or more ragged plastic tarps strung at shoulder-level. And the alley stretched in front of us for blocks. A twenty-first-century shanty town, tucked behind buildings polite society ignored. "Jesus." I couldn't stop it from slipping out.

I'd read everyone's coverage of the overdoses. Nobody had this. I put one hand into my pocket. My phone had a decent camera.

Brooks kept his foot lightly on the brake, the car crawling past cocoons of coats and blankets that I assumed concealed people.

"These are the folks who don't have the money for a room," he said.

Drugs will get you booted—sometimes even blacklisted—from a shelter. "Damn," I muttered. "There are so many of them."

"When people say 'epidemic,' they're not kidding." Brooks shook his head. "It's just not a socially acceptable epidemic. If they were dying from some kind of virus, they'd be in hospitals." He stopped the car. "Stay put. I'll be right back."

I didn't argue. He locked the cruiser's doors and rounded the hood, ducking under a blue tarp with as many holes as I had shoes, leaning over the still form huddled on a wide, flat sheet of cardboard. This one didn't have nearly enough blankets for as cold as it was.

The person moved, and Brooks said a few words before he stood and returned to the car. He didn't get in, leaning into the back seat and pulling a sleeve of crackers from the Dollar Tree bag. "Two more seconds." The dimples still bookended the grim line of his mouth.

He hustled back to the makeshift tent and tucked the crackers into the blanket, patting a thin shoulder through the fabric before he hustled back to slide behind the wheel of the cruiser.

"He forgets to eat. It's too cold, and he's too skinny." His eyes said his matter-of-fact tone was forced.

I shook my head slowly. "You are a good man, Griffin Brooks."

"I can't ever get ahead of it, you know?" His voice was quiet, the words heavy with regret and responsibility. I pulled out my notebook and jotted it all down.

Thirty feet of slow-rolling silence later, we passed yet another tarp, this one held up by posts fashioned from what looked like wooden chair legs attached end-to-end. Under the tarp, a young woman sat leaning against the broken vinyl slats of the fence, chunks of sticky, dull, blondish-brown hair framing a face that would have been striking with another twenty or thirty pounds on her frame. Blankets pooled around her waist and legs, but her torso and arms, poking out of a pink spaghetti strap tank, were a scary shade of blue that also tinged her full lips, half open as her head dropped back to bounce once before it settled against the fence.

I blinked, squinting first at her face when my heart took off at a gallop —Katie?

I honestly couldn't tell.

And when my eyes found the thin tube running from the inner crook of her elbow to a plastic baggie full of clear liquid she'd hung from the fence above her head, I wasn't sure I wanted to.

"Jesus." I hadn't said it so much since last time I was home and went to church with my mother.

"Dammit." Brooks slammed the car into park and flew out the door, not bothering to lock it this time.

I forced my gaze back to the scene. Brooks squatted in front of the woman, blocking my view of her face. My fingers tightened around the pen until I couldn't feel them, every detail making it messily onto the page as my eyes stayed locked on Brooks's shoulders and what I could see around them.

Was that Nate DeLuca's widow, hooked to a makeshift IV of God only knew what in a forgotten alley in the city that still revered her husband? I couldn't say.

Did it matter?

It shouldn't. That was the best I could do.

Brooks's profile was tense as he reached for his radio and spoke into it. He stood and rushed to the trunk of the car, retrieving a first aid kit.

Kneeling next to the woman's limp arm, he donned gloves before he opened an alcohol swab and pressed it over her skin, pulling the tubing slowly. It fell to the pavement, still dripping liquid into a slowly spreading puddle as he scrubbed at her arm with the swab before he pressed gauze over it and held pressure, his other hand going gently to her face.

Her head fell to the side, eyes still closed.

I pulled my phone from my pocket and opened the photos, swiping to the file on Katie DeLuca. Her last mugshot showed sallow, yellowish skin, dull hair, and hollow eyes and cheeks.

I held it up, looking at the profile of the young woman slumping on the cardboard pallet next to Brooks.

Her nose was pointed where Katie's was rounded, her ears small and tight to the sides of her head where Katie's curved out.

Not her. But it could've been.

Brooks pulled out a small purple box and ripped off an outer casing and a red safety tab, tossing them before he punched the dark end of the device into the side of the young woman's thigh and held it for a five count. Dropping the whole unit to the pavement, he tucked a tattered blanket around her shoulders, lowering her the rest of the way to the ground.

Her eyelids fluttered. Opened. He leaned over her, his lips moving.

And she landed a punch square in the middle of his face.

Notebook and pen flying, I scrambled out of the car as her pale bluish arms and legs flailed into a storm cloud of fury. She kicked the pole out from under one side of her makeshift tent, and landed a couple more good ones on Brooks before he got her pinned.

"You okay?" I took two steps toward them.

He grunted, jerking his chin back toward the car, blood trickling a thin trail from his nose.

I backed up and laid a hand on the door just as sirens pierced the eerie gray quiet.

Lights flashing, the ambulance crawled our way from the far end of the alley. Brooks was still restraining Miss Tasmanian Devil, so I stepped forward and waved to the driver.

The paramedics made quick work of getting the young woman strapped to a gurney and loaded into the back, the driver backing out the way he came in. Back in the passenger seat of the squad car, I watched Brooks lower the baggie and tubing into an orange-emblazoned evidence bag. He sealed the bag and slid back behind the wheel.

"And here I was worried you wouldn't see anything you thought was worth writing about."

"Will she be okay?"

"Depends on your definition of the word, I think." He barked a harsh, low laugh. "If they can get more meds into her at the right intervals, she won't die today."

"Aaron White told me the PD is working with the fire department to train officers in administering emergency overdose meds." I gestured to his nose as he retrieved a tissue from the console. "You're on the front line of that, I guess?"

"Do me a favor and keep that to yourself, if you would. I'm not supposed to have the injectors on me yet, but I have a good friend who's a medic."

"Because of that?" I pointed to his nose.

"Dosing that stuff is tricky. People get hurt."

I clicked out my pen again. "I haven't read anything about it being a risk to patients."

"Not the patients. The doctors. Or nurses, or medics. If you give someone too much too fast, you bring them crashing down and it pisses them right off. They'll fight back with whatever they have handy. The university hospital in Charlottesville had a doctor and two nurses damn near killed last summer. So the rollout of the injectors statewide was postponed until they could do more research and training with them."

I scribbled it all in my notes, putting a star next to it so I'd remember to look up the incident in Charlottesville.

"What happens to her after that? If they save her?"

"They'll keep her for seventy-two hours and detox her, and then they'll ask if we want to press charges, which we don't because we don't have room in the jail for all these people, and the only person she was hurting was herself. So, by Saturday, she'll be right back over there hooked to another bag." He started the car and we rolled forward.

Still no sign of Katie DeLuca. I wasn't sure how to make people care about the other folks out here, but they would care about her. Probably Tucker Armstrong, too. And that was at least a start.

Brooks stopped to check on or feed half a dozen more folks before we made it out of the alley. I noted every minuscule detail, because I needed to paint people a picture so vivid they could see the gray cloak of despair heavy over the space, feel the hopelessness that seemed to crawl further into my skin the longer we stayed, smell the sting of urine mixed with the sickly-sweet decay that I couldn't confidently source to the dumpsters as opposed to the huddled masses of sleeping humans.

"I work in the news business and I had no idea this was so bad," I murmured as we turned onto 32nd Street, sunlight slanting through the windshield and making me reach for my shades.

"It gets worse every week." Brooks pointed to a gas station. "Coffee?"

"Please."

He parked in front of glass doors sporting thick iron bars and cut the engine. I followed him inside, smiling at the clerk when he called Brooks by name.

Coffee in hand, I went to the register.

The stooped little man behind it smiled and shooed me away with a wrinkled hand, shaking his close-cropped silver-haired head. "Your money is no good here, miss. Any friend of Brooks is on the house."

Brooks walked up behind me. "Thank you, Miles." He put two fingers on my forearm. "Nichelle is from the newspaper. Writing an article about what I do."

"You tell people this boy here is an angel walking among us." Miles stood up, his back more hunched than when he was perched on his stool. "He takes better care of this community than anyone. Watches out for our kids. He's good people, miss."

Back in the car, Brooks shook his head. "Miles remembers when this was a neat, manicured-lawn little working class neighborhood and his dad ran the corner store and a bakery in the back. He wants that back, and nobody can convince him he should sell and retire to somewhere he's not in danger."

"Danger?"

"I met him my first day on the job here," he said. "Robbery. He managed to hit the alarm before they got across the counter, but they almost killed him. Broke his back in three places with a bat and fractured his skull. Over a hundred and thirty-four dollars. That's all he had in the register."

Holy Manolos. "And he's still here."

"His life is here. I try to talk him into retiring, but I honestly don't know if he'd survive long without his store. It's his reason for getting up in the morning."

"I can relate. My mother isn't near retirement age, but she's a florist with her own shop, and it's definitely the center of her universe."

"So she just makes a habit of making the world a more beautiful place, huh?" The dimples deepened.

Uh oh.

"Thank you." I started to say something else and couldn't put the right words together, so I dropped my gaze to my hands folded around my coffee cup.

"Could I maybe buy you a cup of coffee for real sometime? Without the vests and sidearm?" His tone was light.

I pulled a slow breath in through my nose. "I have an ironclad rule against dating cops." It wasn't untrue, even if I had bent it occasionally. It was also way easier to say than telling him I had a boyfriend, because we had hours to go yet. He was easy to talk to and sharp as a four-inch stiletto, and I really didn't want to talk about Joey. Or where he was. Or how long it had been since I'd heard from him.

"Ah," he said. "No mixing work and play?"

I looked up. "It keeps my life simpler."

Or it had, back before I'd met Joey.

"Offer is open if you ever change your mind." He turned out of the parking lot.

"I appreciate that." I sipped my coffee.

I wouldn't. I was decidedly a one-guy sort of girl, and my guy, for better or worse, was in hiding from the mafia and maybe the federal government, too. I didn't like the situation, but I wasn't looking to move on.

My cell phone binged a text arrival.

Pierce. I clicked the box.

How about that coffee?

I touched the bar and tapped back.

It looks like my afternoon is spoken for. Tomorrow?

I watched the dots bounce around the gray bubble on my screen as he typed.

If we talk tomorrow, will you still have time to get something else for the cover if you need to?

Boy, I'd give Pierce that he doesn't give up easily. I could get something else, but it wouldn't be necessary. The wider this story spun, the more interesting it got. And the more convinced I became that I had a mission here more important that Evan Connolly's P&L charts and a fast talking, well-dressed consultant who wanted a slick, sexy story with splashy cover art.

I will have a cover-worthy piece. Promise. And I will let you know when I'm free. I tapped send before I slid the phone back into my bag. I glanced at Brooks, his profile relaxed, eyes still sad and trained on the road.

I tapped my pen on a blank page in my notes. "So, you said Tuck had a roommate some of the time. How recently? Do you remember anything about her?"

"You really don't ever stop working," he said, steering into a neighborhood. The houses were small, many of them in disrepair, with various stages of rust on the vehicles scattered across yards on blocks. "Her name was Kay. Or at least that's what she went by. Sweet girl who fell in with a bad crowd. She was quiet, and Tuck never said much about her." He turned right at the next corner and parked a few feet down from the intersection. "She was a sports fan. Had a Generals cap she wore so much I thought she must be bald under it until I happened by one day when she was coming out of a shower."

No.

Seriously?

"What did she look like?"

"Tiny little thing, light hair, pencil skinny. Soft-spoken until you get her mad," Brooks said. "She has a temper, that woman."

I reached back through my memory, pulling up a slight, frail, screaming young woman with flames lighting her tear-washed face. That could fit. I had nothing for the temper, but she sure could scream.

Mostly, though, I'd bet my whole shoe closet the hat was Nate's. I jotted it all in my notes. "How long ago did she leave? Did Tuck say where she went?"

Brooks shook his head. "No, she was there one day, leaving to get a bus to the capitol to deliver more letters to the state senate for Tuck, and then she wasn't there the next time I went by. I took a pass through the city lockup looking for her, and then asked Tuck when I didn't find her. He said she was doing research. But wouldn't tell me anything else. I didn't push." He tapped his fingers on the wheel, throwing me an appraising glance. "You think she might know who killed him?"

I shrugged. "I think if he was living with someone recently, that person is worth finding and talking to."

"I wish you luck." Brooks settled back in the seat. "People disappear and reappear around here like ghosts walking between astral planes. But maybe Landers will be able to track her down. Everyone says that guy is like a dog with a bone."

"If something happened to me, he's the cop I'd want on the case," I said. "He's difficult for me to deal with at times, but he's damned good at his job." I followed Brooks's line of sight to a ramshackle little shingle-sided house that faded from white to gray-green thanks to a thick layer of moss-riddled grime on the lower tiles. "What's that?"

"Dealer house. A traffic stop, a search of the car, and I might get lucky if he knows what happened to Tuck. Either way I'll probably get him off the street for a few days."

I settled into the cold leather of the seat.

He had said himself it wouldn't do any good to arrest the dealers. But he wanted to feel like he was doing something. Because of Tuck. I got it. I hadn't even met the guy before he was dead and I felt the same way.

6

Nobody came or went from the house in the four hours we sat there. I learned that Brooks was the oldest of three boys, the only one of his father's sons who followed him into law enforcement, and an Aries who loved football because he'd played it in high school and college.

When the silence began to stretch and I grew bored of watching the door, I pulled out my phone and made story notes for a while before I texted Aaron to say I'd be later than I thought, and could I drop in tomorrow. *Sure*, came the reply.

I played a word game until Brooks finally pulled his eyes from the house.

"This is the boring-ass, frustrating part of what I do." He started the engine as the sun sank low behind a wall of gray clouds. He jerked the gearshift to drive and slammed his foot on the gas so hard my shoulders pressed back into the seat. My fingers closed reflexively around the handle on the armrest.

"Sorry," Brooks muttered, easing his foot off the gas.

"No need to apologize." I let go of the door. "I get it."

He just nodded, quiet until he turned into the back lot at the second precinct.

"I hope you got what you needed for your article." The dimples sank deep with the first genuine smile I'd seen since we found Tuck. "And let me know if you change your mind about that coffee."

I followed him inside and handed him the vest, stretching my arms over my head and pulling in a deep breath as he hung it back in the closet. "Thank you for letting me tag along, Officer Brooks. Watch yourself out there."

"Same to you, Miss Clarke."

I swallowed hard at the affection cloaking the words. He was attractive. Time was, I'd have been tempted to break my own rule and go to coffee. Or dinner. But the lump I was suddenly trying to swallow wasn't regret, it was worry. Joey called me "Miss Clarke" for months when we'd first met, and he said it with the same sexy undertone that made the formal address more familiar than it had any right to be.

In early November, I got a small box in the mail with a single, perfect piece of cerulean beach glass. No return address, postmarked in Baltimore. A scrap of white paper had a heart scrawled on it with a standard blue ball-point pen. I'd gone over every millimeter of the note and the packaging with a magnifying glass and a blacklight. Nothing. I'd driven three hours north to the central Baltimore post office, but no one could tell me where the package was mailed from or who might have seen the person who dropped it off. I'd gone to Ocean City, walking the chilly, nearly-deserted beach until I couldn't feel my nose and my legs ached, thinking maybe it was a clue. Or an invitation.

He wasn't there.

I did more staring at my ceiling fan these days than I did sleeping, and I couldn't ask for help. My hotshot ATF-agent ex, Kyle Miller, was cool with me and Joey these days, it seemed, but was that because he wanted me to be happy? Maybe. Or, maybe it was because for the past half-decade, his whole life had been about chasing the Caccione family and Joey had helped him get closer in eighteen months then he'd been able to get on his own in so many years.

Motivation notwithstanding, I didn't see a universe in which Kyle wouldn't be pissed at Joey for sending me something when he was supposed to be in hiding.

But why would he be in hiding in Baltimore? That was the question that threaded through every cell in my brain. Joey had lived there when I first met him. I assumed—though I'd never asked—that his "business" with the Caccione family was rooted there. Which meant they were there. So why in the ever-loving Birkenstock hell would Kyle "hide" him there?

And when that thought crept in, usually right before my alarm went off, I had to get up. Because I couldn't breathe.

Months of overthinking it hadn't gotten me closer to an answer on how Joey had become such a big part of my world in two short years, but here we were. I checked the mailbox with my heart in my throat every single day. Nothing else had ever arrived.

The beach glass lived under my pillow.

And the adorable cop smiling at me in what was now officially an uncomfortable silence didn't have any idea why I was suddenly batting my eyes at him to keep tears from spilling over.

"I always do." I managed to force the words around the lump, spinning and striding to the exit before I started blubbering at him. I could think of few things more mortifying than crying in front of one of my cops.

Two deep breaths, and I crossed the parking lot. It was odd, not needing to rush back to the newsroom to get my story ready for the web before Charlie could get the murder on the air. Months into this gig, I still wasn't used to that part. But that was assuming Charlie knew Tucker Armstrong was dead—iffy assumption, according to Landers.

I pulled the door open and slid behind the wheel as the first snowflakes drifted down.

My kitchen light was on.

I slowed my car to a crawl when I spotted the soft yellow light. I never leave lights on, even when I'm going to be out late—I read something once about the polar bears that would be saved if everyone just shut off their lights when they weren't in the room, and I like polar bears. From a distance, anyway.

I checked the alarm system app on my phone. Not armed. But I knew I'd set it when I left, because Kyle had practically threatened me with arrest the day he showed up on my porch with the crew that installed the thing if I forgot. And even he didn't have the code. Joey had been gone three days when the system was installed.

My stomach closed around the long-ago coffee. I flicked the windshield wipers, sending snowflakes skidding to the edges of the glass as I leaned forward, peering at my driveway, gripping my phone tighter. My breath let out in a *whoosh* when I saw the pale blue Subaru.

I parked next to it and took the steps carefully in case they were already getting slick, opening the door to the smell of garlic and lemon pepper and a very content toy Pomeranian lying across my best friend's foot while she stirred something she had simmering in a giant pot I didn't recognize.

"I know I set the alarm." I locked the door behind me, laughing when Darcy raised her furry head for a split second before she dropped her chin back to the yellow linoleum.

"The code is my son's birthday." Jenna put the spoon on the edge of the sink and rolled her eyes. "Took me three tries: your mom's, Gabby's, and then Carson's. I admit to a moment of panic when I wondered if it was captain hottie's, but then I got it right." She shook her head when my face fell at the mention of Joey. "Sweetie, a breakup is a shitty thing, but it's time to pull yourself out of this hole. It's been three months. You don't return phone calls. You're not eating real food. Darcy is tired of hanging out with you. And I miss my friend."

She took my bag, putting a hand out for my coat. "Sit. I opened wine. We are going to get you through this if it takes all night." Her eyes went to the window. "Another hour of snow and I won't be leaving until the plows come through, anyway."

I took my coat off and handed it to her before I swept her up in both arms and squeezed until she squeaked. "You're doing the psychic thing again." I let go and stepped back, the knotted muscles in my shoulders relaxing almost painfully. "I didn't realize just how much I've come to dread opening that door to an empty house until I saw your car." Especially today. But I didn't say that out loud for a lot of reasons.

"I've missed you, honey. Have a seat. The dumplings just need a few more minutes here."

I dropped into the little black bistro chair at my tiny kitchen table and reached for the open bottle of Moscato. I filled the glass more than I usually would and swallowed half of it while Jenna fussed over her great-grandmother's famous chicken and dumplings. In the South, comfort food cures all. Probably would've even worked, had there been an actual breakup for me to get over.

If I shut my eyes, Kyle was still sitting across from me, autumn sunshine giving his thick hair coppery highlights as he leaned forward and pleaded with me to see things his way.

"Why can't he just be away on business?" I had asked.

"People need to think he dumped you and took off." Kyle's voice was low. Insistent. The longer he talked, the less he asked and more he ordered, and it had pissed me right the hell off.

"People need to? Or you'd like to?" The words slid through my teeth before I could stop them, and the look on his face said they'd hit their mark. Kyle stood.

"This isn't up for discussion, Nichelle." I flinched at the hard edge in his tone. "A bad breakup. You have no idea where he went, and you don't care, either. If you have any concern for his safety, that better be your story to anyone who asks, be it your editor, your mother, or your priest."

I hadn't seen or spoken to Kyle since. I got a card from his mom at Christmas, and I'd picked up my phone and clicked to his name in my favorites list half a dozen times that day, but I was too chicken to call him. Days stretched on, and while I watched the ceiling fan spin at night, I talked myself into being scared I hadn't heard from Kyle because Joey was dead and he didn't want to tell me. I didn't really believe it—just like Jenna knew I needed her tonight, if something had happened to Joey, I would know it. Wouldn't I?

I tapped a fingernail on the tile tabletop. No room for that right now. I needed to focus on something that had nothing to do with my fake breakup story.

"We found a dead guy on my ride-along today," I said. Jenna had always harbored a borderline-macabre fascination with the ickier aspects of my job.

"Really? Like the gross dead guy in the dumpster the joggers always find on *Law and Order*, or like, a skeleton?"

She settled a lid over the pot and laid the spoon down before she poured herself a glass of wine and fixed me with an expectant look.

"Like a guy who'd been shot in the head in a freezing little shithole motel room with his brains splattered across the wall behind him." I picked up my glass and swirled the wine around, trying to keep the image off the backs of my eyelids. "He was a recovering addict, staying in one of those places over off Hull Street that you can rent either by the hour or by the week. The cop I was shadowing was trying to take him food." I shook my head. "It's been a weird day."

"Who do they think killed him?"

"That was the other thing: Landers showed up when Brooks—that's the guy I was with today—called homicide. But he was weird, too." I watched the snowflakes drift down outside the window, a small pile starting to form on the sill. Growing up in Dallas, I didn't see much snow as a child, and it was one of my favorite things about living in Virginia. But right then, even the snow didn't make me less uneasy.

Jenna sat back in the chair. "Oh no. No."

My eyebrows lifted at the sharp urgency in her voice. "What?"

"Uh-uh. I know that look. That's the look you get when you're about to try to get yourself killed. You let the homicide detective detect the homicide, okay?"

"That was part of the weird thing. He asked me to help. Sort of. Landers, who generally doesn't like me all that much." My fingers went to my hair, twisting a long, thick lock into a knot and then letting it go.

"Stop it, Nicey." Jenna backed toward the stove with eyes so wide I could see white all around the brown. "You haven't talked to Kyle in months and your mystery hero is..." She paused. "Honey, you don't have any help. Your safeguards are MIA. I know you're looking for something to lose yourself in, to focus on, but I don't think your options ought to include charging into a murder case and getting yourself hurt. Have you ever tried knitting?"

I bristled at that, even though I knew her heart was in the right place. She wasn't criticizing me, she wanted me to keep breathing. I got it. But I'd done my fair share of detective work in the past couple of years, and my fair share of being the hero, too. I didn't need Joey and Kyle, or Brooks or Landers, to get to the truth about what happened to Tuck. I liked Brooks.

But the patrolman didn't have the kind of clout it takes to push for a deeper investigation, and we hadn't made it an hour out of Tucker's room before he had a new crisis to manage. He would trust Landers to run the case. The thing bugging me was that Landers hadn't seemed to trust himself.

Since I knew he disliked unanswered questions as much as I did, I needed to know why, but I needed to know a whole lot of other things first. And right then I needed to not scare the hell out of my kindhearted suburban soccer mom best friend.

"I have no intention of getting myself hurt. It's just weird, that's all." My stomach had impeccable timing, for once, letting out a gurgle so loud Darcy sat up and yawned. "Is that about ready?"

She went back to the stove and lifted the lid, the smell of chicken and spices that wafted out making my mouth honest-to-God water. My stomach growled again. Jenna laughed, her face smoothing back to its relaxed but concerned mom expression. "When was the last time you ate a decent meal? Not Pop Tarts and coffee or something from a drive thru, but like actual food?"

I just shook my head.

Joey liked to cook. He liked teaching me to cook. I didn't enjoy the reminder that he wasn't around to make it fun, so the closest thing I'd had to real food since Christmas was a turkey sandwich. "You don't want to know." I couldn't keep the thick cloak of melancholy off the words.

Jenna crossed the kitchen and laid a hand on my arm. "Sweetie. It really is okay. And it will only get better." She turned back to the counter and pulled deep bowls from a cabinet before she ladled chicken and dumplings into them. "Comfort food got the name for a reason."

I breathed deep when she put the bowl in front of me, smiling up at her. "Thank you so much, Jen. I might never know what I did to deserve a friend like you, but I'm sure glad I did it."

She took the chair across from me. "It was a good day for us both when you wandered into the shop." Jenna ran a used bookstore in Carytown where I fed my collection of first editions of beloved books, she displayed her incredible artistic talent in a small gallery in the back, and we'd gotten to be fast friends when I'd first moved to Richmond. A decade later, I wasn't sure I remembered exactly what my life had been like without her, and I'd be forever grateful I'd noticed the little ivy-covered storefront that Saturday.

The rich, savory mixture of herbs and chicken and perfectly-sized dumplings melted across my tongue and I sighed. "This is incredible, as always. I'm not sure how Chad doesn't weigh four hundred pounds."

"His crazy metabolism. I'm glad you like it." She took a couple of bites, watching mostly as I plowed through my bowl and got up for seconds.

"I love you, Jen. And I know you're right. I'm just looking for my footing." It was a good track—put the blame on my job. Don't talk about Joey, but in a way that didn't make it obvious I was avoiding the subject. I didn't want to lie, and if I could shift the focus, I didn't have to.

Finally, something useful from my years of deciphering cop and lawyer double-talk.

I took my wins where I could get them.

"Anything I can do to help you find it?"

"You're doing it, doll. I haven't been a stellar friend lately, yet here you are, making sure I'm fed and reasonably well-adjusted and offering me a shoulder if I need it. Thank you." I raised my wineglass.

She picked hers up and touched it to mine with a soft *clink*. "I worry. I think babies activate some sort of gene that makes you fret over everyone you care about."

"My mom would agree with that."

"How's she doing? Y'all had a nice Thanksgiving, right?"

"She's good." Lord, had I not talked to Jenna since Thanksgiving? No wonder she was sneaking into my house to make dinner—it was a wonder she hadn't come armed with tequila and Godiva instead of soup. "My grandmother is something else. Swept right into Mom's house like they last saw each other thirty days and not thirty years ago, refurnished both bedrooms, and had the entire holiday choreographed and catered by the events staff at Neiman's."

I nodded as Jenna's eyebrows disappeared under her fluffy bangs. "For real. She said Mom looked tired, declared the beds unacceptable, and had delivery people there with new furniture and drapes the next morning. Super fancy plush furniture and drapes. My childhood bedroom could be in *Southern Living*."

"And your grandfather?"

"Didn't come." I swallowed, tapping one foot. "She said he had a work emergency."

"You don't believe it." Jenna didn't bother with a question.

"It occurred to me that there's always a reason I can't talk to him. And Grandmother only calls me in the middle of the day. My mom's original blowup was mostly with him, from what I gather. I think maybe he still blames me for ruining my mom's life. Or the life he wanted for her."

"You know your mom doesn't feel that way." Jenna's chilly fingers closed over my arm.

"I do. And my grandmother is cool. She wore my mom out, but we had a nice time. And in case you ever need to know—the chefs at Neiman Marcus roast a mean turkey, and the chocolate chip pecan pie is to die for. I ate my whole slice and half of Mom's."

Jenna's eyebrows scrunched. "But your mom's health is good?"

"Eight years and counting. She just went for scans in November." If she just wasn't so worried about me, but I didn't say that part out loud. Mom would never come right out with it, but her texts had gone to four daily since October, and she called me more often, too. When I got out of her car at DFW on December first, I thought I might miss the plane, she held on so long and tight.

I really was trying like hell to fight my way back to myself—I didn't like them worrying over me.

My gut said maybe Tucker Armstrong was the road to normal I'd been looking for. As much as I'd always talked about wanting to write politics, the free rein to cover whatever struck my fancy had shown me that politics on the daily is tedious and boring. And that's when I wasn't wading through piles of bullshit. While Pierce was right that I lacked the kind of sources in politics that I had in law enforcement, the people at the statehouse liked to talk—cops didn't. The real trouble was that most politicians care more about making their detractors look bad than serving the people who elected them, and I'd grown tired of being their mudslinging vehicle.

A murder tangled up in a drug war nobody was really covering wrapped in a face I could put on these opioid deaths—maybe it was the wine, or the awesome friend, or the snow, but I felt more content than I had in months.

I didn't want to think about what that actually said about my life.

"How are things with you?" I hedged the question. It had been less than a year since her marriage hit a rocky patch, and I didn't want to dredge up bad memories, but I worried, too.

She put out her right hand, the overhead light flashing a rainbow off a row of large diamonds set in platinum. "Chad got me an anniversary ring for Christmas." Her soft smile said things weren't so rocky anymore. "It's been good lately. I think our cruise in the fall was a turning point. We had forgotten how to be us, without the kids and the bills and the everyday bullshit. It was nice to get to know him again. He's smart. And funny, too, when he's not so tense."

Her words glowed, relief and joy plain on her pretty, heart-shaped face. "There's someone funny and sweet and just the right kind of goofy out there for you, too."

I didn't say anything. I knew my perfect guy was out there.

I just wished I knew where Kyle had stashed him.

7

Snow coated the roads as deep as Darcy's legs and we'd finished a second bottle of wine by the time Jenna was satisfied that I was well and truly on my way out of my funk.

I was just about convinced of it myself, smoothing a sheet into place on my overstuffed sofa. "I'm glad you came over." I shook out a blanket and laid it over the sheet.

"Me too." She perched on the edge of the sofa, her feet swallowed up by my pajama pants, and hugged me before she slid under the blanket. "Chad got the kids down with minimal bickering, and I have missed you. Remember when we used to do girls' night every other week? I think that needs to be our resolution this year. To reinstate girls' night."

I settled the blanket around her. "Sacred girls' night. No matter who's dead." I grinned. My face hadn't stretched into a grin that big in so long it hurt a little.

"Or puking. Or has a project due Monday." Jenna snuggled into the covers.

"It's a date." I flicked the lamp off. "I'm going to work for a while if it won't bother you."

"Just don't forget to go to bed," she said. "And please don't get yourself almost killed again, okay?"

"Better than actually killed."

"Not funny."

"Who's being funny? It's true." I padded out of the room, pulled my laptop from my bag, and settled back at the kitchen table.

The key to most murders lies with the victim. Aaron had told me that my first month at the *Telegraph*, and it had turned out to be one of the most valuable things any cop had ever said to me.

Landers said he had two other victims, so the obvious answer was in how they were connected. I opened my notebook, then pulled up a blank file on my computer and started a list.

*Three victims

*Two men, one woman

*Different locations

*Drugs?

*WHY?

I stared at the cursor flashing in and out behind the question mark. "Why?" is always the million-dollar question with murder. The psycho who slaughters indiscriminately is entirely too feared in pop culture—the vast majority of murder victims are killed by someone with a reason. Someone they know.

The most visible common thread would be a person who linked all three victims, which Landers ought to be looking for already. But just because he was looking didn't mean I shouldn't. First up: who were they?

I clicked to the police department's online records database and entered search criteria: homicide, December 1 to today, go.

A little silver wheel spun for two blinks.

One result found.

Um. What?

I clicked back and double-checked my search parameters. Clicked "go" again.

One file. A grandmother in Church Hill killed during a robbery. Patrol officers responding to the scene picked up the perpetrator a few blocks away. I remembered that one—it happened the night *RVA Week* went to press and was too stale by the next edition for me to cover.

Tapping one finger on the edge of my keyboard, I clicked to the *Telegraph*'s website. Landers said these were in the blotter, didn't he?

My eyes scanned three weeks of miscellaneous reports, mostly burglary, larceny, and domestic disputes: the ugly underbelly of the holiday season nobody notices except victims, cops, and reporters.

No murders. The home invasion gone wrong in Church Hill had a story on the metro front the day after it happened. But where were the others? If someone stuffed the reports, Landers would know it. Wouldn't he?

Tucker Armstrong's murder wasn't showing up in the PD reports, either. Yet, anyway. I made a note.

Three murders in two weeks is weird. Three murders the PD seemingly has no public record of in two weeks?

There's a story there. But I still needed the names. So who else had them?

The Medical Examiner, but their database isn't searchable online.

I plucked my phone from the tabletop and checked the time. Ten forty-five. Late, but not ridiculous for an important question about a murder.

I opened my contacts, found Jacque's name, and started thumb typing. *I need insider intel on three corpses nobody's talking about. Any chance you've seen a fatal GSW lately that you didn't later see on the news?* Send.

I watched my screen for a good minute, willing the gray dot bubble to pop up.

My phone stayed dark. Okay—until I could find out who else was dead, I'd work up a background worthy of a biographer on Tucker Armstrong.

I flipped pages in my notes and opened my web browser, typing his full name into the search bar. No social media—not surprising given that Brooks said the car accident that altered his life happened before the age of Facebook and Instagram. Four journal articles, also not a shock from a former professor. I clicked the blue links, finding two pieces on climate change, both with a specific focus on fossil fuel dependence, both on sites with paywalls to view more than the abstract.

I didn't figure Connally would be interested in paying $140 for a year of access to a couple of obscure science journals without a hugely compelling argument for why it was the key to a murder, so the abstracts would have to do: Armstrong cited core sample research from tidewater to the Blue Ridge showing that heavier presence of fossil fuel byproducts in the soils was associated with a variety of negative outcomes, from higher summer temperatures to fewer of the minerals farmers depended on to feed their plants.

Interesting, but the studies were all more than a decade old. If someone was going to kill him to keep this quiet, conventional wisdom said it would've been before today.

I bookmarked the pages and clicked back to the search results.

Three ads from people finder services, his court records—which a few clicks confirmed were just as Brooks said—then an old MySpace page.

Huh.

"I didn't even know this was still a thing," I muttered, tapping the trackpad.

Tuck—younger, thicker, with better coloring and the top of his skull intact—filled half my screen, hugging an attractive blonde woman in a red sundress and strappy beige sandals.

Last updated, August 2010.

He looked just like me, my mom, or any of the dozens of academic experts I'd interviewed over the years.

I scrolled.

A link to one of the journal articles I'd just read. A note about writing a syllabus for a new politics of the environment class he was co-teaching with a professor from the political science department. I jotted the name of the class and the other professor and kept reading.

Photos, one behind his desk in a small but cozy office, the walls papered with topographical maps of Virginia. One with the blonde woman on the boardwalk at Virginia Beach. One at a Virginia Tech football game outfitted in so much Hokie gear even Bob would raise a brow.

I noted his presumed alma mater and opened another window, clicking to the Tech alumni association and using the login credentials Bob had given me long ago when he got tired of me asking every time I needed to find someone on the site.

Search all classes, all programs. Armstrong, Tucker C. Go.

Our victim was a smart, determined guy: he graduated with a dual bachelor of science in political science and biochemistry in 1993, then returned to complete his PhD in environmental science as part of the program's inaugural class in 2001.

I jotted a note to find out where he got his master's and clicked to a list of his undergrad classmates, my eyes scanning for any familiar names. My gut said Landers's peculiar behavior was rooted in whoever wanted these murders kept quiet, and it would take power to clamp down on something hard enough to get Chris Landers to ask me for help.

Nothing jumped out at me.

I copied the list and pasted it into my notes file, then went to a list of the first doctorates granted in the environmental science program.

Nothing there, either. Back to the search results.

Halfway down page two, there was a link for a press release. From one of the biggest law firms in the state.

I clicked it. January 1997, Alexandria. *Tucker Armstrong joins Heller, James, and Nowitzki as a junior associate.*

Huh. I touched my phone screen and found the photo of the letter he'd written me, my eyes sticking on the three little letters after his name. He did have a law degree. But somewhere after he earned it and got a job at one of the most prestigious firms in the country, he went back to school to save the planet.

I noted the date and firm name and bookmarked the webpage with the press release before slumping back in my chair. I rubbed my eyes and contemplated my Keurig. If I wanted any prayer of even a wink of sleep, I didn't need coffee at eleven o'clock. But it might help me think through something I was missing.

Darcy's nails scratched on the wood floor in the hallway, her head peeking around the doorjamb.

"Just a few more minutes, Darce." I stood, opting for stretching over caffeine. Darcy flopped onto the floor half in and half out of the kitchen, resting her chin on her front paws and fixing me with a tired stare. I returned to my chair and clicked back to Tuck's MySpace.

Several shots of a Rottweiler puppy, two more of the blonde. She wasn't tagged in anything, though, so I had no way to know how important she might be or how to reach her. I paused on one of Tuck with a group of what had to be students, taken that May. They were in the woods at nearly sunset, by the slant of the shadows from the trees. I clicked on the picture and scrolled down to the caption.

Great weekend in Shenandoah with these brilliant young activists. These kids are going to change the world. You heard it here first.

I read it twice, tapping my finger on the edge of the keyboard. It didn't say what they were there for. But I noted the word "activists" and zoomed in for a closer look at the photo. Not an RAU logo on any of their clothes. Including Tuck's. Huh.

I dragged my fingers up, leaving the picture zoomed in, and studied faces.

Wait.

There, fourth from the left in the back.

Was that...?

I clicked up a blank window, my fingers flying over the keys and then tapping restlessly while the state senate website loaded.

Myers, Nickerson, Pohl...Rowley.

I clicked back to Tuck's old MySpace photo.

Yeah. If that wasn't Dakota Rowley, the hotshot new state senator from the 65th, I'd eat my Louboutins.

Tucker Armstrong had written me a letter he never got to mail.

Had he written Rowley, too?

I clicked to the notes file and typed reminders and theories until the screen was full of text.

Clock check. 11:27.

Landers was one of the only people I knew who was as much of a workaholic as I was.

I picked up my phone and opened my texts.

Hey. Are you awake?

The gray dot bubble popped up almost immediately.

I don't think I'm ever not these days. What?

I rolled my eyes at the abrupt reply. I'd learned long ago not to take it personally with him.

Do you have Tucker Armstrong's computer in evidence?

Buzz. Of course. Why?

I'd like to know who he was writing letters to.

The reply buzzed as the message went out. *Besides you?*

Smartass.

Besides me.

The gray bubble's dots flexed up and down for more than a minute.

Buzz. *It's going to take some work, the thing is password protected and once they got through that, they found that every single file is encrypted and passworded.*

I slumped into the iron back of my chair, pain shooting five directions from my tailbone. These chairs weren't designed for lounging.

Every one?

Buzz. *We can't even see the filenames.*

Damn. Needle, meet haystack.

I stared at my phone. I should have learned by now, nothing is ever simple.

I'd just have to pay Senator Rowley a visit, then.

Darcy sighed, and I looked back at the window.

After the plows came.

My phone buzzed again.

Landers: *Why did you ask?*

My brow furrowed. He'd told me something he maybe wasn't supposed to. He'd asked for my help.

But I'd ridden this carousel more than a few times now, and until I knew what was actually going on, the fewer people who knew what I was looking into, the better. Not that I was worried about Landers blabbing to the TV reporters. But especially with the silence that even seemed to have him suspicious about these murders, I wasn't sure I needed to tell him Tuck had a connection to this politician. It might be nothing. I might be totally off base and cost Landers time. And besides, it was right there on the internet. He could find it himself if he was handy with Google.

Brooks said the vic had been writing to people, that he'd moved into the motel with a woman (friend), she sent things out for him because he didn't like to leave the room. Something about saving the world but not being able to save themselves. Just wondering who else letters were going to. Send. Every word true. I just left out a few key points.

Buzz. *Well now I'm wondering who this woman was, why Brooks didn't put her in a report or mention her to me, and why Tuck didn't want to leave his room.*

I typed notes. Landers was a good cop. Brooks hadn't really said why Tuck didn't go outside, come to think of it. I assumed he had some sort of phobia, or paranoia brought on by the drugs. But what if it was way simpler than that?

What if he was just scared of someone?

I picked up the phone again.

We have a lot of questions.

Buzz. *And this storm is fucking with my ability to find the answers.*

At least it's pretty.

Buzz. *Clarke, you let me know if you get anything on this. Immediately. It's important.*

I bit my lip. Important for who? Tuck? The residents in the area of the second? Or Landers's career?

You got it. Goodnight, Detective.

I sent the message and turned back to my laptop. Brooks's story about the ball cap gave me decent reason to think Tuck's mystery woman was Katie DeLuca.

If Landers knew that, he wasn't sharing.

I would tell him. As soon as I knew what it was that I might have. I closed the computer and stood, clicking my tongue softly at Darcy. "You ready for bed, princess?"

I left the computer on the table and plugged my phone into the charger on the counter. Crawling between chilly sheets, I pulled the heavy down comforter to my chin and slid my hand under the pillow, my fingers closing around Joey's beach glass.

My objectivity was my single biggest asset when I worked a big story. All the facts had to be laid out to find the ones that mattered to the incident at hand. Just because Tuck was a college professor, just because he knew Dakota Rowley, didn't mean any of that had anything to do with why he was dead.

Landers had flat told me he had two likely related victims cooling at the morgue. I closed my eyes, calling up his face.

He didn't say drug-related.

He said related.

It might be drugs. Aaron always said the easy answer was usually the right one.

But Landers had asked for my help. As much as he ever would, anyway.

And the cases where I was useful to them were usually the complicated ones.

I needed all the facts. But as I drifted to sleep before midnight for the first time in weeks with Joey's gorgeous, stormy eyes dancing on the backs of my lids, my gut said Tucker Armstrong had a bigger enemy than a random drug dealer.

Always, the most important question is: why?

The plows rumbled past just after daybreak, and Jenna and I got our workout in digging her Subaru out of ten inches of snow so she could get home to spend the day with her family. She hugged me tight through our bulky coats before she climbed into the car. "You'll get your feet back under you."

Unraveling a murder sounded like a good start—and since most everything in the South shuts down when it snows, my chances of finding people I wanted to talk with at home were excellent.

I retrieved my laptop and set up the kitchen table as a makeshift desk. With a fresh cup of caramel vanilla coffee and white mocha creamer at my elbow, I picked up my phone and touched Parker's name in my favorites list.

I couldn't recall ever wanting an interview as badly as I wanted one with Katie DeLuca. She had to be the woman Brooks had described, with her Generals ball cap, so she knew my victim better than anyone. And the night Nate DeLuca died in a tragic crash on the James, Parker had carried the star pitcher's young widow away from the river—I'd heard him tell someone he was taking her to her parents' house. Maybe he still knew how to get in touch with them.

"Nicey?" Mel's voice was thick with sleep. "What's wrong?"

"Sorry to wake you, hon. I need to pick your husband's contacts list."

"Hang on." She disappeared.

I opened my notes file and clicked a pen.

"Baby, wake up." I could barely hear Mel, the sound muffled, like she put the phone down on the quilt.

Parker grunted. Mel giggled.

I pulled the phone away from my head.

"Come on, Nicey's on the phone. She says she needs your contacts to help with her story."

"She was going out to do something about drug overdoses, I thought," he grumbled. "What kind of trouble is she trying to find now?"

"I heard that," I said.

"I meant for you to." Parker's voice came through loud and clear, sleep-laden as it was. "Why are you waking me up on a snow day? Don't you sleep?"

I hated telling my friends things I knew they didn't want to hear. But I knew from more experience than I cared to remember the best way was to jump right off the bad news cliff.

Deep breath. Clear words that weren't too rushed. The only thing worse than delivering bad news is having to repeat it. "I think Katie DeLuca is in trouble, Parker. Do you still know how to get ahold of her family?"

Silence. It stretched so wide I pulled the phone back again. Nope, still connected.

"Parker?"

A long sigh filtered through the speaker into my ear. "I know." He was awake now. "I was afraid you were going to latch onto this. Clarke—"

I waited. He didn't say anything else.

"I'm not talking about drugs trouble," I said. "Do you think her parents might know where she is?"

"Wait. You don't know where she is?"

I heard something fall. Break. Mel, in the background: "Grant? Baby, what's wrong?"

"I think we're getting our wires positively tangled here." I drew the words out.

"I assumed you'd seen her yesterday. I figured there was a decent chance of it when you told Wind-and-Money Bags where you were headed at the meeting, and I wanted to warn you, but by the time I got into Bob's office to look for you, you were gone."

I heard a cabinet close. Silverware rattling. The coffeemaker burbling. "So if you didn't see her in the shanty town over off Hull, why are you asking about her?"

Parker knew about the pitiful little makeshift tent city?

"I saw a mugshot because she was arrested a few months ago for possession." I stumbled over the words a little. "I looked for her yesterday but didn't see her, but I'm wondering."

I stopped for five beats, pulling in a deep breath. I was wondering a whole fucking lot of things. Which was the most important?

"Clarke?"

Katie. Finding her mattered most.

"Does she have one of Nate's old ball caps?"

"The one he wore to his last game," Parker said. "It's like a security blanket, she carries it everywhere. Oh, God. What are you not saying?"

"Nothing." I barked it too loud, trying to get the panic out of his voice. "Nothing. I didn't see her, I swear. But there was a guy, a professor—former professor—at RAU, who was murdered yesterday. And the cop I was shadowing said there used to be a young woman who was an addict staying there in the room with him, and she had the hat. I thought maybe it was Katie after I had seen that photo of her, and I really need to talk to her if it was."

"Murdered? Tuck?"

Leaping Louboutins.

I had one thing right. Katie DeLuca did indeed know Tucker Armstrong.

But why the hell did Parker know my dead guy by his nickname?

8

I don't often go into a conversation without expectations. Most of the time I'm pretty spot on, too—I'm good at reading situations and have a knack for knowing what I need to bring to a given table to leave it with the information I want.

I'd called Parker braced to give him bad news about his friend's grieving bride. I'd expected him to be upset. I was ready for him to tell me to leave Katie out of my story. And while twenty-four hours ago I thought she was the key to getting my mojo—and my readers—back, Tuck had taken that spot almost the second I spotted his foot sticking out from behind the bathroom door.

Except now Katie was in the big middle of my story anyway—maybe as the linchpin that could help us figure out why Tucker Armstrong was dead.

Which meant thirty seconds went by with me opening and closing my mouth like an indecisive guppy before I settled on a question for Parker. Sort of.

"Huh?" Need erudite? I'm your girl.

His coffeemaker stopped the snorting sound. "Clarke? Tuck is dead?"

"I—uh—yeah. Yeah, he is. How do you know him?" I let my eyes fall shut, hoping maybe my head would stop spinning. Opened them. Nope.

"I met him in a box at a game. He was Katie's favorite professor when she was in college and Nate invited him once. Nice guy. It's sad what happened to him."

I leaned back in the chair, watching my computer screen go dark. "You know, for a city that seems so big, Richmond is a borderline incestuous little Peyton Place sometimes. Wait—Brooks told me Tucker Armstrong had been an addict for way longer than Nate DeLuca played for the Generals."

"I suppose that could be," Parker said. "You wouldn't have known it to talk to him, though."

I knew Parker well. And I'm good at listening for nuance. It took both facts for me to hear the almost nonexistent undercurrent in his words.

The tiny little uptick that said he was tense. The just-a-hair-too-fast words said it was because there was something he wasn't telling me.

"There's at least some chance that Katie is among the last people who saw this guy alive, Parker. I need to talk to her. Do you know how to get in touch with her?" Landers would probably want to talk to her, too, once he figured out her connection to Tuck. And then there was the possibility that whoever killed Tuck was also looking for her—but I couldn't tell Parker that.

"Why is that your job to find out?" His voice was guarded, but I couldn't tell now whether it was me or Katie that caused it. It wasn't unfair—he'd spent years worrying when I got into a dangerous mess chasing a story, and he didn't love the experience for either of us.

"Didn't you hear Connally yesterday? He wants a Nichelle story. The exposé, uncover-the-truth-in-neon-lights kind that helped the *Telegraph* make money. I kind of thought before I left the office yesterday for the ride-along that maybe Katie was the way to that." I muttered the last couple of words.

"She would make a good human interest angle that would get people talking," he said. "I kind of thought the same thing, but I wanted to talk to you about it before you started."

He paused, sipping his coffee probably. I did the same.

"But now you don't think you need her anymore because Tuck is dead. And your Lois Lane spidey sense is tingling." Parker spoke first.

My brain groped for a reply. A good one, that Parker would buy.

He liked Tuck. He was one of the only people I knew who had as big a heart for helping folks as I did.

"Parker, they're going to write this off as a drug-related shooting, and nobody will even know his name next week, much less anything about what happened to him." I pulled in a deep breath, slowing my words. "I've been researching this thing for a while now. Do you know how many kids right here in Richmond are addicted to this shit? And their parents have no idea. They think they live in a safe neighborhood and send their children to good schools and that's a thing on the news that happens to other people. Poor people. Not people like them. That's why I wanted Katie, because she's proof our audience will relate to that this shit crosses economic and class lines. But I can get around making her the center of my story. If I can find out what happened to Tuck."

Every word true. I just left a few things out.

"You know you want to help." I let that hang in the air for a minute.

He sighed. "Yeah. I do."

"Where can I find Katie?"

"I'm not sure, but I'll call her folks and see if they'll talk to you." One finger tapped on the back of his phone. "I don't know that they'll go on the record. They worry about her. She's—" He cut off the end of the word so sharply I knew he wanted to say something else. "Katie hasn't always been the most stable girl."

"She walked right up into the scene of her husband's death," I said. "I don't doubt that left some sizable scars on her psyche."

"Yeah. Her folks try to keep her safe. But I'll ask them. I'll text you after I talk to them."

"Thanks, Parker."

"Just stay out of trouble, okay?"

"Doing my best," I said before I clicked the end button.

There were two possible scenarios here: one, Tuck got his head blown off by a dope dealer who was pissed at him for some reason. Which could be because Brooks was his friend or because he owed them money or even because he was trying to get clean, especially if he was trying to get Katie or who knew how many other people clean. Dealers don't take kindly to their market being cut.

I split a blank page into two columns and typed all that into one. In the other, I put the letters and the map.

Senator Rowley.

Environmental activism.

That Lois Lane sense Parker mentioned sent butterflies flapping around my midsection as I re-read the words.

I had no proof one theory was better than the other. I had loads of experience that said the easy answer in a run-of-the-mill murder is usually right. What I didn't know was whether or not Tucker Armstrong's murder was outside the mill.

I couldn't get a step further down the drug dealer path without talking to Katie, given all Landers's double talk. So until I heard from Parker, I would look at the other possibilities. The ones I wasn't convinced anyone else was looking at, though I couldn't ever be sure about Landers.

Clicking the browser icon on my screen, I raised the phone with my other hand. My photos of Tucker's map showed two different-colored stars. Why?

Tuck didn't exactly leave a key for me to follow.

I flexed my fingers and put them on the keys.

Google Earth to the rescue.

———

Sort of.

Turned out, a poorly lit cell phone photo of a wall four feet away wasn't fabulous source material.

It was pretty easy to figure out this wasn't a hiking trail. But way more difficult to pinpoint what it actually was.

I spent half an hour zooming in on my pictures, identifying towns marked on Tuck's map and measuring the distance between them. Pretty sure I had a decent scale, I pulled up the drone's-eye view of the area around the first gold star.

It was a hillside in the mountains, trees stretching spindly branches up and out to get sun on their leaves. Save for the trees, all I saw was rocks and dirt.

I took a screenshot, numbered it, and went to the next one.

Two hours later, I sat back in the chair with a furrowed brow scrunched so hard I'd need extra wrinkle cream tonight to prevent permanent evidence of it on my face.

Best I could tell, Tuck's stars marked vacant fields of all stripes for more than three hundred miles.

I pulled up the last location—this one noted with a black marker on his map—and blinked when my computer returned its satellite image.

I picked up the phone, stretching two fingers in opposite directions across the screen. I couldn't zoom in any more. That was all I got. But it sure looked like that was Suffolk, and by my not terribly scientific but accurate enough to get me in a shoe's throw scale, that was a swamp. Which snipped any common thread I could even vaguely see. No woods, no rocks.

Why would Tuck care about all these places? Better question: why would Tuck think Senator Rowley might care about it? Or that I would?

In abstract, I could see where an environmentalist who was passionate enough about the planet to take college kids out on activism trips would easily get on a soapbox about keeping land safe. But I'd be damned if I could see what this particular land had to do with me or Rowley or why it could have gotten Tuck killed.

I asked Brooks about it and he said it was a hiking trail, but it wasn't. At least not one I could find. Nothing I could see above the ground gave the line any sort of meaning—but what if the answer was under the ground? It wasn't a coal vein coming that far out from the mountains. But what if I was looking at it backwards? Not out from the mountains, but in from the Atlantic? I opened another window in the map and a second browser tab and typed.

A flood of thumbnails and news links dotted my screen. Pulling up the first map, I lined it up on my screen next to Tucker's.

"It's the oil pipeline," I said out loud, sitting back in the chair with my eyes on the screen. "I'll be damned."

The planned route ran right along the path of Tuck's stars.

One answer. A dozen questions right behind it.

I drummed two fingers on the edge of the laptop.

"Why did he think anyone would care that the pipeline was set to run through these particular places?" I dropped my head back and stared at the ceiling like Tuck was going to pop down and explain.

In a place where there's a Civil War or a Revolutionary something or other in spitting distance pretty much everywhere, plenty of people might have a problem with a pipeline digging through history.

I found a map on the historical society's website and put it next to Tucker's. The black line snaked through almost a dozen marked sites—all of them close enough to gold stars for me to think I could be onto something.

I shifted in the chair, resisting the urge to pump my fist in the air. If Tuck really had something that might stop the pipeline, it definitely could've cost him his life. And the coroner's offhand comment about the bullet trajectory had haunted me all day. Whoever knelt down in front of Tucker Armstrong to shoot him in the head wanted to look him in the eyes as he died. That was decidedly not normal drug dealer MO.

Before I could find my notes on the body to consider that further, my phone binged a text arrival. Parker. Finally. I snatched it up and touched the message.

They haven't heard from her in weeks. Her mother is borderline hysterical and her father is talking about buying a gun and going over to Hull Street.

9

Holy Manolos.

What the hell is going on here, Clarke? Is your street clear yet?

I tapped letters with my thumbs. *Street, yes. Driveway, no.*

Buzz. *My car has all-wheel drive. I'll be there in 15.*

I stood, sliding the phone into my pocket and moving to the front of the house to look out the window. A winter wonderland sparkled in grayish, low-cloud-filtered sunshine. Smooth, pillowy snow covered my front steps and yard, and every neighbor's yard as far down the block as I could see. It never got old, and I couldn't imagine ever not loving it. But I didn't own a shovel, and I didn't have time to be trapped by it.

"Where are all the broke teenagers when you need them?" I muttered, going to the bedroom to get actual clothes before Parker arrived.

I pulled on sleek, stretchy black slacks and a soft pink sweater before I slipped my feet into low, chestnut Nicholas Kirkwood booties and went back to the kitchen to brew more coffee. Snow days are good for coffee.

I added an extra pump of my favorite sugar-free white mocha syrup to Parker's cup as he opened my kitchen door and stomped snow off his boots, a blast of frigid air following him into the house. He pushed the door shut and pulled off the navy knit cap covering his blond hair.

"You read my mind." He took the cup with a smile, wiping his feet on the mat before he stepped onto the faded yellow linoleum floor.

"I wish I could do that with my cops," I said, waving my free hand at a chair. "How is it that you can wear a stocking cap and not have it screw up your hair?"

He flashed the grin that made every woman I knew who'd passed puberty want to call for smelling salts. "Good genes, I guess."

His brow furrowed over the rim of the cup as he tested the temperature and took a sip.

"This is about more than Katie having a drug problem." I didn't bother making it sound like a question, taking the chair opposite him and crossing my legs at the knee before I set my mug on the table.

Parker set his down too, his chest puffing out with a deep breath. "I tried to tell Nate," he began.

Wait. What?

"Did she have a drug problem before he died?" Boy, had I read this all wrong.

Parker just stared back at me, his eyes wide and sad.

Oh, hell.

"Before he married her," I said. Puzzle pieces rained into place. "Damn, Parker."

"It would've ruined his career for people to know. He sent her to the best hospitals in the country, always during the off season when he could make sure it stayed quiet. Every time, she did great for a few months, and then..." He ran his long fingers through his hair. Every strand fell right back into place. It would be annoying if I weren't so fond of him. That's what his wife said, too.

"Did he know about this before they got married?" I asked.

"He loved her. I didn't get it until I started seeing Mel, but honestly? I'd do the same."

"Except your job doesn't require you to be gone for six months of the year anymore," I said. "That was the thing, right? She did well, and then the season started and he was gone all the time and she backslid."

"Yep. Nate tried cutting off her avenues, he notified every pharmacy in the state, threatened to sue so many doctors he could've put a hospital out of business, but she'd just find other places to buy. It's fucking ridiculous how easy it is to get that shit. It seems her old teacher had some connections."

Tuck.

Parker called Katie's parents his friends. Parker was my friend, and I wanted to keep it that way. Tread carefully.

"Did her parents know that?"

"About Tuck? Sure they did. Not until after Nate died, though—she'd learned to do a good job of hiding it. But after the funeral, she spiraled. They moved her home. It lasted a few months and she took off."

I reached for a pen.

"This is off the record." Parker put his hands up.

I rolled my eyes. "Of course. I just want to make sure I'm keeping my facts straight."

He pinched the bridge of his nose between his thumb and forefinger. "I'm sorry. I just...I'm not sure how to handle this, you know? If it's all over the paper that Nate's widow is a junkie, what does that do to his memory? To the foundation the Generals set up for him? He was a good kid, Clarke. We weren't best friends or anything, but I liked him and he had a hell of a promising future."

I knew all that. It was why I'd told Bob yesterday I might piss Parker off with the story I'd had planned. Watching the way he'd cradled Katie in his arms when he carried her away from the scene the night her husband died was the first time I'd realized he wasn't just a superficial self-centered asshat.

But my gut was coiling around the coffee in a way that made me squirm in my chair because I was afraid I might not have a choice now. Or at some point, at least.

"And did they know she'd been staying with Tuck and helping him with some sort of project—at least I'm pretty sure she was—until a few weeks ago?"

Parker shrugged. "All I know is that they can't find her and they're worried sick over it."

"Did she talk with them regularly?"

"They pay for her phone, so they can track her with the GPS. When it disappeared off their radar for several days in a row they panicked. But what cop cares about a missing junkie, especially when the department is running on holiday manpower?"

I tapped a finger on my phone. "I know one who does." Brooks hadn't seemed to think it was out of the ordinary for Katie to disappear for days at a time, and there were a million possibilities for why her phone dropped off the map: maybe she traded it for a fix, maybe she lost it or dropped it in the toilet or didn't have a charger.

But the likely answer there kind of depended on which one of us was right about Tuck.

Because listening to Parker, my gut said Katie DeLuca's father might have cause to want to look the man in the eye as he put a bullet in his head.

Coming up on a decade covering cops and courts—with a handful of homicide collars to my credit—I knew one thing for sure: murder is the most personal crime there is.

Even in murder-for-hire, there's an intimate element mixed up in the case somewhere. Hitmen usually have a broken compassion receptor or five, but the people who pay them are almost always fueled by passion—be it fury, jealousy, or the ever-popular greed.

What I couldn't tell, sitting at my kitchen table staring down my worried friend, was which of the geese congregating around this case I should chase first.

Brooks thought it was a simple drug addict issue, not much different to him than the overdoses that had claimed three lives since Christmas. He cared about Tuck, and I had no doubt he was working his ass off hunting for a lead on what had happened to him. But I didn't know if he was looking in the right place.

Landers thought he had some sort of serial/vigilante situation, best I could tell, but his suspected motive was also drugs.

And then there was me: not convinced this was related to either of the things the cops were looking at.

Drug dealers talk a big game to make sure they get paid, since they don't have the most financially stable or trustworthy clientele. But when it comes down to it, killing a customer isn't in their best interest—a dead customer means lost income. If it's going to happen it usually follows the same lines as a pimp murdering a prostitute: violent, bloody, and very public. Whoever killed Tuck wasn't looking to make an example of him with one shot clean through his head in that locked motel room. So my gut said Brooks and Landers were wrong.

But my guys weren't exactly bumbling idiots, and most cops like their secrets. Not knowing what I didn't know left me with too many trails—standing at the mental intersection wondering which led to the killer.

Finding Katie DeLuca seemed to be the key to blocking a couple of them off.

So that's where we would start.

I picked up my phone and stared at the favorites list on my screen for so long it went dark.

"Clarke?" Parker put a hand over my free one.

I swallowed, as much as one can with a mouth drier than an El Paso creek bed in August, and touched Kyle's name.

Three rings. I started to hang up before it went to voicemail when he picked up.

"Nicey? Is everything okay?"

He sounded worried. Which immediately sent my thoughts to Joey. But I couldn't talk about Joey in front of Parker.

"I'm okay. But I could use your computer access to check on someone," I said. I didn't want to ask my guys at the PD about Katie until I had more than a hunch she might know why or how Tuck died—and until I knew where she was and why her folks couldn't find her. The holidays are hard when you're grieving. If she was on a bender somewhere, Detective By the Book Landers would feel compelled to book her on possession. Shelby might have missed one arrest report, but a second one with "DeLuca" on it skating by her was unlikely. She'd proofread Parker's columns and my stories for too many years to not recognize it. Damned if I was doing the legwork on this so she could print it first.

"What's up?"

"There was a homicide yesterday at the Hideaway Motel on Hull

Street," I said. "The last person to see the victim alive besides the killer is missing. I'd like to talk with her, but I need to find her first."

"Credit cards?" I heard keys clicking in the background.

I covered the mic with my hand and whispered the question to Parker. He shook his head. "Her dad said she used to have a card on one of his accounts, but he canceled it because he was trying to make her come home or go back to treatment."

"Is that Grant?" Kyle asked.

I removed my hand. "Kyle says hi, Parker."

"Hey man, you shouldn't be such a stranger," Parker called. "Come hang out sometime. I'll even watch the Cowboys with you and Nicey."

Kyle let it pass without comment.

"He works too much," I said.

"Look who's talking." Parker snorted.

"Hey now." I laughed. "Besides, Kyle doesn't like watching football with me. I yell too much."

"You really do," Parker said. "But I spent a lot of years on the pitcher's mound ignoring screaming fans. I tune you out."

Kyle laughed in my ear.

"Anyway. No credit cards." I steered back to Katie. "And no car."

"Then we'd need a last location to know where to start," Kyle said. "Because we're trying to piece together a timeline from photos and surveillance footage. Do you know when and where she was last seen?"

I started to shake my head and stopped.

"What?" Parker asked.

"Her parents could tell us the last place her phone was before it went off the grid. That has to help."

"It's a starting point," Kyle said. "But you know, White and Landers could run these same checks."

I pinched my lips together and stayed quiet.

"Except you don't want to ask them to," Kyle said after five beats. "How come?"

"It's kind of a special case," I said, my eyes on Parker. "I'd rather not pull her into their investigation if I'm wrong and there's no compelling reason to."

"That's not a whole answer." Kyle sighed. "But I have a pretty good handle on what it took for you to call me today. Find out where the phone was and send it to me with a recent photo. I'll see what I can do."

"Thanks, Kyle."

"No promises," he cautioned.

"I appreciate you trying." I forced sunshine into my voice. "Everything okay there?"

Kyle knew me well enough to know that "there" didn't have a damned thing to do with him. I shouldn't have said it at all, but I couldn't make myself not say it. "As far as I know," he said. "I um...I don't know how to..."

"It's okay. Me neither." Kyle and I would have time to work through our personal bullshit later. "I'll send you the location when I have it. Thanks, Kyle." My voice softened. Whatever I might think of his methods, Kyle hadn't spent a breath of his whole life not trying to do the right thing. We were in a weird place, but we'd find a way past it just like we always had. "I really appreciate it."

"Always here for a friend."

I clicked off the call.

Parker stood. "I'll drive."

"Probably best. Most Texans know as much about driving on snow as I know about comfortable shoes."

Buckled into the passenger seat of Parker's BMW, I listened to the melodic computer voice direct him toward Katie's parents' home and drummed my fingers on the armrest.

This would work. Katie DeLuca was the person closest to Tuck, at least lately. So if someone was after him—no matter what the reason—she should know. We just had to convince her to tell us.

Ward and Marjorie Olsen were quite possibly the nicest, most quintessential middle-aged suburban couple I'd ever met.

Marjorie was the more talkative of the two, offering me coffee and complimenting everything from my messy bun to my muted-for-me shoes. I even felt a little bad, watching them for cues—Parker told them I wanted to help find their daughter, which was true. But I also couldn't help wanting to know if one of them might be a murderer.

Sitting in a pale pink Queen Anne armchair in their living room watching Ward nurse a cup he'd treated with a generous splash of Jameson, I couldn't imagine Katie's father swatting a fly, let alone looking a man in the eyes and blowing his brains all over a dingy motel room wall.

"Our Katie is a good kid." Drops of desperation clung to the words like Ward Olsen was trying to convince himself as much as us. His soft gray cardigan was loose enough to look baggy on his thin frame, adding a measure of frailty that made me feel sorry for him.

I leaned forward and took a fresh cup of coffee from Marjorie, the warm liquid welcome in the chilly room. "Mr. Olsen, I'm sure she is. Parker here has a pretty good people radar, and generally doesn't entangle himself with bad ones. It's important for you to understand that my end game here isn't to get Katie in trouble. I just think she might know something about what happened to Tucker Armstrong, and I'd like a chance to ask her about him."

"I want her to come home." Marjorie's voice quavered on the last word. "It's not like her to just disappear. Katie has battled her demons, but she knows how much I worry."

I watched her face so intently I forgot I was holding the cup until it started to sear my fingertips. She wasn't lying. And as someone who also had a mother with a tendency to worry, I was suddenly concerned about Katie in an entirely different way.

"That's what we'd like, too, and Nichelle's friend is a federal agent," Parker said. "He's offered to help us look for Katie and try to get her home safely."

I flicked my eyes toward him. Kyle hadn't gone that far, but I supposed sending a super cop to look for their kid sounded more promising than having a reporter with good taste in shoes and a sportswriter who had once been a baseball star on the case.

"But he's not going to..." Marjorie paused. "You know, take her to jail? Because we can't get her out if that happens. It took every bit we could scrape up the first time, and with Christmas, we haven't had a chance to replenish our savings account."

I shook my head. "Kyle isn't the kind of cop who arrests addicts, ma'am. His job is to go after people supplying dangerous things to the American public and breaking the law in the process. Katie's not in any danger of going to jail because of Kyle."

Ward pulled his cell phone from his pocket. He tapped the screen a few times and then handed it to Parker. I leaned over Parker's shoulder, stretching so far I nearly tipped my chair over sideways.

Ward's thin, older model iPhone had a cracked screen. Under the split, a map pin marked the last place Katie's phone had been tracked.

"I went down there and looked everywhere, every bench, every alley. She had to have been looking for something, being down there that time of the night."

Parker cut his eyes to me as Katie's father spoke, but made no other gesture of disagreement.

My eyes stayed on the screen, because I knew what he was thinking, and I knew what the Olsens were thinking, and it wasn't the same thing I was thinking.

Capitol Square.

The last place Katie's phone was tracked was near the Virginia senate office building. At just after eleven p.m. on December 31.

Maybe she was looking to score, it being New Year's Eve and all.

Or maybe she was looking for a new senator who'd been moving into his office that day, because Tucker knew the senator and wanted to talk to him about the pipeline.

I liked my theory best for a lot of reasons, but I couldn't share it.

"Mrs. Olsen, when was the last time you saw Katie?" I asked.

"Christmas." She cleared her throat, blinking rapidly. "She was sitting right in that chair where you are, opening a new scarf. I knitted it for her. The Generals team colors. For Nate. That boy—" That was all she managed before she pressed one fist to her lips, shaking her head.

"Katie's life would be so much different if he hadn't died," Ward said, taking his phone back from Parker.

Everyone nodded. There wasn't another good reply, really.

I focused on Ward. They were a good match, from where I sat. He was only quiet because she wasn't. But when she couldn't talk, he stepped in.

And he was calmly insightful. Was this really the same man Parker said was talking earlier about buying a firearm and going full on *Death Wish* on the southside opioid scene?

"Mr. Olsen, did Katie say anything about Tuck when you saw her last? Anything at all?"

"She said he was thirty days clean on Christmas Day," Marjorie said when her husband shook his head. "And that he was a good soul who never should have gotten sucked into that mess."

"Katie would know about that."

I flinched at the edge in Ward's voice that hadn't been there before.

Marjorie laid a hand on her husband's arm, and he shook it off.

I let the silence stretch before I eyed them in turn. "What am I missing?"

Marjorie shook her head. Ward kept his eyes straight ahead.

Parker sighed.

My eyes made the rounds of the room twice more before I got it.

"Oh." It popped out before I could stop it.

Parker twisted in his chair, putting a hand out to squeeze mine. "Nichelle, wait a minute. Let me explain."

"Grant, honey, please—" Marjorie stopped when Parker raised his other hand her direction.

"She'll figure it out. It's what she does best. I promise, it's better to just give her everything you know up front."

Marjorie's fist went back to her lips, but it didn't keep the sob in this time.

"Ward wouldn't hurt anyone, Nichelle. Not really."

"But Tucker Armstrong got Katie hooked on pills? Is that what I'm hearing?"

"Yes," Ward bit out as his wife sniffled a hitching "Not exactly."

"Which is it?" I asked.

"She took some at a party when she was in college without knowing what she was taking," Parker said.

"Goddamn fraternity parties." Ward's voice had gone from calm and pleasant to a downright gravelly growl. And his face was red. Maybe I could see him swatting that fly after all.

"It would be highly unusual for her to be addicted from one dose," I said.

"But it wasn't one. It was several, at different parties," Ward said. "She thought it was recreational. They smashed them down into powder and put them in the girls' drinks to..."

"Yes, sir," I interrupted. "I get it. But was Tuck at a fraternity party?"

Parker shook his head.

"He was her favorite teacher," Marjorie said. "Our Katie—she started a neighborhood recycling contest when she was in the third grade, and saved up her allowance to buy the prizes with her own money. God help me if I ever walked into the house with a Styrofoam cup. Saving the planet was her thing. She should have been nominated for the Nobel Prize by now."

"Except that Dr. Armstrong was her favorite professor," Ward cut in.

"But you just said she became addicted to the painkillers from exposure at parties."

Marjorie nodded. "She started buying them from a boy in the fraternity."

I didn't need to know who Katie's dealer was. I needed to know why this mild-mannered, sweet little man who managed a grocery store for a living looked ready to kill someone now that we were talking about Tuck.

"Armstrong was already hooked. He found out Katie was too and started sharing his stash with her because he didn't want her..." Parker paused. "Well, she could have gotten busted, dealing with the frat kid."

Ten-four. I looked back at her parents.

"He was an adult. A teacher. He could have called us, tried to get her help," Ward spat. "Instead, by the time we found out about this, it was way too late."

"It's not too late," Marjorie said. "Don't say that."

Ward's Adam's apple bobbed with a hard swallow and he stopped talking.

Before I could get another question out, the doorbell rang.

"Probably the Peterson kid wanting to shovel the drive." Ward's voice was flat. Resigned. "I'll remind him that we have a snow blower." He stood and disappeared.

Marjorie leaned across the table, her coffee cup shaking in her hands to the point of spilling over before she set it down.

"I know what you have to be thinking, Miss Clarke, but my husband has been home all week. Ward couldn't kill anyone."

She'd likely be surprised at how easy it can be in the moment for a person to lose their shit and not be able to pull it back before they land a fatal blow. But I had bigger things to worry about.

Like Chris Landers and Brooks following Ward back into the living room.

"Told you she was good at this stuff," Landers muttered to Brooks.

Ward didn't even look a little ruffled. Was he about to go to jail on suspicion of murder?

"Nichelle, Parker," Landers said, putting out a hand to shake Parker's extended one. "I'm afraid I'm going to have to ask you to leave. Open investigation."

He didn't give one damn about the open investigation. And I was already sitting there, talking with the Olsens, which meant he didn't even care what I knew. Besides, if he had some evidence he was about to use to arrest Katie's father, I wanted to see.

Parker stood.

I kept my seat, folding my arms slowly over my chest.

It wasn't Landers's house, and the Olsens hadn't asked us to go anywhere.

Landers held my gaze until he blinked. "Whatever."

He reached for his pocket. But instead of cuffs, he produced a notebook.

"Mr. and Mrs. Olsen, I need to speak with your daughter. Right now. If you know where she is or she's in this house, please either tell me or bring her into the room."

"What's this about, Officer?" Marjorie's voice wobbled, but she held it together.

I couldn't look away from the envelope I'd just spotted in Brooks's hand. Landers took it from him and opened it. "She's a suspect in the murder of Tucker Armstrong. We have a warrant for her arrest."

10

Few things can suck the air out of a room like an arrest warrant.

We could have heard an ant sneeze for a full minute before all nine rings of hell broke loose.

"Get the fuck out of my house!" Ward Olsen bellowed, leaping to his feet with speed and strength I wouldn't have given him credit for if I hadn't seen it with my own eyes.

"No. No, Katie wouldn't have. She couldn't have." Marjorie's thin arms wrapped around her chest tightly, her fingers sinking into her shoulders.

As Marjorie began to rock back and forth in her seat, I stood and put my hand out. "May I see that, Detective?"

"Do you live here, Clarke?" Landers shot back.

I shifted my weight to my back foot and folded my arms across my chest, arching one eyebrow. I didn't need to add the "really?" to make my point.

Landers ran one hand through his unruly bronze curls and glanced around the room before he thrust the papers at me. I skimmed the first page and flipped to the second, looking for the evidence they'd used to get a judge to issue the thing.

There.

"I said, get out of my house." Ward Olsen was a bit quieter that time, but his veins were pulsing. I flicked my eyes toward him as Parker stood and laid a large hand on the older man's arm when he started toward Landers. "Nichelle? What does it say?"

"They found a gun," I said.

"And the prints all over it are definitely Katie's," Landers added. "Where is she?"

"We don't know." Marjorie's half-whisper was so faint I almost missed it.

"Mrs. Olsen, harboring a fugitive is a very ser—" Landers began, and Katie's father bristled again.

"My wife is not a liar," he said. "Call her one again and I'll throw you out myself." He shook off Parker's arm and Brooks's hand landed on the butt of his gun.

Shit.

I shot back to my feet, extending hands to both sides of the room and focusing on the cops first.

"Gentlemen, there are a lot of emotions running high here, and everyone needs to breathe for a minute so we can sort this out."

"We?" Landers echoed.

I wasn't at a crime scene or in police headquarters, I was an invited guest in the Olsens' home and he didn't have the authority to make me leave. I needed to get a handle on what the hell was happening here. Right quick.

"Officers, the Olsens don't know where to find their daughter. I came here looking for her for a different reason, and I believe they're telling the truth about that."

"Keeping her hidden keeps her out of jail," Landers said, his eyes on Ward.

"If I thought she was going to go to jail for long enough to really detox I would happily hand her over to you." Ward's calm, flat words snapped his wife's head up like it was on a spring.

He shoved his hands into the pockets of his cardigan, sending Brooks's back to his gun. Ward clearly wasn't hiding a weapon in his Mr. Rogers sweater, so my eyes lingered on Brooks. He hadn't stricken me as quite so high strung the day before.

Brooks stayed so still I couldn't have sworn he was breathing, glancing at Landers before he let go of the gun.

Maybe I ought to go get that coffee with him after all.

I returned my attention to Ward, who didn't seem bothered by the daggers his wife was staring at his throat.

"I just told you I didn't want your federal agent friend to arrest her because it didn't do any damned good last time," he said to me before he shot an angry glare at Brooks. "You picked her up and kept her for less than a week before she was right back out."

Hang on. I felt my jaw loosen. Marjorie's small hands balled into tight fists.

Parker said it first. "You had your own daughter arrested?" He dropped Olsen's arm and stepped back like he wanted a shower on the basis of proximity.

"We sent her to hospitals. Nate sent her to hospitals." Ward swept an arm wide at the threadbare carpet and aging furniture. "There's no more money for hospitals. But my Katie, she's a strong girl when she has a chance. She can get better. If we could just get her away from it." Ward's chin dropped to his chest, and his entire body deflated, shoulders hunching in to half their width, spine slouching forward.

Before anyone could speak, Marjorie leapt from the couch and swung a wide right hook, laying her husband out in one blink-and-you'd-miss-it motion. Parker jumped backward out of the line of fire. Ward hit the carpet, but not before he caught his head on the scarred oak end table on the way down. A strangled scream escaped his throat as his eyes rolled toward the inside of his skull and fluttered shut.

"Un-fucking-believable," Landers muttered, shouldering past me and kneeling next to Ward while Brooks hovered near Marjorie. "Get me some towels," Landers barked at Parker, who looked thrilled to have a mission that required him to leave the room as he hustled to the kitchen.

I gripped the back of the chair and watched the Olsen family disintegrate right in front of our eyes. Marjorie was shaking so hard I wasn't sure how she stayed on her feet, but she wasn't crying, and she made no move to check on her husband.

I couldn't exactly pull out a notebook or a camera, but I also wasn't in danger of forgetting a detail. This—the years of stress and anxiety and endless, endless worry: this was the story behind the overdoses and the murders. The families and marriages and frayed, broken souls that were the quiet, unseen victims of the opioid crisis.

This was water-cooler-worthy stuff. I knew because my gut was twisted around a million butterflies, and the backs of my eyes stung with a promise that I wouldn't make it through the piece without crying.

It was one of the saddest things I'd ever witnessed. And in my line of work, that's saying something. It's the nature of my job to be an outsider, always observing, recording, telling the story fairly from both sides. But some days, with some stories, I landed in the big middle of intensely personal moments. Things no outsider is ever supposed to see. When observer became intruder, I had to fight the urge to back quietly out of the room. It was a fine line to walk, between what the public needed to know and outright gossip. The hardest part was staying put. Watching as the blood pooled under Ward's head, the threadbare carpet doing little to absorb it. Brooks called for an ambulance.

Marjorie kept shaking, her face twisted by a massive convergence of every emotional wringer her daughter's addiction had ever put her through.

I put my hand out toward her. Observer, intruder, and impartiality all be damned, I couldn't not—my mother would look the same in this woman's shoes. She would worry herself sick and land herself in the poorhouse trying to save me. But Marjorie wasn't looking at me.

Her eyes were locked on her husband. And Landers, pulling off his RPD jacket and using it to apply pressure to the wound when Parker didn't make it back with towels fast enough.

Her face changed. But it happened too fast. I didn't process the raw fury in time to stop her.

Marjorie Olsen—all ninety pounds of her—raised both arms and pounced on Landers, yanking him over backward and clawing blood out of his cheek with her long, yellowing fingernails.

Brooks whipped his weapon free, locking his elbows and bellowing for her to freeze. I wasn't even sure she heard him.

"Brooks, no!" I jumped between them.

His finger flinched on the trigger. "Move, Nichelle." It came out in a growl, his eyes still locked over my shoulder on Landers.

A noise behind me made me spin, and Parker burst through the door to the kitchen with a dish cloth and a roll of paper towels.

"This was all I could—" He stopped when his eyes landed on Marjorie, who had wrapped her legs around Landers's waist and locked the crook of her elbow around his throat in a choke hold.

"What the fuck?" I think Parker said it, but every conscious person in the room was thinking it.

I dove for Marjorie, Landers's reddening face and bulging eyes searing themselves onto the backs of my eyelids. My knees hit the carpet hard, my arm looping around her waist as I rolled away from Landers, dragging her off his back and over my front.

She was not pleased.

A screech worthy of a banshee ripped from her throat, my shins and ribs taking blows from spike-sharp heels and elbows. I locked both arms around her middle and held on. Brooks holstered his weapon and moved to my side, catching her forearm and her eyes. "Mrs. Olsen, I'm going to need you to calm down."

I squeezed tighter when she lunged again, and the fight went out of her with the breath. Brooks pulled her off me and she slumped into a puddle of pink jogging suit and tears on the floor, twisting her hands in her hair and sobbing.

Brooks didn't back up, keeping a wary eye on her but not moving for his gun again.

I sat up, and Parker stepped up behind me and put one hand under each of my arms, lifting me to my feet. I winced at a twinge in my side. "Thanks."

"What the hell happened there?" His voice was low, just for my ears, his eyes flicking between Ward, who was stirring with Landers staunching the blood flow from his head, and Marjorie, who had gone still save for the hiccups shaking her shoulders every few seconds.

"She went after...well, her husband, I think. I think she was trying to keep Landers from helping him." I shook my head slowly. "Years of this had to have put incredible pressure on them both."

I glanced at Brooks. "Did he really come to you and ask for Katie to be arrested before?"

"I liked her. Tuck liked her. We wanted to help her. So we helped him. She didn't go easily, either. She has a temper and a mean right hook." He rubbed his chin at the memory. "But he's right, she just got right back out. Pretty young girl—the judge took one look at her and let her go on bail because she wasn't deemed a danger."

Except maybe to Tucker Armstrong.

"Why didn't you tell me that yesterday?" I asked.

"I didn't really think it was important. It never occurred to me that Kay —Katie, Landers said her name is—would hurt Tuck, or anyone else." He jerked his head to Marjorie's prone form. "Like mother like daughter, I guess."

Was that why he was so quick to draw his gun on a middle-aged mom? Because he thought her daughter was a murderer? I guess from where he sat, that probably made perfect sense. I'd worked closely with enough cops to know they see the world through a different lens than most people. Every encounter, every day, can go sideways and end up with someone dead. When you really don't want it to be you, drawing the gun at the first sign of danger might not be policy, but it's a security blanket of sorts. The problem is, in a crisis situation, split-second decisions aren't always clear-headed. Which leaves a whole lot of room for deadly screwups.

"Where did y'all find the gun?"

"A sweep of the alley last night. It was in a dumpster not far from the back of the Hideaway."

"You can't possibly have ballistics back. Not yet," I said. "How do you know this was the weapon that killed Tuck?"

"The coroner estimates Armstrong was shot with a .38. It's a .38. It has fingerprints of a known acquaintance on it. Whoever killed him locked the door, took the key, and blended in well enough that nobody registered anything out of the ordinary. You get different math there than we do? Or than the judge did?"

I tapped one foot, my eyes finding a photo of Katie, one arm around Nate's waist and one around her dad's, smiling in front of the Cinderella

Castle at Disney World. Could she really have knelt and looked her old teacher and mentor in the face as she killed him?

It takes a special kind of icy blood to do something like that. I didn't see it. Didn't mean I couldn't be wrong—it happens way more often than I'd like—but if they found her first, she'd spend the rest of her life in a cell whether the state decided the cutoff date or not, because Brooks was right. His answer was the easy one. A judge had bought it enough to issue an arrest warrant. My friend DonnaJo at the Commonwealth's attorney's office was plenty capable of making sure a jury bought it, too.

I didn't mind that, as long as they were right.

As paramedics flooded the Olsens' living room and began working on Ward, Landers ambled over, ignoring the blood on his cheek but rubbing at the darkening bruise on his throat. "The whole fucking family is nuts," he said. "You really don't know where the girl is, Clarke? Why didn't you tell us you knew her?"

"I didn't realize I did until after I spoke to you guys yesterday, and I wanted to see if a mutual friend could get her to agree to talk to me about what Tuck had been so worked up about." I jerked a thumb toward Parker. "Mutual friend."

"I don't think what the vic was writing people about matters much at this point." Landers signaled one of the medics, pointing to Marjorie. "I'm going to need her checked out so I can put her in the back of my cruiser."

"Seriously?" Parker blurted.

"He doesn't have a choice," I said. "She attacked a police officer. That makes her dangerous. If he leaves it because he feels bad for her and she hurts someone, he could lose his badge."

Landers went on like neither of us had spoken, pulling out cuffs and kneeling to snap them onto Marjorie's wrists when the medic gave the all-clear. He and Brooks half-carried her to the foyer. Landers looked back. "Clarke. If you find this woman before I do and you don't notify me immediately, I'll take you in for obstruction."

Did he think Katie killed his other victims, too?

Parker slung an arm around my shoulders. "Not what I had in mind when I came to pick you up," he said.

"My days are just a regular bushel of fun." I winced when a deep breath made my ribs twinge.

"Let's get you some ice, there, right tackle." He waved me out the front door behind the medics rolling Ward Olsen out on a gurney.

I watched the snow-washed city blur past the windows as he drove carefully over wet, sometimes still-slick roads. The more I thought about it, the more things bothered me. Landers had seemed convinced yesterday he had a vigilante serial. Suddenly he had pegged Katie DeLuca on the Armstrong murder, and maybe the others, too? Either he'd lied to me yesterday, or he wasn't telling the whole truth now, but something wasn't right.

I had to find Katie before he did.

11

Parker ushered me to the sofa, handed me my computer, and disappeared. Three ticks later, he returned with a big Ziploc bag full of snow.

"Easier to mold around your side."

I took it, smooshing the baggie into place. "Smart. Thanks, Parker. Sorry if I wrecked your snow day."

"I know a thing or two about icing collision injuries," he said. "You don't throw as many pitches as I did without taking a couple of line drives straight back at the mound. A broken rib is a bitch, but better than a broken face." He smiled. "And I'm always glad to help. I think I still owe you a couple hundred before we begin to approach even."

I reached for my water bottle, perched on the end table, still half full from yesterday. "Tell Mel I miss her."

"We should do something soon." He walked to the arch that led to the hallway. "I could find you a date, if you want."

His voice was so gentle it didn't even sound much like him, the way most people would speak to a frightened child. I'd heard it once before, at the river the night Nate DeLuca died: it was how Parker talked to Katie.

It still sounded foreign coming out of his mouth. But I appreciated the words and the intent behind them.

"Not necessary. But if y'all don't mind a third wheel, count me in." I winced when I tried to take more than a shallow breath. "This better not be broken."

"Rest it. And don't piss that cop off. He sounded serious when he said he'd put you in jail."

I couldn't argue that convincingly, so I just waved as he disappeared.

I went to work typing in everything I'd learned since I left the house. The stars of this show were Katie's last known location being Capitol Square, Landers's almost smoking gun, Brooks's seemingly uncharacteristic trigger happiness, and Marjorie Olsen's temper. Leaving the Olsen house, I saw I'd missed a text from my friend Jacque at the morgue, but she'd spent the holidays with her family in North Carolina, so she didn't have an answer to offer on the other two shootings beyond *we're backlogged, but I can ask around.*

I was not nearly as convinced as Chris Landers seemed to be that this case was closing. But thinking that and proving it are very different animals.

I tapped a nail slowly on the edge of the keyboard, my eyes on the screen. Dammit, I missed my sounding boards. I ought to be pacing a hole in the rug and talking to Joey until I figured out which thing I needed to track down first.

Normally, absent Joey, I would've called...

Kyle.

I picked up my phone and touched the text message icon. I had to scroll way down to find his name.

Felt weird. But I didn't have time for my personal issues.

Tuck's obsession with the pipeline, the connection I'd seen to the new senator, and Katie's last known location being near the capitol added up to more than interesting—it was flat-out suspicious. Trouble was, I already knew it wasn't going to be suspicious to anyone but me. Tuck, no matter what else he'd done or how much Brooks liked him, was a junkie to everyone who had say-so in this. Which meant no matter how well-intentioned or kind they were, the conditional biases of their work prevented them from caring as much about his death as they would a lot of other people's. Same for Katie's freedom, when you got right down to it. Landers thought he had it figured out, and maybe he was right—I didn't know enough to argue that either way.

The thing was, Landers didn't either.

The only way I could see to the truth—whatever it might be—was Katie DeLuca. And the only prayer I had of finding Katie without Landers's help was Kyle.

I touched the screen and started typing.

Katie DeLuca's last known location was Capitol Square.

I waited for the dots to pop up.

They weren't there long. *What the hell are you trying to get yourself into now? Haven't you had enough of politicians?*

I'm not sure the politician is the bad guy here.

I had read a fair amount about Rowley. If he was crooked, he was damned good at hiding it, and in the age of the internet wannabe investigative reporters and bitterly divided politics, that's harder to do than people imagine.

But you think this woman disappeared from Capitol Square.

You asked me to get you the location. I got you the location. Beyond that, I'm trying to figure out what I think.

Buzz. *10-4. There is no shortage of cameras in that area. Date and time?*

I looked at my notes. *December 31, between 11 and midnight.*

I'll let you know what I can find.

I paused, just for a second. I didn't want to tell him. But I had to.

Kyle. I hit send before I should have.

The screen was still for a minute before a reply buzzed in. *Nicey?*

The RPD is looking for her, too. They have an arrest warrant. Suspicion of murder. I sighed as I touched the send arrow.

My phone buzzed immediately, not a text but a call.

"Um. What?" Kyle's voice was tight when I lifted the phone to my ear. "You didn't tell me I was helping you hunt a suspect here. I can't piss them off by big-footing their case. It wouldn't be a good thing for anyone if I did that right now."

I skipped right past the worrisome drop in his tone on the last bit because I needed his help to find Katie. I couldn't access state camera footage without him.

"First, I didn't know she was a suspect when I called you this morning. Landers showed up at her parents' home with a warrant while Parker and I were talking to them and everything went straight to hell without passing Go. So I did tell you, as soon as I knew."

"How did he get the warrant? Did you look at it?"

"He's got her prints on a gun, but no ballistics."

"Backlog at the lab?"

"No shells at the scene," I said.

"Ah. So you don't think she did it." He sounded more annoyed than surprised.

"I actually don't know what I think about that. Picking up the casings smacks of professional. But maybe she just watches too much *NCIS*. The only thing I'm pretty sure of at this point is that I need to talk to her."

"Why not just let Landers bring her in and then go do that?"

My head started shaking before he got the last words out.

"He's being weird, Kyle. I'm not sure why I think that's a lousy idea, but I do. Like, past my gut in my bones. I can't even think it and sit still." I squirmed on the sofa cushion like he could see me.

A long sigh hissed through the speaker into my ear. "My boss has been up my ass with a microscope since he found out I had an informant I didn't take through proper channels, so I have to be careful. But let me check the cameras and see what I get."

Joey was the informant. And having been kept in the dark about that arrangement right along with Special Agent in Charge Derek MacAulay, I could understand his irritation. "Thank you."

"You want to talk now?" Kyle's question came out quietly.

Nope.

"We're good." I forced brightness into the words and hated myself for it because I knew he could tell it wasn't authentic.

What I wanted to know was that Joey was safe and warm and as happy as I was, at least, with our current situation. And Kyle couldn't tell me any of that because he couldn't talk to him, either. Joey was working for Kyle as an informant in a case that was bigger than anything I had ever even imagined. And when his chivalrous side got the better of him last fall, he'd compromised everything about the case, put himself in very real danger of going to prison for manslaughter, and put his life at risk as a bonus, if the wrong people found out what he'd really been up to for the preceding year.

We didn't know how much they knew, since Joey was Kyle's inside man and Joey was basically currently on the federal government-sponsored lam. At least I thought the government was sponsoring it—Kyle swore he'd been shut out of the loop, which left me without much in the way of facts. MacAulay was Kyle's version of Bob—a veteran mentor who trusted Kyle and looked the other way when risky behavior caused trouble. Until he found out about Joey. Kyle had come within a breath of losing his career for keeping a high-level informant to himself and covering up a politician's death, and MacAulay had put Joey in hiding, but he wouldn't tell Kyle where—or so Kyle said, anyway. I didn't have the energy to wonder if Kyle was lying to me again. If he did know where his boss had sent Joey or when MacAulay might let Joey come home, he didn't want to tell me, which meant pressing it would only make things more awkward.

The optimist in me wanted to believe there were other cops, other informants, and other agencies in the army of law enforcement at war with the Caccione family—people who could step in and take them down so Joey could come home. Hell, maybe we'd get our happily ever after, even.

But the disappointment loomed so threatening when I let those thoughts creep in, the idea of it not happening was enough to make me lose my breath.

And Tucker Armstrong needed me to breathe today.

So. Kyle and I were as good as we were going to be for now. That was the God's gospel truth.

Kyle didn't pry, just said he'd let me know if he found anything and hung up.

Standing, I tried a moderate breath and a small step. A twinge. Nothing major. I put Parker's homemade ice pack between the ice cube trays and a bottle of Cuervo Silver in the freezer.

Walking just slightly slower than normal back down the hallway, I paused at the linen closet for an ace bandage on the way to my room for boots.

The latter took some doing. I hadn't ventured out far in the snow since last winter, so the clunkiest, ugliest footwear I owned was well and truly buried in the back of my closet.

I dug them out, laced them up, and went to work wrapping my ribs, pulling the bandage snug and hoping for the best.

It felt almost normal when I stood, but I watched my pace and stride on the way to the car.

Parker and Jenna had packed the snow down enough going in and out of the driveway that the peekaboo rays of sunlight melted it almost clean through in the tire tracks.

All I had to do was stay in the lines. I slid behind the wheel and started the engine, not even really sure where I was going yet. What I knew that I knew was there wasn't news breaking or leads happening inside my house, and most of the city was running on skeleton crews because of the weather, which meant fewer hurdles between me and the next lead on this story.

The tires slipped twice on the way to the street, but I didn't panic, and they gripped fine once I was out of the driveway. I hung a right at the corner, heading for Hull Street and the Hideaway Motel.

Someone there had seen something. But nobody without a badge had asked them about it, and in my experience, the kind of folks who frequent places like the Hideaway don't exactly trust police officers, no matter how nice they seem. Landers and Brooks would be tied up with paperwork for a while yet.

Once I made it to Hamilton Street, the pavement was nearly dry and traffic moved at an almost-normal pace. I was probably the most cautious driver on the road, leaning forward in my seat to watch for icy patches hiding in the blacktop and gripping the steering wheel like I was trying to choke information out of it.

The lot at the motel was a pillowy white expanse of untouched snow that fairly begged for a group of kids to build their own Frosty or throw a few snowballs. For me, it was also a blaring, reflective "no parking" sign.

I rolled past to the plowed-but-empty lot at McDonald's and took a space in the front corner, noting the lack of lights on inside the building.

Seriously. Snow closes more things in the South than Christmas.

The police departments, however, aren't among them.

The lone other car in the lot was a marked Chesterfield County patrol unit, straddling three spaces and angled toward the front of the Hideaway.

Wondering if he'd been there yesterday morning, too, I walked a wide arc around the car and waved one arm in front of the windshield.

The officer inside, bundled up in a puffy coat, didn't look up from his phone. I took slow, deliberate steps to the driver's side door and tapped the window. I wasn't trying to startle him, but he flinched anyway, his smooth brow furrowing as he looked up.

I pulled my press credentials from my bag and held them up, smiling. He pressed the button to move the window down.

Leaning in, I tried not to wince when my ribs didn't want to let me bend and breathe at the same time, focusing on the cop peering out a quarter-open squad car window at me.

"Hi there, Officer"—my eyes went to the gold lettering embroidered on the front of his coat—"Hendricks. I'm Nichelle Clarke from the *T*—um, *RVA Week*." Damn. I kept doing that, even months into this new gig.

"What are you doing out here in the snow?" His voice was deep. Not unkind, but more than a little wary with a healthy pinch of curiosity.

I pushed my lips higher into a friendlier smile and lightened my tone. Curious, I could use. "I'm working on a story about the motel." I pointed. "And I hear your job is pretty much to keep the folks there on their side of the county line."

He snorted. "I suppose it is. As long as they stay there, I can't bother them, not that Richmond PD does much to slow them down."

It wasn't so much his words but his tone that made me want to reach for a notebook. But I didn't know him, and that shuts some folks right up, so I kept still.

"I'm wondering if you've seen anything terribly out of the ordinary the last couple of days?" When he wasn't looking at his phone, anyway. I didn't say that part out loud.

He tipped his head to one side. "You mean besides the cops and coroners spread all over the place yesterday?"

"Besides that."

"Couple of fancier cars than I'd drive through this neighborhood, and some guys in suits. They stick out around here."

"You didn't happen to take note of the plates, did you?"

He shook his head. "Both sports cars, one blue and one black, but they didn't come across the line." The look on his face said he'd have found a reason to pull them over if they had.

"You remember how many guys in suits? Or what kind of suits?"

"Dark suits. Two, maybe three guys. Hard to tell them apart from this distance. But one was definitely shorter than the others. Like by a whole head."

Boy, Landers had missed the boat here. He'd pointed this car out to me less than twenty-four hours ago, but he hadn't thought to come ask the guy sitting here what he'd seen? Just goes to show that even the best detectives can miss the forest when they get ass-deep in studying the individual trees in a big case.

"Thank you for your help, Officer," I said. "Stay warm out here."

"Hey, you know, if you're looking for the real story over there, you ought to start with that RPD unit that's in and out at all hours."

I spun back slowly. "I should?"

His lips disappeared into a thin line. "Listen, I'm not one to judge without all the facts, but either that guy knows something or he's doing something he shouldn't be. Or both."

12

My people radar is my greatest asset. More than my cluttered photographic memory, my ability to get people to talk, or my gift for finding gorgeous shoes at bargain basement prices online—I can tell a good human from a lousy one almost on sight. With very few exceptions.

I liked Griffin Brooks. I didn't want to think I was wrong. But I couldn't leave a question unanswered here. Katie DeLuca's freedom, or safety—or both—might depend on it.

"You know the car number?" I asked.

"Six three seven."

The one I'd just spent the day in. Damn. I thanked him again.

It took long enough to wade through the small field between the fast food joint and the motel that I couldn't feel my feet by the time I got to the edge of the parking lot.

I could feel my ribs, though. And they weren't happy with me. But I wasn't turning back now. I started in front of Tucker's room, noting a couple of pieces of yellow crime scene tape still clinging limply to the doorframe.

No answer at the three doors to the left of Tuck's. I backtracked and tried the right side.

The door on number 127 was rough under my knuckles when I rapped on it, a hollow knock reverberating in the still winter air. I took a halting step back, the rotting deck shifting under my feet like the building itself was uneasy.

The curtain over the window to the right of the door shifted. Not much, but enough for me to notice only because I was watching. I fixed my face into a pleasant, open expression and took slow breaths through my nose to tap the brakes on my racing pulse. Brooks had said nobody was here the day before.

Light footsteps. A chain lock sliding back.

I smiled, just a little, and let my arms hang at my sides.

The knob creaked as it turned. The door opened just enough of a crack for me to see a bloodshot blue eyeball almost dead-even with my own.

"Yeah?" I couldn't peg the raspy single syllable as coming from a man or woman.

"Hi. I'm Nichelle, I write for *RVA Week*. I'm working on a story about the neighborhood and am wondering if you might talk to me." Slow, light. Easy. No dead people, no cops. No promise of the fabled fifteen minutes of fame, either—I learned a long time ago that politicians aren't the only folks who don't always want their name in the newspaper.

The door didn't move. "You're not a cop." It wasn't a question.

"Correct."

"You a reporter? Like on the TV?"

"Except I work for a newspaper. I'm just trying to tell the real story of the folks who live around here."

The door slid back an inch, a shaft of gray sunshine falling on a sliver of pale, smooth skin.

I'd never seen a human so gaunt. Not upright, anyway. In the middle of the most aggressive chemo my mother had to endure, she might have approached it—but she was in a hospital bed at the time. And the girl in front of me, shivering in a threadbare T-shirt and baggy sweatpants with four holes I could see, looked like she ought to be in one, too.

She swung one impossibly bony arm. "I can't take the cold. Come in and shut the door. I assume you're asking around about Tuck?"

I slid inside and pushed the door closed quickly, throwing the lock and watching her. The room was tidy, a small igloo cooler on the desk closed tightly, the bed made even though it was clear she'd been lying on it from the rumpled spread and the thick blanket tossed to one side. The TV sat dark, a single yellowish bulb in the lamp on the night table lighting the space.

I was surprised she'd mentioned Tuck. Most folks in a place like this would wait for me to ask before they brought up the dead guy in the next room—oversharing can be particularly dangerous when people are getting shot and the only thing between you and the killer is a paper-thin wall or a half-rotten door.

She must have liked him.

She crawled back onto the bed and pulled her knees and the blanket up to her chin. "Have a seat, please. I don't really have anything to offer you in the way of refreshments, I'm afraid."

I pulled the chair around the desk to the end of the bed and settled into it. My ribs were thankful for about three seconds before they started throbbing in time with my heartbeat.

Her face was drawn, the crater-like circles under her eyes an almost unnatural shade of purplish-blue.

She was sick. I would bet my last Manolo on it.

How did she end up here? What was wrong? Why wasn't she in a hospital?

The questions jostled to be first out of my mouth and I had to bite down on them. Slow. Easy. I needed to know about Katie and Tucker, and she needed to trust me if I had any hope of getting her to open up.

"Tucker seemed like a nice man, from all the accounts I've found so far," I said. Neutral, but complimentary. Let her talk.

She coughed again. The deep, raspy rattle in her chest was loud enough for me to hear it from four feet away, her shoulders heaving in a way that looked painful. The wince on her face when she stopped said it probably was. "Sorry." She reached for a handkerchief and wiped her mouth. "That happens a lot lately. Yeah, Tuck was a good guy. Paranoid as all hell, but he had a good heart. Made for a quiet neighbor except when he took to his soapbox about the oil companies, but he only did that in the daytime, really."

Oil companies. Because of the pipeline. I liked being right, though it didn't much matter in this case unless the pipeline was the reason for Tucker's murder.

I reached into my bag for a notebook and pen. "Do you mind if I take notes?"

"I suppose you better if you want to get your story straight, right?" Her cracked lips curved up.

I returned the smile and opened the notebook to jot down what she'd already said. "Were you here yesterday morning?"

She shook her head. "I heard on the radio that it was supposed to maybe snow, and I walked up to the Stop & Shop to get milk and bread. And eggs. My grandmother used to say everyone in the South has to make French toast in the snow. I think it's a rule." She pointed to a hot plate resting on the edge of the dresser with an oil-stained skillet on the burner.

So whoever killed Tuck could have slipped in and out without being seen? But how would they know where the occupants of the nearby rooms were?

"Do you remember how long you were gone?"

"It was probably an hour and a half. Just up the street to get food and back with what I could carry." She smiled, her skin stretching too tight over her skull. "I'm slower than I used to be."

She couldn't be older than my thirty-one years. I swallowed hard. "And you didn't see anything unusual when you got back?"

"Not until the cops came screaming in there, nope." She shifted under the blanket, rolling her bent knees to the other side and grimacing.

Time to switch gears.

"How well did you know Tucker?"

She shrugged. "About as well as I know anybody." She paused. "Maybe a little better. Some of the element that runs in here, you don't really want to know, honestly. But he was a nice guy. Shitty luck, for sure. But nice. We talked. A couple times last fall we went for walks when I needed fresh air and he wanted to get some sun. He'd say he needed vitamin D to help his mood and it was priced right outside."

He wasn't always afraid to leave his room, then. I scribbled that down.

Did he ever give you any reason to think anyone would want to kill him?

That's what I wanted to say. But I had the feeling I needed to tread carefully.

"Tucker Armstrong came from a place where worrying about things like money for vitamins wasn't probably ever on his radar. But is that a fair assessment for most of the people who live here?" I asked instead.

"Does anyone really live in a place like this?" She coughed again. I waited. "I mean, people are here. They exist. But most of them have had something get screwed up—maybe a lot of somethings—pretty bad to wind up here. The thing that always makes me saddest is the kids. They didn't do nothing but get born in the wrong place. Tuck got that. He always tried to help them, teach them stuff. I think for some people being a teacher is the kind of job that's, like, part of who they are, you know? Like a calling almost. Never goes away no matter what happens to them. Hell, he even tried to teach me things about science and the planet and that kind of junk. But the kids, he wanted them to have a fair shot."

"Kids?" I hadn't seen any sign of children, not even outside in the snow-covered parking lot.

"I haven't seen any in a while, but they come and go. There were two in the room the other side of Tuck for about a week right after school started. He would sit out there with them all day, teaching them math and science stuff. He even did a couple of, like, test things. What do you call them, where they mix up stuff and it makes fizz?" She sucked in a slow breath, probably trying to avoid aggravating her cough.

"Experiments?" I asked.

"Yeah. I remember because one of them was putting some candy into a soda bottle and it blew right the hell up. Their mom was pissed that the noise woke her and more pissed that they wasted the food."

I kept my hand moving as she talked, getting every word and putting a star by the last sentence. In most of the neighborhoods where *RVA Week* had racks, nobody would give two thoughts to blowing up a bottle of soda in the name of science. Here, food—even junk food—was a precious commodity that couldn't be wasted.

I wrote it all down. I wasn't sure where it would fit in my story, but if I hadn't considered how this world affected children before, it was a pretty safe bet a lot of other people hadn't, either. And thinking about children in a situation so bleak made my heart twist in my chest. If I was really going to tell the story of this place, that had to fit somewhere.

"You said Tucker needed vitamin D to help his mood." I looked up. "Do you know what he was looking for help with?"

"I think for him it was about missions he felt like he was failing at. He got dragged under by it every once in a while, you know?" Her lips twisted to one side as canny eyes raked my face. "I got a feeling you do."

"Missions?" I asked, letting her last comment lie.

"The oil thing. His own recovery from addiction. Kay. He was trying to be like Superman, or something, save the day. Life should've taught him there's no such thing as liberty and justice for all a long time ago, but he was a stubborn dude, Tuck." A small smile played around the corners of her lips. "I'll miss him."

"Can you think of any reason anyone would have wanted to hurt him?" I couldn't stop it from tumbling out that time.

She tipped her head to one side. "The three I just gave you, I reckon. I mean, when you give everything you've got to being a hero, eventually you're going to piss off someone who doesn't want one of your causes saved, aren't you?"

My teeth closed over my bottom lip as I scribbled that in my notebook.

The way her dark eyes pierced right through me, I got the feeling she wasn't just talking about Tuck anymore.

I met her gaze head-on. "Why are you here?" I kept my voice even. Curious, but still casual.

"The hundred-million-dollar question." She coughed again, her face twisting as she reached for the tissue box. "I suppose you can tell I'm not exactly running marathons these days."

Sometimes it's hard to keep my mouth shut, but years of experience has taught me that it's best to ask fewer, more open questions than try to lead the conversation. Most people like to talk. They'll tell you more than you'd ever know to ask about if you can manage two things: make them feel comfortable, and stay quiet unless absolutely necessary.

"I won the insurance trifecta at twenty-six. I was diagnosed with cervical cancer after a routine pap smear my senior year in college. But they caught it early, and it took one round of radiation and a surgery and I was cured.

But I graduated and had to stay on my dad's insurance because of follow-up care." She coughed. "Pre-existing condition is a dirty word, you know. Then I started getting sick to my stomach all the time, and they said I had lupus. Nice to know what it was, but the medication and treatments are like stupidly expensive. And that was before they figured out I was allergic to one of the drugs they use all the time. The only other option is an IV infusion that costs two hundred thousand dollars a bag. And you need a bag every two months. I maxed out the lifetime benefits in three years. And then my dad had a heart attack. I got fired from my job for being out too much, and nobody wants to hire and train someone with severe health issues. So I sold my dad's house and I paid off all the medical crap, and I wound up here because it's cheap and they pay the utility bills. You can pay a lease in advance, but the power company won't give you service if you've never had it unless you have proof of income."

"Wow." I didn't miss a word, my hand moving so fast it cramped. I wasn't sure what I could do with that in the midst of a murder and a drug epidemic, but I couldn't just do nothing. She might well have the worst luck I'd ever heard of—and I talk to crime victims for a living.

"Yeah, there's not much else to say, right?" She barked a low, bitter laugh that set off another coughing fit.

"Is that a symptom of the lupus?" I asked.

She shook her head. "It's kind of new, just the past few weeks. Colds linger with me longer than they do everyone else." She pointed to a bottle of hand sanitizer on the table by the door. "Tuck brought that over last week. Said I should be more careful keeping my hands clean in the middle of flu season. Always trying to be the hero."

"Sounds like he was a good guy. What can you tell me about Kay?"

"She and Tuck took care of each other. For as long as I've been here. And then they had a big blowup." She paused, tipping her head to one side and squinting. "Probably a couple of weeks ago now? Took me a minute to figure out I hadn't fallen asleep with the TV on. I'd never heard him yell. I don't even know that I thought he was capable of it. She slammed off out the door into the cold. Shook the walls, because I had a little string of lights up over the door and they fell."

Well, hell.

That would certainly give more weight to Landers's warrant.

"And she never came back after that?"

"Nope. I think more than anything about the last forty-eight hours, I hate that he died without making up with her. No creaking bedsprings coming from over there or anything, but sometimes you find your people when you really need them. Those two, they were good for each other. She was getting along. I'm afraid she'll spin out when she finds out what happened to him."

A valid concern, if Katie hadn't been the cause of what had happened to Tuck.

"You mentioned the oil company a minute ago. I understand Tuck was working to stop the COC pipeline," I said. "Did he talk to you about that?"

Another laugh, another cough. "Seemed like he didn't talk about anything else," she said. "There's some bullshit going on with that deal, I'll tell you. Tuck started off trying to help people last year who were getting like kicked out of their houses or having their farm fields dug up." She shook her head. "I didn't even know the government could throw you out of your house to give it to someone to make money off of. Seems shady as hell to me. And a lot of the people Kay was out there talking to didn't know it either. But they're farmers, or people who live in neighborhoods like two steps above this place. Politicians don't have any incentive to help them. Tuck would really get on his soapbox about it. But he didn't have anything anymore that would make them listen to him, either."

I snorted. "Except that he was right, you mean?" Every addict in that alley was just as sick as she was. But most people see addiction as a weakness, not a disease. There was my way to fit her into the story, and maybe make people understand that at the same time, if I could do it right.

"Are you sure you work in the news business? They don't care about right—they care about what people like you tell them to care about. Tuck was just saying the other day it was time to talk to the press, because he finally had something nobody would be able to explain away, and if it was in the news, then the politicians wouldn't have a choice except to actually do something instead of just talking and then taking the oil company's money anyway."

"He didn't say what that thing was, by any chance?" I knew the answer before I asked the question, but I had to ask anyway.

She shook her head. "Said anybody who didn't need to know was better off not knowing until he could talk to a reporter. Some hotshot who isn't afraid to really nail the kind of bastards who could do that to people."

I wouldn't say "hotshot," exactly. But the guy was trying to ask for help. From me. And he died before I got the message. Maybe it was a coincidence. But it was a hell of a big one.

I couldn't walk away until I knew what had happened here.

And right then, I needed back into Tucker Armstrong's room.

"It takes a lot to scare me these days." I stood and laid a hand on the doorknob. "Thank you for talking to me."

"Amy. I'm Amy. Tell his story right. I know that's what you really came here for. Make him count, Miss Nichelle."

"I hope you feel better soon, Amy," I said.

The half-smile that didn't get anywhere near her eyes said she heard that a lot, and she knew just exactly how much bullshit it was. "Thanks." But she was too nice to say so.

I slipped out of Amy's room, shutting the door quickly to minimize the draft, and moved to Tucker's door. Odds were good that nobody had cleaned yet because of the snowstorm. And even though forensics had been through it with a microscope—it wasn't more than 250 square feet including the bathroom—they were looking for evidence that might ID the killer.

Not that I'd pass that up, but I had a new mission, now that I knew more about Tucker's mission.

There was a whole fucking lot of money at stake where that pipeline was concerned. And dozens of murder stories have taught me that sex is the only more powerful motivator. Since everyone said Katie and Tucker weren't sleeping together, I was more than willing to follow the money here. The forensics crew may well have disregarded something that didn't fit their narrative, depending on when Landers had come up with that gun.

I put a finger on the doorknob and pushed.

It swung inward easily—weird, because Landers should've secured it before he left the scene. I checked the frame again. No padlock. I couldn't figure out why he'd leave it open.

Until I looked inside.

The mattress was leaning against the wall, blankets tossed on the floor, shadows lining the walls at odd angles from lampshades hanging askew, drawers gaping open.

Someone had been through this room with a microscope all right.

But no cop did this.

13

Whoever had blown through here behind Landers and his crew was looking for something.

I put a hand into my bag and closed my fingers around the cool metal of the mace canister Kyle called an occupational necessity when he gave it to me two Christmases ago. To date, I'd rarely had it with me when I actually needed it, but it's handy when I can manage it.

The door was badly in need of some WD-40, so if there was still someone in here, they'd heard it open. And I wasn't winning a footrace through a foot of snow with my ribs burning every time I took a regular breath. Better to be the cat than the mouse.

I spun quickly around the edge of the doorframe, index finger ready on the trigger of the canister. The corner was empty, as was the area behind the curtains. Keeping my back to the doorway, I scanned the rest of the room. Not much in the way of places to hide, especially with the mattress upended and the carpet beneath the bed visible. Looked like the dingy brown fibers under my boots had been red at some point in the distant past.

Behind the mattress and the bathroom were the only available hiding places. I stepped carefully away from the door, pushing it closed and keeping the mace out in front of me and ready.

The plastic file boxes were tossed into the far corner, emptied of stacks of newspapers, magazines, and documents that obscured much of the carpet like there had been an indoor ticker tape parade. I didn't stop to look through the drawers, my eyes on the dark maw that led to the bathroom. Rounding the edge of the mattress, I pointed the mace canister.

Nobody there.

I ducked under it and slid toward the bathroom, my breath speeding.

One. Two. Three.

I spun around the corner and flipped on the light.

It flickered, casting a sallow glow on the tiny room. Dingy tile, toilet, boxy shower stall.

The plastic curtain was pulled across the latter, sticky under my fingers when I closed two around it and whipped it back.

All I saw were broad shoulders and a wall of chest behind a sleek black pistol.

A short scream pierced the silence, but I couldn't tell if it came from me or the large man hiding in the dead professor's shower. I raised the mace and squeezed my trigger just as he let go of his.

"Nicey, no!"

Too late.

I jerked backward, my finger flexing on the trigger of the canister again before I dropped it to the plastic bottom of the shower stall, coughing when my mouth opened into a horrified O.

"Kyle? What the hell are you doing hiding in here?" I punctuated each word with a cough, backing toward the door and closing my hand around the sleeve of his shirt to pull him with me.

Out in the larger room, I pulled the door to the bathroom closed to contain what I could of the mace, wiping at my own eyes with my sleeve and peering up at Kyle's.

Damn.

"At least we know I can aim this thing," I muttered, watching his baby blues turn redder and more swollen by the second.

"You're not supposed to aim it at me." He coughed, flexing his hands into fists to keep from rubbing at his eyes. It would only make it worse, but I could imagine it was a hard impulse to suppress.

I kicked the mattress back across the bed, the impact sending up a cloud of dust so thick I sneezed.

"Sit." I pointed Kyle to the bed, looking around. I couldn't go back into the mace-filled bathroom for water, but if his eyes got any redder he'd have his very own Crayola shade.

My eyes landed on the window. The snow.

I patted Kyle's arm. "Hang in there just a couple more seconds."

I yanked one of the threadbare drapery panels off the wall and dragged it outside, ripping it into three strips. Scooping snow into each of them, I closed the fabric around the bundles and hauled them back inside, dumping two of the loads into one of Tuck's plastic bins. The other, I took to the bed. "Cold. But it'll help," I said, filling my hands and pressing them to Kyle's swollen-shut eyes.

He sucked in a sharp breath and recoiled. "Is that snow?"

"It is, and I have more over there melting. Let me help you get the chemicals off." I pulled my hands away from his face and shook the slush covering them to the carpet before I got more and repeated the treatment.

"What the hell are you doing here?" I asked on the third pass.

"I could ask you the same," he said.

"Working on my story."

"By breaking and entering into a crime scene?"

I scooped the snow off again and he cracked one eye open and tried to glare at me through bloodshot vessels and tears.

"The door is broken, therefore it wasn't locked," I said. "I was surprised Landers didn't secure it, but that's not my fault. It's a public building."

"Actually, it's private property unless you've paid for the room," Kyle said. "And Landers did secure the door. I saw him do it myself." He gestured to the mess. "Whoever did this broke the bolt."

"You saw him? Like yesterday, you saw him? Before I called you about Katie, you saw him?" My pitch rose with every question. If I wasn't trying to undo the damage I'd done to his eyes I might have put my hands on my hips. "Why would the ATF be interested in this?"

"No comment." He said it gently, but I flinched anyway. And then I got madder.

"Fine. Keep your motives to yourself." I wanted to add a "we'll see who gets to the truth first," to the end of that, but I swallowed the petty words before they hit the air. My temper usually leaves me regretting things I say when it gets away from me. Kyle and I were in a weird enough place already. And he didn't yell at me for macing him, which I appreciated given how much pain he must've been in.

"Why did you come back?" he asked.

"Why would I tell you that?"

"Because you maced me?"

"I thought you were a murderer." I pressed fresh snow to his eyes. "What were you doing lurking in the shower, anyway, Anthony Perkins?"

He snorted. "I heard the door open and thought you were the killer. I figured I'd surprise them, pop off a flesh wound if I had to, and make the arrest, all nice and neat, but then you pulled the curtain back and it was... you." He shook his head, his voice dissolving into a gravelly growl. "I almost shot you. Stop going into places you don't belong."

"Your reflexes are faster than mine." I let regret coat the words, ignoring his last comment. "I squirted before I looked up at your face. But on the bright side, you did tell me to not hesitate to use the mace if I was in a dangerous situation. I didn't hesitate."

I dropped the last of the snow to the carpet, stepping back to assess the remaining damage. "Much less puffy," I said, picking up a length of curtain and dipping it in the water. "Lean back."

Kyle obliged. I squeezed the cloth, letting the cold water run over his eye. "Can you open that?"

He managed about halfway. "Sort of?"

When I'd rinsed each eye three times, he blinked and tried to sit up. "Not so fast, cowboy." I flattened my free hand across the middle of his chest and took a clean piece of cloth to blot his eyes, then his forehead. "Don't want to let more spray run down your face."

His lashes fluttered, tears escaping the corners of his eyes.

"I suppose I can rest assured that shit would give you time to escape an actual bad guy."

"It seems." I squeezed his shoulder. "I'm sorry I hurt you."

"You sure it wasn't a subconscious on-purpose kind of thing?" His voice was soft as I handed him another clean cloth for his eyes.

"Uh. No. I can't see ever being that pissed at you."

"But you are mad at me."

I sucked in a deep breath. Face to face, it seemed we were having this conversation. Dammit.

"I am frustrated on just about every level you can imagine, with this entire situation." The practiced words rolled off my tongue just as calm as they'd sounded in my head all these weeks. Go me.

"And you're angry with me." Kyle blinked again and tipped his head up to catch my gaze. "You can just say it. I think it might make me feel better, if you get right down to it."

"You lied to me." The words were out of my mouth in the heat of the moment before I even managed to digest them myself. But there it was. Part of what had kept me awake so many nights, the bitter little seed that had grown teeth and tentacles, gnawing at my insides, making me feel like a lesser version of myself. I couldn't say if I hadn't actually realized what I was feeling or if I just didn't want to think about it. Standing in the dank, chilly little room that a forensics team had washed clean of blood and brain matter less than twenty-four hours before, a lump rose in my throat with so little warning I couldn't swallow it. I swiped at my eyes, glad for a tiny fraction of a second that he couldn't really see me.

"I did." He nodded. "I had to. And I am sorry it upset you, but I have had a whole lot of time to reflect, and I wouldn't do it differently if I had to do it over."

I wasn't sure what I expected him to say, but that wasn't it.

"Y-You," I stammered, "you've always been like the one guy I could always trust, Kyle. How could you lie right to my face for months on end? And how in the bleeding, burning, fiery hell could I not see it?"

The tears threatened again, and I willed them right back where they came from. I wasn't crying in front of Kyle. I was so pissed I could have cheerfully punched him in his maced eye, but I was not shedding any more tears here today.

I paced to the door so I didn't give in to that impulse. "I feel like an utter fucking moron. I know you better than I know anyone. And you lied to me and I didn't even see it."

The weight of the realization hung heavy over me. It had reached deep into and colored my every interaction—with everyone—in the past weeks and months.

"Nicey, I had to." The cool calm cloaking his earlier words was gone, pain leaking into his voice. "I want you to be happy. I saw a way to fix your issue with Joey, and I took it. I never dreamed in a million years it would come to something like this."

"Didn't you? I mean, he's out of the way now, right? I can't even talk to him. And I assume you're closer to your big bust of the Caccione family? Where's the downside for you?"

Even through the swelling and tears, Kyle's eyes widened and he flinched backward like I'd slapped him.

"I hope you know better than that when you get over being angry," Kyle said.

I didn't look up.

I wanted to think I knew better, too. But this whole weird day had served to teach me a precious few things about Tucker while showing me that I wasn't sure what I knew these days, not only with work, but with the people I loved most in the world. And that was an utterly shitty way to feel.

"I just want to know he's okay."

"MacAulay knows what he's doing, Nichelle. Joey is safe where nobody can find him."

"You don't know that. You told me yourself you're in the doghouse and your boss isn't telling you anything."

Kyle put a hand out, squinting and stepping toward me. "I'm earning my way out slowly. I've been busting my ass on this case, and having MacAulay hover has offered the benefit of him seeing that. He's still comfortable in the director's chair calling the shots for me, but I think we're getting close on this one, finally. The old man doesn't fully trust me yet, but he will. Just give me a little more time."

My breath caught in my throat as I looked up.

Kyle shook his head before I got any words out. "It's a conflict of interest," he said. "He won't tell me where Joey is because of you, because he's afraid I might tell you." Kyle sounded more than a little annoyed by that.

"You wouldn't? How am I supposed to believe you, then?"

His fingers tightened around my arm. "Because you can trust me," he said. "At least, you can trust me to do what's best for you. He's safe. I wouldn't compromise our case even if I did know where he was, but I would know if he wasn't safe. Don't worry."

Maybe it was his swollen, almost magenta eyes. Maybe it was my lack of faith in my instincts. But I wasn't sure I could believe that with the same confidence he cloaked the words in. What I was sure of was that we had reached the dead-end portion of the discussion.

"We have time to sort out our personal shit after we locate Katie DeLuca," I said, waving an arm to the mess. "You find what you were looking for?"

He stood, tottering at first as he squinted, looking around the room. "I didn't have a chance to look much," he said. "What did you come in here after, exactly?"

"Whatever was out of place that Landers didn't notice or take," I said. "And a closer look at this map." I stepped toward the wall.

The middle section, the one with most of the stars, was gone, tobacco-brown-stained plaster showing through the gap.

"Huh." Kyle crossed the room to stand behind me.

I looked around the floor, bending to flip over the papers nearest the wall.

"It's gone," I said.

"Not just torn down?" Kyle asked.

"No. Not here at all." I stepped back and began flipping more papers. No maps.

"He hung onto things, this guy," Kyle said.

"He was a scientist. That's kind of their bag. I'm not sure I've ever met one who wasn't a bit of a hoarder."

"What've you got?" Kyle asked.

A strong desire to have him out of the room.

But in my hand, I held what looked like a page of a deposition. Armstrong had been a lawyer for like five minutes long ago. I skimmed the text. Huh. Legal people can be weird and old-fashioned, but the type suggested a typewriter, not a word processor.

A really old deposition.

Kyle moved in behind me and grunted when he couldn't make his eyes focus on it.

He wouldn't let me take it, I knew that without asking. But I slid my phone out of my pocket and snapped a photo of the sheet as soon as he reached into a dresser drawer.

"Not much in the way of clothes."

I kept quiet, picking up more pieces of paper.

Three water quality study graphs and a report on stability of digging near swamps later, I came up with another page of the same old-fashioned-looking typeface. I put it on the bed and snapped a photo, sliding my phone back into my coat pocket with nearly-numb fingers when Kyle turned around. "What now?" He pointed to the papers.

"Random stuff," I said, banking on the fact that he couldn't really see them.

I was looking for anything that might tell me who besides Katie DeLuca might've had motive to kill Tucker Armstrong. Kyle was looking for a thing. Like a specific thing, that someone might have stashed in their underwear drawer because humans are predictable creatures. But if Tucker was predictable, whatever Kyle was looking for was long gone.

"Don't you think that whoever tossed this room took whatever it is you're after?" I asked, laying a hand on his back. "You should go home and get a shower. Wash your face and eyes good with a gentle shampoo. And lie down with an ice pack."

"You too," he replied, ignoring my actual question.

I steered him toward the door, shining my flashlight on the map wall on the way out for a last look. I spotted a corner of a red star. Kyle pulled the door open, letting in a gust of shiver-inducing wind, and I stepped to the wall and bent to get a photo of the torn star and the piece of the map I could still see before I followed him out into the deepening twilight.

"You need to get home before the roads refreeze," he said. "Do you have four-wheel drive?"

"I do not." I looked at the wide expanse of maybe slightly shorter but still formidable snow and sighed. I hadn't realized it was so close to dark.

"I do. If you'll take me home, you can take my truck and I'll get it tomorrow," he said. "I doubt I have any business driving anyway."

Being the reason he didn't have any business driving, I couldn't say no, so I took his keys. My car would be fine for one night—the CCPD was permanently posted five steps from where I'd parked it.

Engine purring, I threw the truck into reverse and eased onto the gas pedal as Kyle turned on the radio.

"Really any information at this time is vital."

My foot slammed back onto the brake so hard we both pitched forward in our seats, our heads turning toward one another at the voice coming through the speakers.

"She could be a danger to anyone she meets. Please use extreme caution and don't approach her, but do call 804-555-8763 if you have any information that might help detectives find Ms. DeLuca," Landers said.

My jaw hung loose, my eyes on the radio.

"Thank you, Richmond Detective Christopher Landers, for joining us this afternoon with this sad, scary warning." The afternoon news program's host sounded appropriately somber. "Listeners, I know the Richmond PD appreciates your help. We'll be back with more headlines after this message."

Four words into a Schwarzschild ad, I punched the button to shut off the radio and let my head drop back against the seat. "He's staging a good old-fashioned manhunt. Womanhunt. Whatever," I said.

"That's a gamble in police work," Kyle mused. "And Landers has never struck me as the bet-the-house type. Something's not right here."

"What do you mean?"

"I mean either Landers has something he's not sharing that has him convinced Katie DeLuca is a menace to society, or he's up to something else entirely, but going on the air asking for leads is like throwing your own sanity on a bonfire: he'll bring the nut jobs out of the woodwork and spend the next six weeks chasing wild geese that lead nowhere."

"Unless he knows what he's looking for," I said slowly.

"Or unless he just wants someone to think he's really hell bent on looking for Katie when it's not her he's after at all." Kyle nudged my hand back toward the gearshift.

"Everything about this has been more complicated than it looks on the surface," I said. "Whether Landers really wants Katie in custody or not, I can't imagine everyone around here is going to take kindly to him calling her a murderer all over the airwaves."

Kyle leaned his head back, keeping his puffy eyes open as I pulled out of the parking lot. He found music on the radio, his words falling too softly behind it for me to swear I heard him right. "Not a bad way to distract people. Not bad at all."

I kept my eyes on the road, flipping the comment twenty different ways in my head on the drive to Church Hill.

And wishing things weren't too weird between us for me to ask what the hell he meant.

14

Kyle's eyes were still an angry shade of scarlet I hadn't even been aware the human body could produce when I let him out of his truck ten minutes later. And we were still in a weird not-really-speaking zone that left a thick, heavy melancholy pressing in until it was hard to catch a deep breath for reasons that had nothing to do with my bruised ribs as I watched him disappear into the building.

Back at my house and settled next to Darcy on the sofa, I opened my laptop and checked the *Telegraph's* website. Landers and his on-air manhunt plea had to have blown my exclusive on Tucker's murder, and I needed to know just how badly Shelby had scooped me.

DeLuca's widow wanted in connection with drug slaying took up my entire screen. Damn. I clicked the headline and started reading.

Hang on. Shelby's entire article—all maybe seven inches of it—was about Katie. A wedding photo of her and Nate front and center, Shelby reported in vague terms that she'd struggled with addiction after his death (I knew better), and she finished by quoting Landers and asking anyone who saw or had seen Katie to call the detectives' desk at the PD.

I shook my head. She barely mentioned Tucker's name, let alone anything else about him.

"At least my story is safe," I muttered, trying to squash the impulse to be glad my weaselly former publisher was getting exactly what he deserved. "For tonight."

I checked Channel Four. They had a similar piece with a byline from "staff reports."

Channel Eight. Dan Kessler had a decent piece that mentioned Tucker's background as a professor, but nothing about his time as a lawyer, and buried the hunt for Katie in the fourth graf.

It was a weird, weird day in Richmond when my biggest competition for a murder headline was Dan Kessler.

I clicked to social media.

The *Telegraph* had a poll: *Should the Richmond PD continue to pursue Katie DeLuca?*

More than three thousand replies in twenty minutes were split pretty evenly, with *No* leading 53-45 and two percent of folks *not sure*. "Two percent," I muttered, scratching Darcy's ears. "I guess that's better than no percent, but anybody who only read Shelby's story doesn't know enough about this situation to have an opinion on what the cops need to be doing here."

The comments served as evidence that more than half the folks who'd voted either way hadn't read a word about the case past the headline, and also that people will say some vile things when arguing over the internet about something that doesn't affect them whatsoever. I closed the browser and reached for my notes, going back over the day in my head. Before I got past the Olsens, my phone started buzzing.

Jordan Pierce.

I clicked the green circle and put it to my ear. "Good evening, Mr. Pierce," I said. "Enjoying the snow?"

"I'm partial to palm trees and sand," he said. "Not to make a pest of myself, but you promised me coffee today, and the day is fading pretty fast."

I checked the clock. Five forty-five. My stomach grumbled a protest at the late hour and lack of food.

"Do you know where Thompson's is, off West Cary?" I asked.

"I'm sure Google can tell me."

"See you there in fifteen minutes," I said.

Jordan Pierce was a slick piece of work. Time to see if he was as good at his job as Evan Connolly thought.

Pierce really didn't want me to write about Tucker Armstrong.

"It's been all over the radio and TV all afternoon, and now the *Telegraph* has it on their social media pages and their website. It will definitely lead their front in the morning. This isn't the story that's going to get Evan back in your corner, Nichelle." His voice was calm. Matter-of-fact.

Infuriating.

"I have a different angle. A better angle. I'm not at all sure Katie is the right person for Landers to pursue in this case. And I'm past beginning to wonder if he might know that. Shelby is barely reporting anything about the murder, and Dan Kessler, the only person who is, doesn't have the whole story and doesn't have my audience." I stirred my coffee. "I know you're new. I know you're trying to help. But trust me. There's a story here. The kind of story I haven't seen since I started working at *RVA Week*. I'm telling you, if you move me off this, you're shooting yourself right through that shiny Prada wingtip I saw yesterday morning."

He shook his head before I even finished talking.

"Evan told you yesterday, I'm the best there is in media consulting, and you are following the wrong story."

"I'm the best of the best at reporting crime in this city, and I say I'm not." I arched an eyebrow.

He sighed, sitting back in the chair. "Bob said you were stubborn."

"Did he mention the part where I'm usually right, too? I like that part."

Pierce flashed a quick smile. "I just bet you do."

I put my cup back on the table. "I'm not trying to be difficult. I just know a great story when it walks up and plops in my lap."

"I'm probably trying to be a little difficult, but it's for your own good," he said. "Jesus, I think that was my mother talking. Look, I don't want to sound like a heartless dick, but..." He sighed.

"In my experience, if you have to say that, you're pretty much guaranteed to," I said.

"If you're going to make me do it anyway, here goes: you are overestimating how much people in your target demographics care about a dead junkie with a record, Nichelle."

"Yep. There it is." I leaned forward. "People care about the things I make them care about. That's what makes me good at what I do. Mister Pierce."

"I'll give you an abnormal ability to humanize your subjects," he said. "It's a good thing to have. But I'm not sure it will work here, and your recent track record says I'm more likely to be right than you are."

"I wasn't working murder for the past three months," I said. "There's something off here, I'm telling you. I just need to find it. And I will."

"Any actual evidence to support that, or am I supposed to take your gut to Connally and tell him he still needs to pay everyone this week whether you're right or not?"

Ouch. I didn't flinch. "I have two more bodies nobody knows about." I kept my voice low. "And I'm going to find out what happened to them and to Tucker Armstrong, and you..." I toyed with the handle on my cup. "You will owe me an apology when I pull this off. A public one."

"You have two days." He lifted one brow to emphasize his counteroffer. "If you're still trailing Shelby Taylor by then, you will take my suggestion for a cover story and not look back. We could discuss the possibilities over dinner."

Damn.

I held his gaze for five quick heartbeats. His face said that offer was the best he was going to make, and he didn't want to be negotiating with me in the first place. Not about business, anyway.

I stuck out a hand. "Deal." I stood, grabbing my bag. "But that means I have work to do. If you're hungry, though, there's a great little place about three blocks down on the right behind the red door. Get the macaroni and cheese."

I walked out ahead of him to Kyle's truck, feeling his eyes follow me all the way to the parking lot. He was cute, objectively. He was also brim-full of himself and rooting for me to fail.

I'd proved smarter men wrong.

I just had to figure out how to do it again. I had one big advantage over every other reporter in town: I'd been inside the murder scene. Twice. Maybe something I'd spotted in Tucker's room would help me unravel his death.

15

The depositions were from two different cases, best I could tell, neither remotely related to environmental law. One was peppered with mentions of the segregation of races from the cradle to the grave in the Jim Crow South. Schools, restaurants, homes, jobs, healthcare. But no names I could use to search for the case file.

I shook my head as I squinted at the slightly out of focus text on my phone. The other was a testimony about RICO violations in Tidewater in 1987.

I flipped back through my notes. "Dammit, Kyle," I whispered under my breath. Darcy's ears perked and she trotted to the doorway, looking through the foyer to the front door.

"He's not here, girl."

Did I think Katie was capable of hurting Tucker? Not the first damned clue. What I did know was that a young woman with a history of drug abuse and a recent falling out with the victim was one hell of a convenient scapegoat, and that her parents had some serious issues, or had been stressed to their breaking point, or maybe a little of both.

I opened my laptop and clicked to the Channel Four website. Charlie didn't have a byline today. Every headline save the one on Katie from staff reports focused on the weather. Which meant Charlie probably wasn't able to get safely to the studio. Score one for the snow.

So I had at least one more day before she might catch on. I would take it. And try to make the most of it.

I touched my bookmark for the *Telegraph*, just in case.

Fourth death in as many weeks could shut down Southside motel stretched across the top of the screen in thick black type.

My breath stopped as I clicked the link and scrolled through the story. The city council was holding a special session—I checked the clock—in seven minutes. At issue was closing down the Hideaway until the PD could complete their investigation into "a string of troubling deaths."

Son of a bitch. Was that why Aaron wanted to talk to me? And who handed this headline to Shelby? My friend Mel was still the city hall reporter at the *Telegraph*—she would definitely take that piece for herself before she'd hand it over to Shelby willingly. Someone had tipped Shelby off.

My own annoyance notwithstanding, I really wouldn't want to be that person when the snow melted and Charlie got ahold of them.

I clicked to the city's website and pulled up the live feed of the meeting before I reached for my phone and opened a text to Melanie.

Did you tell Shelby about this special session?

Buzz. *NOPE.*

I nodded at the screen, turning up the volume on my laptop when the mayor took his seat and called the meeting to order. *I didn't think so. Any idea who did?*

She started typing immediately. *If you find out, please let me know. I've never even heard whispers of the city taking action like this against a private business. I'm not sure the lawyers will let them. They've been in executive session with three cops and the city attorney since 3.*

You're there?

Yep. They're starting. Should be interesting, I'll call you after.

I rooted in the end table for a pen and flipped to a clean page of my notes.

Doris Ellen Lowe, the councilwoman for my neighborhood and several even more affluent areas around it, jumped right in. She brandished a copy of the *Telegraph*, talking about drugs, and then gestured to someone I couldn't see on the video feed.

"These officers are out there every day and the stories they could tell," she said. "This place is a menace to decent Richmonders, and public safety should come first in the minds of everyone on this dais."

"Damn." I scribbled notes. "And she's not even up for reelection this year."

"With all due respect to my colleague from north of the river, this business is in my district." The smooth baritone came from the other end of the dais before the camera had a chance to move. "I'm proud of the job our police force is doing to ensure the safety of the surrounding area, and see this move as alarmist on the part of the council at best, and a violation of the business owner's rights at worst." Russell Milton was himself a successful businessman, founder and CEO of the largest independent contracting firm in the state. He'd won his seat by advocating for business growth in a part of the city where even payday lending joints and pawn shops were disappearing faster than rats bailing off the Titanic. It made sense for him to side with the hotel's owner.

The mayor refereed the bickering for more than an hour, Milton and Lowe getting by far the most airtime. I kept notes, watching their faces as their words got more heated. I'd never covered a Richmond council meeting, but I'd heard plenty of stories from Mel, and one of the things I liked about my new job was the lack of limitations. At a daily paper, everyone has their box. You cultivate your sources and cover your beat. But nobody gets to break out of their box very often. At the weekly, I could write about pretty much whatever I wanted—assuming, of course, that I could dig up something with this cover story that would move papers and make Connolly happy.

Deep breath. The thing about the big stories, the kind I'd had a good run of at the *Telegraph* in the past few years, is I never knew when one was coming. And I could never force one out of something that wasn't worthy.

Sitting there listening to the council argue the legal definition of the term "public nuisance," I realized that was why I'd been twisting myself into knots all week. Because since that meeting Tuesday morning, I'd had a teeny little Evan Connolly on my shoulder, telling me I had to find the magic in this one. And the magic had never been a thing I could control. It was the journalistic equivalent of a lightning strike: unpredictable, illuminating, and cleansing. Trying to pull lightning out of a clear sky had me so busy looking up for a spark, I was beginning to wonder if I was missing something important going on around me.

Like the motel's owner: I hadn't even thought to look up who owned the property before these politicians started talking about closing it. I had assumed the motel was an aging corporate concern that was rundown because it was being ignored due to lack of profitability. But these people were talking about the owner like they meant a person sitting in the room with them. Which made me wonder why anyone would be content with owning a bastion of criminal activity. You'd think it would be bad for business.

The only thing that occurred to me off the top of my head was that you'd have to be into some shady shit to be cool with having your name on file at the courthouse as legally responsible for a building that was part flophouse and part opiate den with a tiny side of violent crime.

I fired off a message to Mel and asked her to grab me a name and maybe a sneaky cell phone photo if she could. I just didn't know if she'd see it before she left. I shut my phone off when I really need to pay attention in court, and I knew she did the same with her meetings.

Back to the screen. I opened a second browser window and went to the property tax records in search of a name.

While the computer hunted, I turned up the volume more. The city attorney had the floor. It seems "public nuisance" is a hard thing to prove in court.

"With the violent crime that took place at the Hideaway earlier this week, the council could certainly make the argument, given the number of minor offenses and calls related to the address in the past twelve months," he said. "But it's not an immediate solution. It will take time and require due process."

A flutter of movement in the lower corner of my screen pulled my eyes from his flushed cheeks and thick, pale neck. A lanky man in a suit that looked two sizes too big leaned over the mayor's left shoulder and laid a folded paper on the dais.

Rhonda Strathmore fancied herself a sort of local answer to Eva Perón. She married into one of the oldest, wealthiest families in the city and, when widowed at thirty-seven, she ran for mayor on a platform of transparency and restoring governing to the people through forums and town halls. Mel wasn't allowed to have a public opinion, but privately, she had said more than once since November that the only person Strathmore wanted to see in power was herself.

The light over the mayor's seat came on in the corner of my screen.

I leaned forward.

"Thank you for your insight, Mr. Clary," she said. "In light of the legal timeline and uncertainty, perhaps we should table this discussion and let everyone get home tonight before the roads get any worse?"

Lowe's mouth gaped and shut like she was afraid to say what she was thinking, her eyes shooting daggers I could even make out on the questionable video feed. The two women on the council usually voted together, and Lowe was obviously the driving force behind this special session being called before the snow melted.

The council members stood, and the screen faded to black.

Back to the tax records.

Not a name. Well. Not a person's name, anyway. I made a note, plucked my phone from the blanket tucked around my knees, and watched for Melanie to call.

It took three minutes.

"Who was the guy? The tall one who passed something to the mayor there at the end?" I asked by way of hello.

"I wasn't sure the camera caught that," she said in hushed tones. "Hang on, let me get in the car. Grant drove me."

"Sure."

I heard a door shut. "Okay," Mel said. "So, that was Josh Dershowitz from planning and zoning. No idea what he gave her, he was gone by the time I got up. But the dude, the owner of the motel, went straight into a huddle with Councilman Milton, and they didn't look happy. What the hell did Clary mean 'violent crime?' I searched and we haven't had anything but overdoses associated with that place. Neither has the TV. But experience tells me if there's a hush-hush violent crime, you know exactly what he was talking about."

Parker hadn't told Mel what happened? Huh. I tapped one index fingernail on the back of the phone. "You can't tell Shelby."

I could practically hear her eyes roll back into her head. "Duh. What happened?"

I hit the big facts, leaving speculation and detail out. Not that I didn't trust Mel—she was a damned good friend. But I knew how hard it was to keep something quiet in a newsroom, and the city attorney had just said "violent crime" on the live feed. While I was probably one of a dozen or so people not in council chambers who had watched the meeting, someone would ask before long. The more whoever that was had to dig up on their own, the safer my exclusive remained.

"But you don't think that would normally be enough for them to pursue action to shut the place down?" I asked.

"I have never seen them do anything like this before," she said. "I've never even heard talk about it. I mean, Google only even has a handful of places in the country where a council has pursued action like this against a private business. It's definitely weird."

"Huh." My fingers went into my hair, flipping and twisting a thick strand into a knot.

"Nicey?"

"She's playing with her hair." That was Parker, in the background. "Trying to figure out why the city council is being weird."

"To be weird they have to care, and I can't figure out why they care. Especially not why my council rep, who has nothing to do with that part of town and therefore nothing obvious to gain from sticking her nose into this, cares." Words tumbled out of my mouth as they popped into my head. "Did you get a look at the owner? Property tax records have the place listed to an LLC and I'm going to have to go deeper than the surface to find a name."

That was interesting, too. Whoever owned the place didn't want anyone to know they owned it. Did Tucker figure that out?

I might not be able to wish a big story up out of thin air, but maybe the universe knew I needed one right now, because this one was sure growing some long legs the more I looked at different facets of it. I needed a chart already, and Tucker hadn't even been dead forty-eight hours.

"I'm texting you a photo," Mel said. "I couldn't get his name, but I will put a call in to Milton's office first thing tomorrow and get it for you. Do you have the name of that LLC?"

I clicked back to the tax bill on my screen. "Decmar Industries," I said. "PO Box address in Loudon County."

"Thanks, Nichelle. No worries, I won't say anything to Shelby. Let me know if you find anything that ties any of my council members to illegal shit, though, okay? If we've got a crooked rod in there, I'd like to know it first."

"Will do." We could synchronize the stories to run on the same day, in a perfect world. A city council scandal wouldn't upstage a murder, so I could remain reasonably sure I was going to get the circulation Connolly wanted without using my friend as a source and then scooping her. "Thanks, Mel. Y'all get home safe."

"Working on it." Parker sounded like he forced the words through gritted teeth. "Let us know if you need anything. Or whatever."

I clicked the end button. Parker hadn't told his wife about our little adventure this morning, which wasn't normal for him by any stretch.

In fairness, he had almost gotten killed rooting around in one of my stories last year. Maybe he didn't want her to worry.

I opened a new browser window and searched for Decmar. Sometimes a business operating out of a PO Box is nothing more than not wanting to pay the overhead for an office space. But sometimes it's a red flag for secrets, because there's no way to trace the mailing address back to an actual human unless you're a cop with a bench warrant: the Postal Service doesn't publish owners of boxes for public use.

Given the circumstances, I figured Decmar ought to be considered guilty of the latter until proven innocent. Which probably meant this was going to take more than a simple Google search, but I had to start somewhere.

No results found.

Surprise, surprise.

Darcy shifted and resettled on my foot.

I reached for my laptop and went back to the city property tax records just as my doorbell rang.

16

It was dark. The roads were a treacherous mess of black ice and frozen slush.

I had exactly zip for who might be ringing my doorbell.

I put the computer on the cushion and went to the door with the dog on my heels.

Pushing up on tiptoe, I peered through one of the windows lining the top of the door.

Oh.

"Aaron. What on earth?"

I flipped the deadbolt and pulled the door wide. My favorite Richmond detective nodded a hello, his genial face set in uncharacteristically hard lines.

"I have beer, wine, soda, and coffee—pick one, and come tell me what the hell brings you out on these roads, because it's not the adorable dog or a lack of excitement in your days."

"I don't miss you that much," Aaron agreed. "Coffee sounds great, thanks. We need to talk. And you never called me back."

Oh, hell. I clapped one hand over my mouth. "There was a dead guy, and Landers was being really weird, and I totally forgot." Which was so unlike me I didn't blame him for coming to make sure I wasn't dead myself. "I'm sorry, Aaron."

I pointed him ahead of me to the living room and went to the kitchen to get his coffee, returning to find the dog curled in his lap and his foot bouncing as he stroked her fur, staring across the room—maybe at nothing, maybe at my laptop.

I handed him the cup and resumed my seat, pushing the screen shut.

"What's going on?" I didn't reach for a pen yet. This wasn't normal, and I wanted him to speak freely. I could always get a notebook after I got an idea of what he wanted.

"The guy at the sleazy motel wasn't the first body this month," Aaron said. "I was reviewing reports and discovered two important ones that were left off the lists pushed to y'all while I was out of town. But I don't know who would do that."

Me neither. Not Landers either, since he'd told me about them.

"You have those reports on you, Detective?"

"Something weird is happening here, Nichelle." Aaron's words were quiet, half-directed at the floor before his bright baby blues rolled up to catch my gaze. "And last time something weird was going on inside the PD, you figured it out before I did."

Oh.

Oh.

"You think there's officer involvement? Like in the actual murder?"

My fingers went to my hair. Aaron shifted in the chair, linking and unlinking his fingers.

Aaron White. The most confident, direct, affable police officer I had ever worked with. Fidgeting.

"I don't know what I think," Aaron said finally. "I don't want to think we've managed to let more apples go rotten. But I guess I also don't want to be blind to it again. I mean, I didn't want to believe it last time and that might have gotten us both killed, you know? The one thing I know is that when I'm not sure I can trust anyone I work with, I can trust you."

Aw. That was maybe the nicest thing he'd ever said to me, and I was too stressed to fully appreciate it.

"What about Internal Affairs? The FBI? There are law enforcement channels for uncovering police corruption, Aaron. Where the people who work there have guns."

"That's true. But I'm not at all sure what the hell is happening here. And I don't know any of those guys, or who they talk to. Until I know what's happening, I'd rather keep it to myself." He sipped his coffee. "I know you. And I know you can keep a secret better than a priest when you want to. So here I am. If we've got a dirty cop in the mix, let's get the bastard. If we don't, I figure we can get to the bottom of what is happening before anyone else dies, and if you're writing the story at least I know it'll get told right. Three murders in a couple of weeks is high—last January we only had three all month."

I slumped back into the sofa cushions and my side twinged. Taking a slow breath, I reached for my notebook. "Do you have names of the other victims?"

Aaron and I went back a fair ways. Under the glowing tan he'd brought back from the islands, his face looked worried. A man who had a nearly perpetual smile, easy manner, and way with pulling information out of folks before they realized they'd been had. He didn't worry about much of anything but his college-age daughters. And he only asked for my help when something prevented him from using his own investigative channels to get to an answer. I knew his concern here wasn't implausible or invalid. As much as I liked Griffin Brooks, I wasn't sure I should trust him, given my recent lapses in people-reading.

Aaron pulled an iPhone from his pocket. My cops used Droids. They were cheaper for the city to buy in bulk and easier to monitor. "The department make a switch I missed?"

He shook his head but didn't speak, tapping the screen a few times before he passed me the phone.

He'd taken photos of the missing reports. He shouldn't be able to get into trouble for that, since whoever left them out of the dailies was violating the Freedom of Information Act. But the simple fact that he was concerned enough to think to use another phone to get these was plenty to give me pause.

I flipped through, looking at the names. Nothing jumped out at me.

Cause of death was a gunshot wound in both cases. Close range, like Landers said.

"Ballistics?"

"No casings at the scenes," Aaron said.

"I didn't see any in Tucker's room, either."

"There were none recovered there," he confirmed.

I looked over the specifics of the reports, scrolling back up to note the reporting officers' names. And dropped the phone on the second one.

"Nichelle? What?" Aaron's voice sounded farther away than it should have.

Brooks.

He didn't work them both, but the most recent shooting—besides Armstrong's—was in his patrol area. He'd written the report. And I spent a whole day with him and he hadn't said a word about it.

The Chesterfield cop had said he was up to something, and sounded pretty grim about throwing a colleague to the journalistic lions.

None of that was damning, exactly. But definitely weird enough to follow.

Just maybe not weird enough to mention to Aaron until I knew more. I liked Brooks. A ridiculous amount for someone I'd just met, actually. Surely I hadn't lost my ability to read people entirely.

Right?

"Just thinking," I said. "Can you send me copies of those?"

"Sure."

"Someone who remembers to grab the shell casings points to a suspect who does this on a fairly regular basis."

"Usually, yes. Most people who get pissed off and shoot someone in the heat of the moment get freaked out by what they've done. They run. They hide or toss the gun. But they don't stop to wipe prints or retrieve casings." Aaron settled back into the chair. "Experience and distance afford the ability to be methodical."

"So like a hired gun?" I asked.

Aaron shrugged. "Maybe. One of about a dozen possibilities I can think of right now."

"Is one of your possibilities Katie DeLuca?" I asked.

His head shook back and forth slowly. "Looking for Katie is keeping your colleagues awfully busy." Aaron's lips settled into a grim line that looked so unfamiliar on him I had to blink.

All the air left my chest in a long *whoosh* when it hit me: the reason he was here, what he really wanted me to help him figure out.

"You think it was a cop." It came out barely above a whisper. "The actual killer? Really?"

Surely not.

It was one thing to theorize about iffy things going on at the PD, but a cold-blooded murderer walking around with a badge and a sidearm— there's a saying about lightning not striking the same place twice.

"I didn't say that." Aaron's tone dripped caution. "There are several possibilities here. The only thing I know is that I can trust you. And I'm adding that I don't want to leave any alley unchecked here. We need to make sure we look at everything. Even things neither of us would like to believe."

I clicked the pen and made a note without looking down at the paper. "So if it's not a cop, who else would have that kind of experience with a crime scene? Someone with a record maybe? Settling a score? Did these victims know one another? Are there any recent parolees who fit the profile or have been seen in that part of town?" I fired questions off as they popped into my head. Aaron raised one palm, the corners of his mouth tipping up.

"Sorry," I said.

"The questions are always good ones," he said. "I'd just like to take them one at a time. The thing is, anyone who's ever watched *NCIS* or *Bones* knows the basics of covering your tracks. It's being calm enough after you've just killed another human to remember to do those things. That's what we're looking for: a person who can keep it together and remember the details in the face of that kind of trauma."

"That sounds like a wide net you're casting, Detective."

"But it's not as wide as you'd think. As you said, we are most likely looking for someone with experience. I've already put in a request for a list of recent parolees from Richmond and the surrounding counties, because it's not uncommon to see detail orientation like this in subsequent offenses.

People pay attention in court. They see the evidence that got them the first time, and nobody really wants to go back to prison."

"The most recent victim had a record," I said. "But not a violent charge. Minor distribution."

"I saw that yesterday. So maybe he made an enemy inside while he was there." He talked as I scribbled. "And a list of folks with violent priors will be a fairly short one, anyway. The parole board tends to be pickier when there's a public safety issue."

"But Tucker having an enemy in prison wouldn't explain these other dead people," I said. "Are we going on the assumption that they're connected somehow? Brooks didn't mention anything about Tucker Armstrong dealing."

Aaron shrugged. "I learned a long time ago not to ever assume anything." He held up three fingers. "What I want to know is why these people are dead, who killed them, and who told my department to keep a lid on it."

I seesawed the pen back and forth between my fingers, eyeing my chart.

A whole lot of stuff had happened in the past forty-eight hours, and I needed to untangle the events at least enough to figure out which theories might get me somewhere.

"Did you see the warrant for Katie DeLuca's arrest in this case?" I asked.

"Seems a gun with her prints on it turned up in the alley behind the Hideaway." Aaron steepled his fingers under his chin. "Her mother was booked today on an assault charge when they went to serve the warrant in question, too."

I got three things from that: he didn't know I'd been there when Landers showed up with the warrant, he was telling me everything he knew, and he didn't care quite as much about who killed these people as he did the possibility of corruption in the RPD ranks.

I flipped my laptop back up and dragged two fingers across the trackpad to wake the screen. I may have hit a wall on Decmar, but Aaron had research channels I couldn't access.

"Any chance you've ever heard of a company called Decmar Industries?" I asked.

"Nope. Why do we care?"

"The deed to the Hideaway Motel is registered to them."

"Google can't help you?"

I shook my head. "All I've found is a PO Box address in northern Virginia. But the city council held a special session tonight threatening to shut the place down, and there was someone there who Melanie Parker says purported to be the owner."

"Why go to so much trouble to keep your name away from it and then show up at the council meeting?" Aaron asked.

"Exactly. Though at no point during the meeting did anyone call the guy by his name, and Mel didn't get to him before Councilman Milton pulled him into a conversation."

"So he was at a public meeting tonight and we still don't know who he is?" Aaron wore his why-does-this-not-surprise-me face.

"Correct. But I'm hoping you have ways of finding out."

He clicked the screen on the iPhone. "Spell it."

I obliged.

"I don't have ways I can pull out of the cell network, I'm afraid, but I will get back to you."

He clicked the phone off. "I'm not sure what I'm pulling you into here, Nichelle," he began, and I raised one hand.

"I'm already in it, Aaron. I saw that guy's brains splattered all over the wall. I read a beautiful essay he wrote about conserving forests in an environmental journal, and a letter he wrote asking me for help that he didn't get to send before he died. Even when I thought it was drug-related, I thought people ought to care more than Shelby does. And if there's some more sinister reason he's dead, well...I'm in too deep now to go wading back for the shore before I find an answer, you know?"

He chuckled. "Yeah. I've met you." He stood. "That's why I came over."

"Thanks for trusting me, Aaron."

"Thanks for being so committed to getting to the truth that you make it easy, Nichelle. I gotta tell you, this job isn't the same, not talking with you every day. That Taylor woman makes me want to scrape out my eardrum with a car key every time she calls. And I think she can tell, because she calls a lot."

I snorted. "I don't envy you that. Speaking of Shelby, which I'd rather avoid, have you heard from Charlie since the holidays?"

Aaron stopped in the doorway.

"I have not." He tipped his head to one side. "Some detective I am, I hadn't really noticed. What do you figure is going on there?"

I shook my head. "Because we need another mystery right now. I have no idea. But I will see what I can find."

17

I locked the door behind Aaron at 8:30 and yawned like it was 3:30. Darcy bumped her head against my ankle and trotted back to her bed.

I followed, my legs slow and my brain racing.

Charlie Lewis had been my drive to research harder, make the extra call —even occasionally go into offices I hadn't been invited to enter—since I was a cub reporter who barely knew the difference between grand theft and armed robbery. I missed the daily competition with Charlie as much as I missed talking to Aaron nearly every morning.

New normal. I just needed time to get used to it. That's what I'd been telling myself for months, and I was catching the wafts of bullshit in my own self-talk.

Time wasn't the answer. I needed a new mission.

Tucker Armstrong needed me to tell his story. Maybe we could help each other.

I checked my email and found one from a Gmail address for Aaron. He really wasn't leaving anyone knowing he'd sent me these to much chance.

Opening the first report in my PDF reader, I clicked up a browser window and typed the victim's name into the search bar. Not that Aaron would have skipped this step, but I notice different things than he does.

Social media was all locked down except the profile pictures. Instagram had only one: of a Charlie Brown Christmas tree. No help. Facebook's most recent was a skinny young man sans shirt posing in a knit skull cap with duck lips, flashing a sideways three sign at the camera. I scrolled down, watching him morph from that to a teenager in a private school polo with a wide, Invisalign-commercial smile and a crew cut.

"Another guy who came from an upper middle class family, had an education," I muttered to the dog. That was a weird common thread for murder victims in a dangerous part of town, but I couldn't ignore any similarity, no matter how silly it might seem. Not yet.

I started a list, added the guy on my screen, Tucker, and, after a minute of staring at the screen, Katie. She wasn't dead; on the contrary, Landers thought she was his killer. But if he was right, maybe something about that link explained why.

I noted the name of the school—it wasn't one I recognized—and clicked to image results. A newspaper article from the *Pilot* on a high school football game. State parochial championship, seven years ago.

"Bingo."

I went back to the police report to check the scene of the crime. Another motel, this one out off Jeff Davis, just inside the city limits. Kind of like the Hideaway.

Clicking the button for a new browser tab, I started typing the tax office address before the screen loaded. Backspace. Try again.

When it loaded I typed in the name of the second motel.

"Holy Manolos." Decmar Industries for the double.

I went back to Aaron's email and opened the other report, checking the crime scene.

An apartment complex in a part of Oregon Hill even Joey didn't go into after dark.

I was pretty sure who owned the apartments before the tax record came up.

I wasn't wrong.

Three buildings owned by the same company—a company with no internet presence I could locate, and no board of directors I could find listed with the state.

I picked up my phone and opened a text to Aaron. *Three guesses who owns your other two crime scenes, and the first two don't count.*

Decmar Industries didn't have a registered board of directors with the state of Virginia because there wasn't one. Fifteen years ago, it started off as a pharmaceutical distribution company. But the license records with the state board fell off two years later, just as the opioid flood was really hitting a stride. Somewhere after that, Decmar had morphed into a DBA shell company—for a North Carolina property management outfit with a dozen more Hideaway-type motels on the balance sheet.

I was on my third cup of coffee Thursday morning, the drip-drip-drip of melting icicle droplets pinging off the gutter downspout outside and Darcy curled in her bed in the corner of the living room, when I found the reason it was so carefully camouflaged.

"Leaping Louboutins." I stared at the screen.

I'd woken up to sunshine streaming through the windows, less bleary eyes than I could remember in weeks, and a text from Aaron that even his police sources had nothing on this company.

Normally, when my cops had nothing and I'd hit a dead end, I asked Joey.

Since I couldn't do that this morning, I made coffee, opened my computer, and tried my damndest to think like him. I sat with my eyes closed and called up every memory I could muster of every time he'd half-cryptically told me something important or tried to warn me away from danger.

And then I started searching surrounding states.

Listening when people talk is a damned handy skill to have. Joey had mentioned offhand once that Virginia is a safe haven for shelter companies because the DBA registration laws aren't as strict as they are in other places.

I started in Maryland and worked my way around. By the time the "no results found" came up from the office of the Tennessee Attorney General, I sighed and refilled my coffee a second time.

I clicked to the website for the North Carolina Department of Business and Agricultural Oversight, typing Decmar Industries into the search bar.

And there it was. Right in the center of my screen, little black letters. Monavida Property Services.

The name of the company was a blue text link on the government website in front of me. I clicked.

It took me to a list of officers and an address.

My eyes stuck on the first name on the list.

President. Chief Executive Officer.

Mario DelAmico.

I pushed the computer back across the table almost involuntarily.

One, their records were outdated, because I'd watched Don Mario die a year and a half ago on a manicured emerald lawn in the foothills of the Blue Ridge. Two...

"Holy fucking shit, Darcy." I almost choked on the words.

Mario DelAmico was the longtime head of the Caccione crime family, the most powerful American mafia syndicate outside New York.

The one Joey was tangled up in trying to get away from by helping Kyle bust them. The reason I knew him at all, and the reason he wasn't here.

My fingers curled into fists.

It made perfect sense: that's why Kyle had been in Tucker's motel room blathering about things he couldn't tell me. I jumped out of the chair fast enough for my ribs to remind me that was a bad idea. I had to fold my hands behind my back to keep from grabbing my phone and calling Kyle. He was up to something. I'd known him since I was fifteen, lost my virginity to him at seventeen, and damn near given up my dreams to stay in Texas and wait to marry him when I was eighteen, only to have him show up in Richmond ten years later and help upend my quiet little world.

All that history was a large part of why I'd been avoiding him, really. I was mad at him—but I still loved him, so the anger twisted back and made me mad at myself.

But the letters on my screen made me think maybe I didn't know as much about what was going on as I thought I did. Again.

All of a sudden, my anger at Kyle felt justified. Driving, even. But it wasn't helpful.

Deep breaths. Being pissed at Kyle—or anyone else—wasn't going to help me figure out where Katie went or who killed Tucker or what the hell Aaron thought might be going on at the PD. Journalism since before there were newspapers 101: emotion makes it easier to do stupid shit and harder to see the situation clearly.

I had time to be angry later.

If anything around this had a Caccione connection, it changed the whole game. I had spent two years of my life studiously burying my head in the sand where that word was concerned. Kyle had told me little things here and there, but I avoided knowing any more than was absolutely necessary to keep people alive.

I let a long, shaky breath go and went back to my chair, unwrapping the bandage around my torso and pulling it tighter. Clearly, Kyle didn't want me knowing this. Aaron wouldn't have come to see me if he thought there was mafia involvement in these murders. He also wasn't sure who we could trust at the PD—not that the mob was the local PD's area of expertise.

I pressed the Velcro end of my bandage down tightly and reached for the computer.

Two years of dodging my every instinct, not asking, ignoring, looking the other way, because I loved him.

Two years of carefully building myself a shaky little happily ever after in my imaginary future where this wouldn't ruin us someday.

It crumbled and crashed down around me so hard I could practically hear it, the dust from the implosion fogging my brain as I opened my browser and typed *Caccione crime family* into the search bar.

18

Google had so much on the Cacciones, I wasn't at all sure how the hell Kyle even had a job.

An hour of hunching over the computer later, I knew the names of two bosses, three underbosses, and even a handful of suspected foot soldiers.

I knew that the organization stretched from the Outer Banks to southern Pennsylvania, with a storied history that included cameos by people like Bugsy Seigel and John Gotti, and it was apparently common knowledge that they had their hands in everything from underground gambling (I'd seen that for myself once) and moonshine (that, too), to cement and construction work, interstate trucking, and waste management.

And drug trafficking. Of course. That was the free space in the center of my Tucker Armstrong murder bingo card.

"If it's all right here on the internet, why has it taken Kyle years to build his case?" I asked Darcy. She turned a circle in her bed before resuming her nap.

I grabbed my notebook and jotted down the names on my screen.

The thing Google was missing was the name of the new big boss, the Don. Wikipedia knew Don Mario was dead, and had a pretty damned accurate description of what had happened that day, given that as the only journalist on site, I had vagued up the details at the request of the two most important men in my life at the time.

"*New family members are made in a ceremony usually involving a blood oath taken over a gun or a religious artifact,*" I read.

My brain threw up an image of Joey cutting his arm and swearing allegiance to criminals before I could stop it, bitterness rising in the back of my throat.

I even figured I knew the scar. It wasn't big, on the inside of his right forearm, faded in the winter and almost obscured by his easy, deep tan in the summer.

Jesus. Part of me wanted to slam the computer shut and open a bottle of wine. At nine o'clock in the morning. Another was realizing just how little I'd learned about Joey's life, and even though I'd done it on purpose, the more I read, the more I needed to know. I had asked, of course, eventually. But he was careful with his words when he talked about them, with that look he got on his face when he was intent on protecting me, so I didn't press. He worked in transportation. He helped fix problems for Don Mario. I had seen business cards and even been to his office, so I knew the trucking company was a real thing. But the screen in front of me said the Cacciones were into transportation. And the short description Joey had given me of his connections with Mario sounded an awful damned lot like the definition of a consigliere on my screen.

"The boss's right-hand man." I shook my head. "He couldn't be. Right?"

There was a blue link on my screen that read "law enforcement and informants."

I put my finger on the trackpad and dragged the arrow in the center of the screen over. Hovered over the "and."

I couldn't click it.

I pushed the computer away.

Nothing good would come from clicking it. If his name wasn't there, it wouldn't convince me that the boss didn't know Joey was working with Kyle just because the internet didn't. And if it was...I might never sleep again.

I needed to focus on what I'd jumped off into the center ring of information hell looking for in the first place: how this might lead to Katie, or to whoever killed Tucker.

And that was simple: the names.

I walked a slow lap around the kitchen, stretching my sore side gently, reached past the Moscato to grab a Diet Dr Pepper from the fridge, and returned to my chair.

Closed that window and opened a new one.

Since Mario DelAmico was still listed as a principal in the North Carolina property company, I went back to their site to search his name for involvement in any other company. The way things like this worked in the criminal underworld, possibly questionable but strictly legal, above-board businesses were registered to the bosses, because there had to be a place they got all their money. And there was income from those ventures, of course, that taxes were properly filed and paid on. But the real money came from the cut the boss took of every single family operation—money that was earned or taken by foot soldiers with no obvious connection to the bosses, which was how they stayed insulated from prosecution. It was often laundered through the legit companies to the family's credit, and distributed to the other members in cash.

Two hits: a concrete company and a port management company.

I blinked at the screen. This had taken Kyle years? It was so obvious I wanted to scream at my screen. Selling stolen cargo, importing illicit merchandise. I wasn't really sure what the concrete had to do with anything except that in the movies, they always say Jimmy Hoffa is buried in it somewhere. But there was mention of cement even on the Wikipedia page, so I'd ask Kyle. When I could talk to him again without shouting.

Virginia was harder: the company name was required to find informa-tion on officers, not the other way around. And none of the companies registered to Don Mario in North Carolina had a Virginia business license. Same with taxes: there's no option to search the county by name for proper-ties owned, it has to be an address search. Great if you're an average citizen who values your privacy. Irritating as hell when you're a reporter looking for a pattern that might lead back to a murderer.

Wait. I opened a new window and went to Maryland's state attorney general's site. The Cacciones had reach all the way into southern Pennsyl-vania? And Joey's office was in Bethesda?

Mario wasn't listed as a director in any company I could find in Maryland. Maybe they were quicker to reconcile death records there?

I backspaced to erase his name and went to the next on my list. Cucinelli, Edward. An underboss. Search.

A rainbow wheel spun in the center of my screen as the computer worked. I tapped my index and middle fingernails on the edge of the keyboard and stared, unblinking, waiting for the results.

One result: Martinsburg Transportation, Inc.

Joey's company.

I pulled a lungful of air in through my nose.

I needed to know, at this point, even if knowing was scaring the everloving shit out of me.

I'd done plenty of scary stuff in the name of a story. I'd just always been afraid the worst that might happen was I'd get shot, and losing Joey for good would hurt a whole lot more.

I added the name to my list and went to a fresh search window, typing it in first.

Journalism in the age of the Internet 101: the answer to anything you want to know can always be found online. The trick is knowing where to look.

If the Cacciones had something to do with these murders, there was a good reason. Maybe even one that meant Aaron was right and we had a new crop of dirty cops in Richmond. But the heart of it had to be money.

The very existence of any organized crime, from a street gang to the original five families of the Italian American Mafia in New York, is fed by two things: money and power.

It's a lot like politics when you strip away the guns and blood and get right down to it. Hell, in my experience, that wasn't even really always necessary.

Nobody was after power killing a drug-addicted former professor in a quiet motel room hit. I didn't think. But I hadn't had a chance to talk with Senator Rowley, either.

That, I could remedy. Maybe before lunch, even. I picked up my phone and clicked the computer to the state senate site, dialing the number for his office.

The snow was melting. The new session was starting next week.

Come on, pick up.

"Senator Rowley's office, this is Marcia, how may I help you today?"

"Hi, Marcia, this is Nichelle Clarke from *RVA Week*. Is the senator in his office today?" The words came out so bright I might even call myself chirpy.

"Oh!" She hadn't been around the capitol much if she wasn't used to reporters calling. "I...um...can I place you on a brief hold, Miss Clarke?"

"Of course." My eyebrows drifted toward my hairline. Surely he'd been interviewed before.

Before I could figure out what to make of how badly I'd flustered her, she was back. "I'm sorry to keep you waiting." She sounded a bit calmer. "The senator has appointments throughout the day today, but he'd like to know if you're free to meet him for an informal discussion this evening. Perhaps Capital Ale House at six-thirty?"

Informal.

Read: off the record.

Hell yes. I didn't say that, though.

"I will see him there," I said. "Thank you so much for your help."

I swear her voice shook as she wished me a nice day before she hung up.

I opened a text to Aaron. *Can you find out if cyber has gotten into Tucker Armstrong's laptop yet? I know they stay covered up with cases these days, but I'm crossing my fingers.* The branch of the police department that once dealt mostly with white collar crime had extended into every investigative division in the past several years. Murderers, rapists, thieves: everyone has a computer and cell phone.

The gray dot bubble appeared before I could put the phone down. *Sure thing. I wouldn't advise holding your breath, but I can try to fast-track it. Anything special you're hunting?*

Letters. I tapped. *He wrote me one Landers has in evidence, but it didn't specify what he wanted. I'm wondering who else he was asking for help. And with what.*

Buzz. *He was an interesting guy with a colorful life. From his file anyway.*

Wait, what?

He has a record? I mean, besides the drug prescription forgery from a few years back? I didn't bother with the all caps, adding a fair number of exclamation points before I sent the text instead.

I watched the little dots juggle around for what felt like ten years.

Buzz. *Goes all the way back to college. Willing to do anything for a cause, this guy. You want me to send you this? Off the record for now, of course.*

I typed *Yes please*, putting the phone on the table.

Anything for a cause.

Had Tucker finally given his life to this one?

And was I chasing the Caccione lead because it went somewhere, or because I wanted Joey back so badly somehow I was hoping that would help me find him?

I truly didn't know. It wasn't like I could go up to Cucinelli's office and ask him—Don Mario had plucked me out of a crowd easily once, and I was sure anyone connected to Joey knew about me and didn't like me. I might be out of sorts, but I wasn't looking to get myself—or anyone else—killed today.

Which left me with one option.

Kyle.

I didn't have time for anger or grudges, especially with people who might be able to help put some of these puzzle pieces in place.

He'd spent years chasing the Cacciones and he was into Tucker's murder for a reason I was pretty sure I didn't need him to tell me anymore. Probably just as well, because I doubted he would.

But maybe I could get him to tell me something else that would be helpful.

He didn't answer his phone.

Or his door.

I drove his truck to his office trying not to panic, looping back through my brain to all the times he'd ignored me in the past few months.

He wasn't in trouble. He was just busy. And maybe still a little pissed at me for the mace thing. I couldn't blame him there, even.

Kyle was a lot of things, but reckless wasn't one of them. I was just worked up because of the reading I'd done that morning.

That was it.

Stuck at a light on Grace Street, I picked up my phone and sent another text before I dialed his office phone.

No answer. And the texts weren't even marking themselves as delivered.

John grinned when I walked into the federal building and laid my bag on the conveyor belt for the x-ray machine. "Miss Clarke! I thought you'd grown bored of us, we haven't seen you in so long. You here to see Special Agent Miller?"

I nodded at the kindly security guard, stepping through the metal detector. "Getting my feet under me at the new place, John. How was your holiday?"

"Too much pie and not enough running." He patted his midsection, about ten Christmases' worth of too much pie stretching his shirt forward over his belt, and winked.

I laughed and took my bag and the plastic visitor's badge he handed me, striding to the elevators with a wave.

I didn't wait for the doors to open all the way before I charged off the elevators on five. I made a left down the first hall and stopped outside Kyle's office when the door was shut tight.

I flicked my eyes to the floor. The light was on.

Deep breath. I raised my hand and moved to rap on the dark-stained oak.

"Miller's not here." The voice was deep and smooth, behind my left shoulder. I spun to find myself eye level with a broad chest under a starched button down. I looked up. Silver hair. Lined but attractive face, clean-shaven.

"Special Agent in Charge Derek MacAulay." He extended one hand. "Miss Clarke."

I didn't miss the absence of a smile or a "nice to meet you," but I went with it, shaking his hand and meeting his somber gaze with a tight smile.

"Thank you for your help, sir." Not that he had been any, really, but I had to say something and I knew better than to offer up any information to a federal agent without being asked specifically—especially when the agent in question was Kyle's boss and didn't strike me as my biggest fan.

He let his hand drop back to his side, his eyebrows lifting as he tipped his head back toward the elevators.

I stood still, refusing to look away from his eyes or blink. I wasn't leaving this building until I knew Kyle was okay.

We stayed that way until another tall man in a dark suit—it's almost like there's a federal agent cookie cutter hidden in the bowels of the justice department—stopped short next to me and lowered the file folder he was perusing. "Excuse—oh. Hey, Nichelle," he said before his gaze landed on the commander. His spine went straight, eyes shifting to dead ahead. He didn't salute, or anything, but it wouldn't have surprised me. "Sir."

"Can I help you with something, Pinkston?" The edge in the words could have sliced steel. Dude really didn't like me.

"No, sir, just going back to my desk, sir."

The commander turned his icy stare back to me. "And you?"

"I need to speak with Agent Miller," I said. "If it's all the same to you, I can wait for him. It's urgent."

"It is definitely not all the same to me." MacAulay leaned in close enough for me to smell the coffee on his breath, keeping his voice low. "I'm not sure what the hell Miller even thinks he's doing, giving a reporter of all people the idea that you can just waltz past security and roam around up here like you own the place, but that will have to be a conversation for later. Right now, I will remind you that this is a federal law enforcement agency, and as such, you need an appointment and an escort to be on this floor. You have neither. The elevators back to the lobby are this way."

There wasn't really anything else to say unless I wanted a couple of Kyle's colleagues to have to toss me out on my ass—which I did not. "I know how to find them, thank you. Have a nice day."

I tapped my foot and fumed until the elevator opened to the lobby. An escort. While it's true that those are the rules, I've helped with enough cases over the past few years and knew enough of the agents that I assumed the relaxed atmosphere that greeted me in this building had been earned.

Not with everyone, it seemed.

Good to know.

I was almost to the doors when I paused mid-step, pivoting on my heel and striding back to the guard desk.

"That was quicker than usual," John said.

"He's not in." I flashed my brightest smile. Nothing is wrong, just want to ask my friend a question. Calm. "Did you happen to see him leave this morning?"

"Oh sure, I just figured he came back in through the garage when you came in to meet him. He was headed over to the capitol with Special Agent McCarthy."

"Thanks, John. Could you help me out with something?" I handed him Kyle's keys. "I left it in a visitor's space out front. Tell him I said thank you for letting me borrow it."

"Sure thing."

"Have a good one."

"I'm counting down to spring. It's too cold out there for my old bones these days, Miss Clarke."

"Mine aren't that old, but I hear you." I turned for the door.

Kyle wasn't in any danger if he was at the capitol, so yay.

Senator Rowley's assistant had said he was in a meeting. And he wanted to talk to me off the record later.

Maybe I knew who he was talking to?

What I didn't know—about any damn thing relating to this whole mess —was why.

And that was getting more frustrating by the minute.

19

"What has you all uptight? Grant didn't say much about where y'all went yesterday, but he's being weird, too. Should I be worried?" Melanie's brow furrowed above her slim rectangular black glasses. We sat on a bench in Byrd Park, her thick coat making it hard for her to fold her arms over her chest.

I shivered when the wind picked up. The local weather guys said a monster cold front was dipping down from the arctic tonight, dropping temperatures to dangerous levels. When I wasn't worried about the mafia and the murder victims, I had trouble thinking of anything other than the people sleeping in that alley behind the Hideaway in single-digit temperatures. It had been all I could do to get out of my Uber and drive my car away from the McDonald's without going back there to check. Brooks had training and a weapon, and it was his beat. A part of his beat where he'd ordered me to stay in the locked car. And I couldn't buy that the concern I'd seen that day was a show. Not without more evidence.

"Did you happen to get a name for that guy who was at the council meeting last night? The motel owner?" I asked.

She pulled a notebook from her bag. "Well, for starters, that's weird, too," she said. "Councilman Milton said he just met this guy yesterday, after the notice was posted about the emergency council meeting."

"He sure did a lot of arguing on a stranger's behalf last night."

Mel pointed her finger at me. "Right. And that's not like him. He's the king of research, generally speaking. So this guy shows up yesterday claiming to own the motel and having a fit about this, and a guy like Milton apparently throws everything I've come to know about his personality to the dogs and jumps up to go toe to toe with the mayor and her right-hand girl over this seedy motel. I know we had a story on overdoses, but I'm pretty sure you wouldn't be in this up to your precious little pom pom hat if there wasn't more to it than that."

I reached up to tap the giant pom on top of my hat forward and smiled. "You sure you don't want Shelby's job?" I shook my head. "Never mind. That makes my life harder, not easier. You stay with the council."

"I'm not sure how much longer I'll be there." She folded her gloved hands over her abdomen. "I'm pregnant."

I let out a whoop that sent half a dozen cardinals soaring out of a nearby tree. "Why didn't Parker tell me yesterday? Congratulations!"

"He doesn't know yet," she said. "I'm waiting for the perfect time to tell him. I found out on Christmas Eve, and I didn't want to say anything in case I jinxed it, you know? But now I'm not sure how to tell him." She fixed me with a flat stare over the top of her glasses. "But I don't want him running off into one of your crazy stories and getting hurt again."

"In fairness, that one was way more his crazy story than mine. But I hear you. I don't need Parker to track down a sleazy motel owner for me. This one, I can handle."

"But that's the thing, he doesn't own the motel, some weird company nobody I can find has ever heard of owns the motel, like you said last night," she said. "There's no board of directors, nothing but a PO Box... Milton was really upset when he heard all this earlier."

"But did he give you the guy's name?" I asked.

"He gave me that name the guy gave him. But I don't think anything about this dude was on the up and up."

"A fake name? Why would you risk going to the city council with something like that?" I asked. I thought I might know, but this was way too weird for me to be sure of anything. "What was it?"

"Yeric Jones." She flipped her notebook around and pointed. "But the state has no record of such a person. Social media has nothing on anyone by that name. I can't find him anywhere. What the hell is going on here, Nichelle? I'm not used to dead people and fake IDs—should I be worried about Milton?"

I pulled out my own notebook and scribbled the name down like there was a snowball's chance in the sun itself I might forget it.

"I honestly don't know, Mel." Every word true. I didn't want to freak her out, but it was probably better for her—and Parker—if they stayed as far away from this as I could keep them. At least until I knew what the mafia might have at stake here and how far some folks would go to protect it. "Let me see what I can find out and I'll call you later." I leaned forward to put the notebook back into my bag, itching to ask her what Shelby was working on today but refusing to scratch that one. Putting Mel in a spot of choosing between our friendship and professional ethics would be a shitty thing to do.

I squeezed her arm as I stood and hurried back to my car, my side feeling more normal the longer the day wore on. Three hours still before I was supposed to meet Rowley. I texted Kyle again, but his phone was either still off or otherwise lacking a signal.

I touched the phone app on the screen and then Aaron's name in my favorites list.

He picked up on the second ring. "White."

"How's your day going?" I asked.

"About like my day went yesterday," he said. "You have anything interesting?"

"A guy who might have given a city councilman a fake name." And a couple other things I could mention later if they led to anything.

"Milton, by any chance? He was here this morning, in with the chief."

"Maybe after he talked to Mel," I muttered.

"Huh? Who's Mel?"

I shook my head, clicking my earring against the phone. "Nothing. Just trying to piece this together. Anyone say what Milton wanted? Would Mike know?" My old friend the former narcotics sergeant and current deputy chief was about as straight as arrows get. For that matter, I thought the chief was, too. If Aaron's suspicions about crooked cops had legs, they didn't climb that high.

"From the hour Landers spent in there with them, I gather he wanted a briefing on the Armstrong murder. Isn't that motel in his district?"

"It is."

"Want me to run your possible pseudonym and see if I get a hit?" Aaron asked.

"Please," I said. "Yeric Jones. No idea really on the spelling, I think Mel guessed by how it sounded."

Aaron grunted.

"What?" I asked.

"Well, it's not impossible, but it's normal for a person picking a fake name to choose something super common. Like I'd expect Tom Jones or Joe Smith before something like this."

I reached for my notebook. "Some kind of a code?"

"For what purpose, though? Who is supposed to get the message?"

"I haven't the first damned clue. Maybe it's not fake, for all I know. Mel is a city hall reporter, she doesn't have to run stuff like this down on the regular."

Computer keys clicked in the background. "Let's see. Stand by."

"You don't think Landers is doing something he shouldn't be, right?" I asked the big question neither of us wanted to say out loud.

"I don't want to," Aaron said.

"I've been fighting like hell to avoid it." I sighed. "But then you showed up talking about suspecting corruption and I found Mario's—" I stopped, stumbling over the last word.

"Mario? Like as in DelAmico?"

Too late.

Aaron gave it four beats. "What are you not saying, Nichelle?"

"The Hideaway Motel, that company, Decmar Industries? It's a Virginia DBA for a North Carolina company. Their state attorney general's website has DelAmico listed as chairman of the board."

"He's really working remotely these days, huh?"

I snorted. "Clearly their records department is a bit behind."

The clicking stopped.

"Anything?" I asked.

"I don't see any sort of government ID issued to that name, no," Aaron said. "Hey, where did you find the name of the parent company for the motel? Tax records?"

"Yeah. Reporter's best friend."

More keys clicking.

"Except in January. Last year's tax addresses are still on the records for all properties sold in the last weeks of December."

"Sold?" I sat up straight and dug in my bag for a pen. "Someone closed on a building three people overdosed in?"

"No, it looks like they closed before the overdoses happened, actually." Aaron let the words trail, like he was reading something on his screen. "I can't see the buyer though. It says 'pending update' for now."

"So the Caccione crime family owned a motel known for drug activity —no surprise there. But they sold it a couple of weeks ago, and people started dying almost immediately? First overdoses, then shootings? What the fuck is going on over there?"

"But not all of the shootings were at the Hideaway," Aaron said.

My brain stuck on the "not all" part of that and played it over and over on a loop in my head.

Not all. Not all.

Not all of the victims at the Hideaway were shot.

Brooks was taking Tucker food because he was trying to get clean.

"Shit, Aaron, I think we've been looking at the wrong victims. Or maybe just not all of them."

"I'm sorry?" he asked.

I was stuck back in the alley with Brooks, watching him load the young woman from the tent into the back of the ambulance, the vial from the Narcan injection still in his hand.

"The overdose victims. There were two young women and a man. What if someone let them die?"

"How do you figure?"

"Narcan injectors."

"The rollout of that program is hung up in red tape," he said. "Sometimes people come out of that shit half-crazy. It's not always a good idea to use the injector even if you have it, and especially if you're solo responding to a call because it's Christmas week and nobody is at work."

"Or if you wanted to make it look like they killed themselves when they really didn't. Who responded to those calls? Was it the same unit?"

"Getting there." More keys clicked. "I'll be damned."

"Please don't say it was..." I didn't finish the sentence.

"Griffin Brooks."

My head hit the back of the seat with a *thunk*. He had injectors in his car, red tape be damned. But the victims were all still dead.

"He's a third generation cop," I said. "I spent the whole day with him and didn't get any indication that he wasn't a hundred percent the genuine article." Damn, what else had I missed?

"This report I'm looking at says the first victim was dead when he arrived on the scene," Aaron said. "Cold already."

"That takes hours."

"Less in this weather and a building that drafty, but still a while."

"Did they perform autopsies on them?" I asked.

"Everything is always backed up around the holidays. Overdoses like this are the very bottom of the totem pole. So my guess is not yet. Why?"

"Just wondering what they might have taken that they didn't know they were taking."

Which wouldn't have worked on Tucker and Katie if they weren't trying to get clean.

"Aaron? Any leads on Katie DeLuca?"

"Not a single credible one."

Damn.

"I'm starting to fear it might already be too late for her," he said.

There I was trying to avoid thinking that, and then Aaron had to go and say it.

"Yeah."

And all I'd been able to get from Charlie's producer was that she was on assignment and the station couldn't give me her cell number.

I liked every possible scenario less the more I thought about them.

The obvious connection for the overdose victims and Tucker was the motel, but if they were all murdered, that couldn't be the only one. Maybe I was overcomplicating it. If the Caccione family had owned the place and sold it, it wasn't exactly to Marriott. Maybe the quality of the drugs being distributed there changed when the ownership did and it was as simple as that.

My bigger question was why would a crime family in the drug trade decide to offload such a perfect distribution point? They had to make a shit ton more on the dope they sold through the place than they were getting for the rooms.

"I'm going to look into Mr. Brooks's record with the department," Aaron said. "If you're thinking about chasing down one single question to do with the mafia, stop thinking it right now and find another focus. If you're right and these other three victims were murdered, there's a reason. You find the why for your readers, and I'll let you know if your new patrolman friend is worthy of your sympathy."

"I'll call you when I have something," I said.

"I'm not kidding, Nichelle."

"Thanks, Aaron." I paused. "I heard you."

I just wasn't sure I could swear I'd listen, that's all.

20

Twenty minutes of trying to talk myself out of chasing down the mafia without Joey or Kyle later, I was in line at the courthouse, the form requesting the title transfer for the motel in my hand.

It's easy to see organized crime involvement in pretty much anything as an easy arrow to the guilty party. Particularly with dead people all over the place. If Aaron was right and all these murders were connected, we were looking at six victims—twice as many as I'd ever written about in a single story. But the most surprising thing about the mafia I'd learned from watching and listening to Joey and Kyle over the past couple of years is that organized crime generally frowns on killing people. Murder is difficult for authorities to ignore, and draws the kind of attention to profitable activities that professional criminals would rather not have to deal with.

By the time I got to the front of the line, I was wondering if I was looking in the easy place instead of the right one. Nobody had died before the Cacciones were vested of the property. So maybe Mr. "Jones" from the council meeting was a better goose to chase. He had to be a safer one, at any rate. So the title office it was.

I smiled at the harried clerk and handed her the form. She checked off three lines with a red pen, looked at my driver's license, and tapped a few keys on the computer in front of her. "Be right back."

I looked around the room, my eyes stopping on stooped shoulders beneath a head of spiky black hair bent over the far counter, hands filling out a form.

Shelby.

Damn.

And she could get this story in front of readers four days sooner than I could. The inability to beat Shelby to a headline and utter lack of control over that situation was enough to drive a girl batshit crazy.

And there was less than nothing I could do about this, short of throwing the computer in front of me to the floor or kneecapping Shelby on my way out. Which would be frowned upon even by cops who liked me.

"Here you go." The clerk returned with my paper.

"Thank you," I said. "Have a good one."

"That's a popular one this week," she said.

I froze mid pivot. "Really?"

"You're the third person I've printed it for since this morning," she said.

I shot a glance at Shelby's still-turned back, betting that was about to be four. "You don't happen to remember any of the other people who asked for it, do you?"

"Sure. But for really different reasons. The first guy was here at the crack of dawn. Dan Kessler from Channel Eight. I've watched him on the news since I was a little girl; it was fun to meet him. And the second guy was..." She fanned herself. "Well, our heat hasn't been working so great, but he made that difficult to remember, if you get my drift. I think his picture must be in the dictionary next to tall, dark, and handsome."

My throat closed up around the next question I was going to ask.

I was projecting. Surely.

I coughed my airway back open. "That striking, huh? Not something you see every day."

"Oh honey." She leaned forward, a conspiratorial giggle escaping her suddenly flushed throat. "I'm talking three-piece suit, thick, dark hair, all the muscles—even under the suit—and the sexiest voice I've ever heard."

I swallowed hard, my brain trying to form a puzzle piece that put Joey in Richmond looking for this particular information. No way. He'd have come to see me. Wouldn't he?

On one hand, her description was sure as hell dead-on. On the other, a good suit and an expensive haircut will sexy-up almost any guy, and both are common in the circles Joey moves in. Muscles are also plentiful, as they come in handy when trouble presents itself. For that matter, all of those things, except maybe the third piece of the suit, are common among federal agents, too, and Kyle is no slouch in the sexy department. So my anxiety hinged entirely on how much I trusted this woman's knowledge of proper men's fashion terminology.

That was ridiculous. Which is where I chose to stick my landing: it could have been anyone, and until I saw Joey with my own eyes, I wouldn't assume otherwise.

"Sorry I missed it."

"Why do so many people care that this place sold?" she asked. "The health department is about to shut it down anyway."

The last word tumbled all the way out before she dropped her eyes to the keyboard. "I mean...um...shoot. I shouldn't have said that."

"Said what?" I winked, tapping the paper on the counter. "You have a nice day now, Kerry."

Gratitude beamed blinding-bright. "You too, Miss."

I ducked my head so my hair fell between me and Shelby and bent my knees so my height didn't make me stand out as I hurried out the office door, pulling it shut tight behind me and pausing for a breath before I went back to the parking lot.

My phone set to buzzing before I made it back to the car. I pulled it from my pocket and checked the screen. Jordan. "Hey there." I put it to my ear as I cranked the engine and turned up the heat. "Are you missing your palm trees and beaches yet?"

He chuckled, warm and low. "I'm having too much fun to mind a little cold weather. Your two days are half up."

I sighed. "Is that all you wanted?"

"It is not. Did you see the *Telegraph*'s piece this morning on Katie DeLuca? People are going apeshit on their Facebook page, outright threatening each other in the comments. Seems half the city thinks this Landers guy ought to be fired for harassing her, and the other half would happily attend her hanging on the capitol square. You people get worked up over your sports here in Dixie, don't you?" He sounded positively gleeful.

"Why are you so excited that Shelby's story is getting a shit ton of clicks?" I pinched the phone between my cheekbone and shoulder and put the car in reverse. "That doesn't make me see my story as less appealing."

"I know. But I think it might give us a truce point—because those clicks are going to keep Shelby focused on the wrong thing. And with Charlie Lewis somehow out of the picture, that gives you an exclusive lane to the real story at the heart of this whole mess."

"I wouldn't count Charlie out," I said. "I don't know why she's been so quiet, but I know her. If there's something this big going on and she's not in the middle of it somehow, I will eat my shoes. The station said she's on assignment. She'll find something. Even Dan Kessler was at the title office before I was today. So please, if you have any earthly idea what the real story at the heart of this mess is, please share."

"Finding the story is your job, star reporter, not mine. If it's the late great Mr. DeLuca's bride, find her while these people are busy fighting over whether she ought to be found. If it's something else, get to digging. I'm working on an ad pricing structure that might allow us to post excerpts of larger stories in a breaking fashion and charge reduced rates for the ads on those pages."

Hot damn. I stopped at a light and smiled. "So I can compete with Shelby and Charlie?"

"Maybe not head on, but certainly more effectively than you've been able to since you started here. The test is, will people pick up the paper or come back to the web for the whole story on Tuesday? And the only way to find out is to try it. When you have something I can use, shoot it to Jeffers."

"You're my hero. Give me a few hours," I said, reaching to the passenger seat for the title transfer record and glancing at it. "Oh, for fuck's sake."

Not Yeric Jones. Eric. How the hell Milton and Mel had both flubbed that, I couldn't guess. And why I hadn't thought to search the sound-alikes, I would blame on lack of sleep to avoid wasting energy being annoyed with myself.

Whatever. I knew it now.

I pulled into the parking lot at Thompson's coffee shop and held my gloved fingers in front of the heating vents, looking back at the title transfer for the date. Three days before the first OD death.

Which meant I couldn't tell conclusively whether the new owner was passing out bad dope, because those victims could have been using a stash. Not likely on the sort of budgets prevalent in places like the Hideaway, but possible.

Eric Jones. Common, like Aaron said. A search would take hours, and even then I'd have to get lucky.

But maybe I was due for a little luck.

I stepped off the elevator into the newsroom with my shoulders squared, smiling when Parker looked up.

"How're the ribs there, Sean Lee?"

"Better. Is Connolly here?"

"Haven't seen him since Tuesday." Parker leaned back in his chair, lacing his fingers behind his head.

I frowned. "Where's he been? I need to ask him something." Evan Connolly was the best-networked businessman I'd ever met. Halfway between the courthouse and my office, I'd realized that my Eric Jones haystack might not be so impossible after all. If he was really on the up and up, my new publisher might know him.

"I don't ask questions about such things, Clarke. I just enjoy the peace and quiet."

Fair, coming from him. I made a beeline for Bob's open office door.

"Hey, kiddo, Parker said you had a rough one yesterday." Bob swiveled his chair from the monitor and beckoned me inside. "Please tell me if it was rough anyway, it was the kind of rough people are going to want to read about."

I settled in my usual chair. "I think so. There's definitely more to Tucker Armstrong's murder than you can see on the surface. In the immediate running, Pierce wants something we can maybe put online tonight, and I think the mayor is working a political end-around on the Hideaway. She called off that meeting so abruptly last night because someone told her the health inspector could shut the place down faster than the courts could and she decided she didn't have to play fair."

"And you can prove this?" Bob's eyebrows went up.

"Working on it. Do you know anyone at the health department, by any chance?"

"Nichelle." It landed like a five-hundred-pound anvil. "God knows I'm the first person to appreciate responsible advocacy in journalism. Nobody who's worth a damn at this job gets into it for anything short of wanting to save the world. But I'm beginning to wonder if Connolly is second-guessing his noble cause of saving traditional journalism, here. It's one thing for us to be on a crusade. He's fronting the money. I need a cover story from you that's going to move papers. I'm not sure the health department shutting down a motel where four people have died in a month is it. Why should anyone who lives and works in the heart of the city give the slightest shit whether or not Madam Mayor is being fair about that? If you're going to challenge her to a duel, pick a better sword."

I sighed. Not because he was giving me a hard time, because he was right. I was grabbing onto any thread I could because I hadn't cracked the real story here, which was Tucker. All the drama of the past couple of days, from political theater to *Law Enforcement Confidential* in my living room, had me looking at the wrong things—which amounted to anything Shelby wasn't looking at.

"Aaron White thinks Katie DeLuca is a scapegoat," I said.

"White didn't give you that on the record or you'd have led with it instead of that health department bullshit." Bob's voice was flat.

"He didn't," I agreed. "And with her mother being arraigned this afternoon for assaulting a police officer, it's going to be hard to get anyone to consider it. But I don't think Tucker Armstrong wrote me a letter asking for my help because he was afraid of Katie, or worried about her, or whatever. I've read it like 950 times, and it sounds to me like he knew something he thought other people needed to know, too. He had files and maps and all kinds of stuff in his room. Like he was building a case. He was a lawyer, once upon a time."

"That I hadn't heard. A case against what?"

I shrugged. "By the time I got there someone had ripped everything all to hell searching through it. So I don't know for sure. But a good lawyer who got into the law for the right reasons doesn't ever really leave it. It's in their blood as much as this is in yours and mine. And I have found a few things I think might be worth killing someone over."

"Such as?"

Here we go. The last time I'd said anything to Bob about the Caccione family it was indirect, and he was recovering from a heart attack. And he still yelled at me.

"Until a couple of weeks ago, the head of the Caccione crime syndicate was listed as the chairman of the board of the company that owned the company that owned the Hideaway Motel," I said. "They sold it before this latest round of overdoses, before Tucker Armstrong died. But best I can tell, this DBA they were running it under is a shell company for drug distribution."

"Drugs like crack, or drugs like prescription?" he asked. No yelling. No chastising. He didn't even blink.

"Prescription. I did a lot of reading on how these pills have been making it to addicts by the hundreds of thousands, and there's been very little regulation, until just recently. The numbers the drug companies were turning in to the government are years behind, so they're no help."

"How long did the mob own this place?"

"Since '05. The same year Decmar Industries was incorporated and licensed as a pharma resale company."

"Quick on the draw, weren't they?" Bob shook his head. "People never saw what was coming for them."

I pointed. "That's the central point of my story, I think, is getting people who have never struggled with addiction to understand that. I've talked to doctors about the biology of addiction, and I'm solid on that. But if Tucker was murdered because he knew the Caccione family was behind this whole thing, and they sold the motel and then killed him to keep that quiet, then I can show that he never had a chance of getting away from it even though he was trying to get clean. That's something Shelby can't give people. And if I can find Katie DeLuca and get her story, too..." I raised my eyebrows.

"We'll blow everyone else out of the water." Bob nodded. "But in order to do that, you're going to have to write about the Caccione family committing a dozen felonies you think they might have killed this man to keep quiet."

His eyes were hard, unblinking.

"That part, I haven't found a way around yet," I said. "But I'm working on it."

"What does your friend Miller have to say about this?"

"I haven't talked to him since I found it."

"I'd feel better if you'd run it by him. He's not stupid, that kid." Bob leaned back in the chair and sighed. "Listen. This is a good story. The whole city is talking about this murder because of the DeLuca connection. But I need you to come to work next week and the week after to write the other big stories."

"I've pissed off powerful people before," I said.

"Which is why I'm not telling you to back off or be fired, I'm telling you to be smart. I think you've earned that," he said. "See where it goes, nail it down, and then we can decide if it's worth the risk to you if we print it. But you be careful."

I could live with that.

"Yes, sir. I think I have a cocktail date this evening that might be able to shed a whole lot of light on what Tucker Armstrong knew and didn't know."

21

Senator Rowley was late, hustling through the crowd in the bar with an apologetic grin lighting his handsome face.

"Miss Clarke, it's a pleasure." He sounded a little winded, sliding into the other side of the booth. "I'm so sorry I'm late. There's definitely a learning curve to this new adventure, and I'm figuring out that rule number one is that every meeting is going to take twice as long as I think it should—especially the ones that could have been emails."

"It's a hard reality of politics, I'm afraid. Thank you for coming to meet with me on such short notice."

"'Young man, you don't turn down a meeting with Nichelle Clarke, no matter what you think you might have done wrong.' I can't tell you who told me that, but it's advice I've taken seriously." He winked.

I felt my cheeks heat with the blood rushing to them and met his grin head-on with one of my own. He was cute. And he knew it. I could work with that.

"I suppose I've earned that reputation." I sipped my water.

He gestured to the glass. "Can I get you something else?"

"Drinks are on me—that's advice from an old editor I take seriously," I said, raising one arm and signaling to the server.

She slid between two customers and stopped at the end of our table. "What can I get you folks?"

"May I please have a glass of the California Moscato, and an order of truffle fries?" My stomach growled at the thought.

"And I'll have a Jack and Coke and a burger, hold the onion, please."

"Be right out."

Three beats. "So what do I owe the call to?" he asked. "I'm pretty sure I haven't been here long enough to have done something wrong, but I have to admit, I'm a little nervous." There went the grin again. He could give Parker a run for his money in that department, with his wide brown eyes and warm, deep voice.

"Not that I know about. Unless there's something you want to confess."

Guys like Rowley speak fluent flirting. I needed him to get comfortable enough to start talking. He was a lawyer by trade, and in my experience, they come with two modes: tight-lipped and glib, or tell-you-where-every-body-might-be-buried overshare. I couldn't tell yet which one Rowley was in this evening.

The waitress set drinks down on the table between us. "Your food will be a few minutes," she said.

"Thank you." I didn't take my eyes off the senator.

He raised his glass. "No confessions here," he said. "But how about a toast. To new beginnings."

There were so many entendres in those three little words I got a little dizzy trying to count them. I raised my wine glass, touching it to his with a soft *clink* and taking a sip.

"I found old photos of you with Tucker Armstrong on his MySpace page." When I get this far and can't get a clear read on a subject, it's usually best to jump in with both Manolos.

Rowley's eyes lost a bit of their sparkle, his smile faltering a millimeter or two. He put the glass on the table, his shoulders rising under his well-cut suit jacket with a slow, deep breath. "I was sorry to hear about that. He was a great teacher, and a brilliant man."

"So I understand." The remorse rolling off him was genuine. Which meant he'd want to help me. Now if only he could. "When was the last time you heard from Mr. Armstrong, Senator?"

"Around Thanksgiving, not long after the election," he said. "I got a letter that said he was proud of me, and he wanted to talk with me about an important issue. I called the phone number he offered and got a woman who said she was helping him. She said he didn't go out, but he needed me to come see him."

"And did you?"

He shook his head slowly. "My campaign manager said it would be a bad idea for me to be seen at a place like that. He...uh...he said the media could paint it like I was a junkie looking to score, or like I was paying for sex. And I should ask him to come to me."

Except sometime between September and Thanksgiving, Tucker stopped wanting to leave the room. Was that when he started writing the letters? I was increasingly convinced the shut-in behavior was about protecting something.

"But he couldn't do that," I said.

"Yeah. I called back and the woman, she said he couldn't go out. I asked if it was a transportation thing or a mobility thing I could get someone to help with, and she said no. She came by instead."

The phone ping. I reached for a notebook. "And when was that?"

"Early December, probably? I'm thinking it was around the first, because they were just putting the tree up in the hallway outside my office."

Not New Year's Eve, then. Or at least, not yet.

"Can you tell me what she wanted to talk with you about?" I asked. "Her name was Katie, right?"

"Kay, she said. Tuck was all worked up about the COC pipeline project. I can't blame him; it's one of the issues I ran on. I'm just not sure exactly what can be done about it now. I wish I'd decided to jump in and run for office two years ago."

"Was the pipeline even an issue back then?" I reached for my glass.

"Not one anybody knew about—which was by design." Disgust crept around the words. "Everything was planned to have it hit between election cycles, when people wouldn't have the opportunity to elect officials who might oppose it. Tuck had figured that out already, but he was still trying to find a way to stop it."

My brow furrowed. "Is that even practical at this point? I know people protested the offshore drilling for years, I even have a friend who covered the woman from Henrico County who chained herself to the buoys when they were moving the equipment out to start the work on it. But it's there. It's producing. And what I've read—which admittedly isn't a whole lot—says it's safer to move the crude to the plant in Winchester via pipeline than it is to truck it over the roads like they have been."

"In theory. Because you're not at as much mercy of human error." Rowley knocked back a long swig of his drink as the waitress put our plates on the table.

I looked up to thank her.

"Sure thing. Can I get y'all anything else?"

Rowley shook his head.

"We're set, thanks," I said.

She left, and I picked up a fry and returned my attention to Rowley. "But not in reality?"

"I'm sorry?"

"You said the pipeline is a better way to move the oil 'in theory,' like the reality is different," I said. "Just trying to follow that trail."

He bit into his burger, nodding as he chewed. "Sorry, I'm starving. Busy day. So, the thing with this particular pipeline is more about where it's going and how than the danger of spills."

"Like the path?"

He tipped his head to one side. "Among other things."

"Do you mean, like, who's building it?" I leaned forward and half-whispered in the crowded room.

He winked as he swallowed.

Transportation. Concrete. Construction.

"The oil company awarded their construction contract to the mob?" I said it so low I wasn't sure he could hear me.

He nodded slowly. Maybe he was good at lip reading.

"And Tucker Armstrong knew this?"

Something tickled the back of my brain. I closed my eyes for a five count, letting my cluttered brain throw up an image of a web page. Heller, James, and Nowitzki. Tax law. Municipal zoning legal navigation.

The firm Tucker Armstrong, Esq. had worked for specialized in construction and taxes.

And the paper I'd found on RICO violations in Tuck's room—was he trying to stop the pipeline by taking down the Cacciones? Maybe because as a long-ago legal associate he'd seen behind the curtain on some of their operations firsthand?

"I could've told him all he was going to do was get himself killed." If I'd gotten a chance to talk with him.

"I tried." Rowley dabbed at the corners of his mouth with a black linen napkin. "And he knew, really. Anyone around the legal game here for as long as Tuck was knows you don't nose around in certain things. He cared more about his cause than he did about his life. Kay, she told me that when she came to see me. She said neither one of them gave one damn about getting killed, they just wanted to win this one. It's what bonded them, she said. She was awfully young to be so hopeless."

My heel thumped on the floor under the table. The only way Katie killing Tucker achieved that objective for her was if he'd changed his mind. And if he'd backed off, why was he dead? There was no logic in the idea that she'd kill him if she got scared—much less messy and less risk of prison time to just take off.

Which brought me back to New Year's Eve. "Was that the only time you saw her?"

Rowley's forehead bunched. "Who? Kay? Yes. I told her to tell Tuck to let me fight the good fight for a while. Lord knows he did it for a lot of years."

"She didn't come back to see you on New Year's Eve?"

"I wasn't at work on New Year's Eve." He let the silence ride. "Why do you ask?"

"Did she talk to anyone else at the capitol besides you?" I ignored his question. Hearing that Katie had been willing to give her life in pursuit of this cause had me more worried about the late-night holiday phone ping near the capitol. Tucker wouldn't go out with her. No cop would have taken her even half seriously. If someone had lured her down there when that part of the city would've been literally dead with everyone in Carytown for the ball drop, she would've been a sitting duck.

The whole city was looking for Katie DeLuca, but Aaron said they hadn't had a single credible lead in forty-eight hours.

Was she hiding? Or was it already too late?

─────────────

Something about Rowley bothered me, but I couldn't lay a precise finger on what. I didn't think he was lying. And I was confident that he meant every word when he said he was sorry about what happened to Tucker Armstrong. But there was something else he wasn't saying. And while I didn't figure he'd have clued me in to the Caccione involvement in the pipeline construction if he was in cahoots with them, I couldn't swear to it.

"So what's your top priority for the new legislative session?" I switched topics when the waitress hurried away after she dropped the leather check folio on the table.

"To save the world." He dropped his napkin on the empty plate in front of him, stretching one arm along the back of the booth. "Of course."

I picked up my pen. "And just how do you think you're going to do that any better here than you could in a courtroom?"

"Well, the thing I never lost after my days climbing mountains with Tuck was my passion for the natural world, and frustration with the effect man has on it. In the real world, the only way to make a living in environmental law is to go to work for the EPA. But they're not often hiring, so I work with boring shit like taxes and will probate. But hopefully this will give me the ability to really make a difference in environmental policy. Like, for generations to come."

"You have kids?"

"I want to someday. When I meet the right woman." His voice dropped a full octave.

I circled back. "Tax law, huh?"

He offered a slow nod that said he got more than just the question. "Only the fun stuff. Rich people will do anything to hide their money from the government."

Hang on.

"People like Mario DelAmico?" I asked. It was a shot in the very dimmest, grayest pre-dawn darkness. Based on nothing but a gnawing feeling that Rowley was hiding something. But not necessarily something awful. The mafia needs lawyers more than your average citizen.

His lips curled up again, in a different kind of smile. Rueful, I might call it. "You are a smart lady, Miss Clarke."

"Did Tucker Armstrong know your firm handled Mr. DelAmico's affairs?"

He shrugged. "It was the first thing out of Kay's mouth when I saw her. I only worked on that account as an intern, basically getting coffee for the lawyers and carrying papers back and forth."

I tapped one finger on the edge of the table. "But someone there has their financial records."

Rowley's eyes slid to the door and back, slowly, to me.

"I'm afraid that's privileged information," he said, nodding so slightly a fast blink would have obscured it.

I held myself still in the seat, resisting the urge to look around. So was the fact that they did work for DelAmico at all. And I'd bet his estate was a massive monster of offshore accounts and corporate interests that would be in probate until the attorney's fees had eaten up better than half of it.

But Kyle wouldn't care about any of that. He'd been looking for a crack in the armor surrounding the Cacciones since before he'd moved to Richmond. A truckload of illegal weapons passing through Dallas on their way to the Rio Grande had gotten his attention, and for a reason he'd never even told me, he hadn't let go.

Had he found his key in a young senator with a passion for saving the world?

Just how many ways was Rowley looking to do that?

"When I called your senate office today, your assistant said you were in a meeting," I said.

"I was."

"Were you by any chance discussing something related to this conversation?"

"No comment."

He didn't have to nod that time.

"Thank you for your time this evening, sir." I tucked my MasterCard back into my bag, standing.

"Sir." He frowned. "That doesn't sound like I'm getting a less formal meeting anytime soon."

"I appreciate your candor, and your time. Good luck to you this session —if you really do save the world, give me a call. We've always got room on the cover for a superhero."

"I'll remember that. Keep fighting the good fight and scaring the shit out of politicians and crooks, Miss Clarke."

"I'm not sure I'm good at anything else anymore." The sadness in the words surprised me as I shrugged into my coat and walked ahead of him to the door.

22

I've done some crazy things in pursuit of a story in the past couple of years: broken into homes, pretended to be several people I'm not, been shot, drugged, kidnapped, almost died a handful of times.

I have never considered—seriously, not so much as thought about—going head to head with the mafia. In much the same way I've never considered driving my car off the Nickel Bridge, or feeding my favorite sapphire Louboutins into a wood chipper.

"And at this point, that's what this has become," I said to the empty car, sitting in my parking space in the garage at Joey's riverside condo. I needed to check on the plants. That's what I kept telling myself was the excuse for dropping in here every week—like I could keep a houseplant thriving with a truckload of Miracle-Gro and a degree in agriculture. My mom's green thumb gene had decidedly skipped this generation.

But we were limping along, the plants and I, and this way I didn't have to admit to myself that I was really there because I wanted to make sure the key still worked, the furniture was still there, and he might still be coming back.

I leaned back against the wall as the elevator shot skyward, wishing for the millionth time that the doors would open and he'd just be there, sitting on the long, black leather sofa with a fire going and that sexy smile that always made me forget whatever might be aggravating me about the day. I'd been just fine on my own for seven years before I met him, but damn it was hard to go back to that. And to be fair, I hadn't covered too many things that tried to kill me before Joey showed up in my living room. Doing it without him really did suck.

The doors opened to a dim hallway, the door to Joey's penthouse directly across from them.

Open.

My heart leapt into my throat, my feet freezing in place with my eyes on the door.

I could see him just showing up, that adorable mischievous look he got flashing across his face when he saw the surprise on mine.

But wouldn't he go to my house and not his?

Stepping out of my shoes, I tucked one into my bag and raised the other, stiletto heel out, as I crept across the hallway.

Voices. Deep. Definitely male.

Tucker Armstrong's ransacked hotel room flashed through my thoughts.

Shit, shit, double shit.

Deep breath.

I guess I didn't have to decide to go looking for the mafia if they came to me. Well, sort of, anyway.

I flattened my back against the cool plaster of the hallway wall. My crazy escapades have taught me that my shoes make decent weapons in a pinch, but a Manolo Blahnik doesn't beat a Sig Sauer in anything but a beauty contest.

I should leave.

But what if whoever was in there was trying to find Joey so they could hurt him? I couldn't just take off without giving Kyle a chance to warn him.

"Why is that door open?"

I knew that voice.

"Sorry, I thought I closed it." That one wasn't familiar.

I scooted back along the wall as the door shut. The lock slid home. They hadn't noticed me.

But what the actual fuck was Griffin Brooks doing in Joey's apartment?

I sat in my car with the engine still cold, my eyes on the elevator doors inside the glass and chrome vestibule across from me.

I'd walked both floors of the garage in the bitter arctic wind. Not an RPD squad car in sight. Leaning out to survey the street, I didn't see one there, either.

My phone rested in my palm with Aaron's number queued up on the screen, my thumb hovering over the talk button. But I hadn't dialed it yet. I had only heard Brooks, I hadn't seen him. I was upset. And how many times had I sat in a courtroom and watched video or experts dismiss someone's sworn testimony concerning eavesdropping as flat-out wrong?

Enough to be watching the doors before I called in the cavalry, that's how many.

Aaron had told me he thought something was off around this. That there might be officer involvement on the criminal side.

Brooks had worked every overdose scene, but hadn't saved anyone with the Narcan I knew he kept in his trunk. He'd worked two of the three shootings. He'd arrested Katie at her father's request, then pulled a gun on her mother while she was attacking both Landers and her husband.

He'd been out the morning I went to meet him. He'd said Tucker was cold, but I hadn't touched the corpse myself because...ew.

That Chesterfield officer had even told me flat out that something was off.

I didn't want to believe that. If Brooks had been bullshitting me when he told the story about wanting to help the community, clean up the area, how the dealers just fell in as replacements so he didn't see a point in arresting them because the enemy you know is better than the one you don't...the guy had seriously missed out on what would have been a very successful career in Hollywood. The catch in his voice, the genuinely stricken look on his face when he saw Tucker propped up against the wall in the corner of the motel room, the bags of groceries in the back of the squad car—I was good at catching people in lies, and I couldn't throw him under this bus until I had seen him diving for the wheels with my own eyes.

If he was here, I had nothing that could possibly be the reason short of a tie-in with the Cacciones. Joey hadn't done anything to warrant having his apartment searched by anyone else, because he hadn't been here. And who would they have served a warrant to?

No way anyone was up there legally. If Brooks was Aaron's dirty cop, we'd know before the evening was over.

I rested my head against the back of the seat and waited.

23

They didn't come out for an hour and fifteen minutes, the *bing* of the elevator rousing me from an uneasy half-doze.

I shrank back into my seat, sliding toward the floor and opening the camera on my phone. I double-checked that the flash was off, and fired off six rapid shots of the three men striding across the garage to the street exit.

Brooks walked in the middle. I didn't recognize the other two, at least not at first glance in the dim light, but my new patrolman friend was still wearing his uniform.

Dammit.

I stared at the doorway until my eyes burned after they'd vacated it, a roaring and then receding engine telling me they were gone.

I wanted to go upstairs.

I needed to call Aaron.

I pulled up his number and hit talk.

Five rings later, my hand closed around the handle on the door to the elevator vestibule, and I got his voicemail. I hung up and called right back.

No answer. "Aaron, it's Nichelle. I have a development in the situation we were discussing and I need you to call me back as soon as you get this." I was surprised at how calm I managed to sound, stabbing the up button on the wall frantically with my other hand.

In the elevator, I leaned back against the wall and breathed the way I remembered Jenna breathing when she was in labor with her son. Nobody was still up there.

But if someone was looking for Joey hard enough to break into his apartment, I needed to know why.

The door was closed. Locked.

Not broken.

I used my key to open it and swung it wide, flicking the light on before I stepped inside.

To...not a thing out of place.

Joey didn't do clutter or knick-knacks, so the whole penthouse was a sleek study in clean lines and austerity that focused attention on the gorgeous view of the river, gleaming silvery-white.

I went to the kitchen. Checked the fridge and freezer.

Empty. Clean. The microwave, dishwasher, and oven were the same.

"This is the most polite ransacking I've ever seen," I muttered, heading for the bedroom.

Brooks had come from back there. Maybe what they were looking for just wasn't out here. If they'd left with anything, if it was small enough to fit in a pocket—would I even notice it?

The bed was made, the covers not so much as wrinkled.

I checked every drawer and didn't find a sock out of order. The bathroom still smelled like bleach from the last time the cleaning lady had been in.

Were they looking for something? I braced one arm on the cool marble of the counter and studied the mirror, barely recognizing the red-rimmed, bloodshot eyes staring back at me.

What was I missing?

Objectivity is the most valuable skill I bring to a situation like this one —the ability to step back and see the whole picture, not just my corner of it, is vital. What did I know different from anyone else involved in this case?

I knew Joey was in hiding. I assumed the Cacciones knew it, too.

But Brooks had no way to know that. He wasn't a federal agent, he was a local patrolman. A local patrolman with some odd behavior patterns and a personal interest in investigating a case involving drug dealing the

Caccione family had been doing on his beat. Or maybe money coming in from them. But I could give him the benefit of the doubt for now.

Joey was connected to the Caccione family. I wasn't sure how much of local law enforcement knew that, or how deep an understanding of it they might have, but Kyle had been pretty clear that nobody but him and MacAulay knew Joey was serving as an ATF informant for the past year and a half.

So could Brooks have had a legit reason to be up here? If he was looking not maybe for a thing, but for Joey? And that was why nothing had been touched?

Maybe. Questionable methodology, coming in without a warrant, but he would've needed a key or some damned solid lock-picking skills. Maybe I'd been too quick to jump to conclusions about him.

Maybe not, of course. I nodded at the haggard-looking Nichelle in the mirror. She missed her old life. The one where the deadlines were constant and the pressure unrelenting, but the process and the guidelines clear. I shook my head and shut off the bathroom light, stepping toward the main bedroom door back to the hallway before I paused.

I shouldn't. But I couldn't help it.

I stepped into the closet and stopped dead.

The smell. Cologne and linen and leather and ... Joey. I swallowed hard and closed my eyes, pulling in a long, slow breath. I'd have sworn on a whole stack of Bibles I could feel his arms around me, just for a second.

Swiping at tears leaking from the corners of my closed eyes, I pressed my face into the rack of Armani suit coats hanging to my left, the fabric brushing buttery-soft over my face and the smell putting me into a hundred memories of finding refuge from a crazy story in Joey's arms, his strong heartbeat under my ear always a sign that everything would work out. Somehow.

It still would. It was just my turn to make it work out on my own.

By facing down the mob. Maybe.

Because here, in this little box of a room, Joey was still real. I didn't dream him, and he could come back. As long as he didn't come out of this dead or in jail.

With the Richmond PD joining the list of large organizations with an interest in where Joey was, that fear was getting harder to keep at bay.

And I didn't fully trust Kyle to make sure of either of those things. Not until I knew more about what was going on here, anyway. The problem there was, Kyle might be the only person who knew more than I did.

Kyle's lights were on. It was stupid that I was nervous about going up and ringing the bell. This was Kyle. The same Kyle who'd held me when I cried the day my childhood dog died, who'd shot people to keep me alive, who'd laughed through pain when I'd used a lacy lavender bra as a makeshift tourniquet when he'd ended up on the wrong end of a gun.

Things might be weird, but they weren't ever so weird that I didn't know in my bones that Kyle Miller was a good man. Honorable, honest, kind—he could legitimately have his face on a poster of the words in the ATF academy classrooms.

Stubborn, pigheaded, opinionated—those too, and they were the ones I was worried about.

By the time I talked myself out of that feeling, my finger was on his doorbell. I pushed it before the nerves came back.

He had his phone to his head when he pulled the door open, his eyes still red and just a touch puffy around the edges.

"Let me call you back." He lowered the phone and clicked the end button, taking a step back and waving me inside. "You okay?"

"Why was Griffin Brooks in Joey's apartment tonight?" The words fell out before I could consider or think better of them.

Kyle put a hand out to help me out of my coat and froze with his fingers around my collar. "Huh?"

I stayed still, his hand on my shoulder, my eyes searching his face.

He was surprised by the question. So he hadn't sent him there. Or talked to him, either, from the look on his face. "Who is Griffin...what did you say? Brooks?"

I sighed, spinning out of the coat, which he tossed over a chair. "The

RPD patrolman I was with when we found Tucker Armstrong's body. Why the hell didn't you tell me the Caccione family owned the Hideaway?"

"They don't," Kyle said.

"Anymore," I added, my eyes narrowing. "Is Joey in trouble, Kyle? I know more about what's going on here than I'm sure I want to, and I'm starting to get scared."

My voice cracked on the last word, furrowing his brow and pissing me off. I didn't come here for sympathy. I needed answers.

"I can't talk to you about that." His voice dropped low, his eyes pleading. Trust me, they begged, as his fingers wrapped my wrist tightly.

I glanced around like my eyes were going to light on a camera. Or a G-Man hiding behind a curtain.

He squeezed my wrist hard, twice. Once for yes, twice for no. That was how we used to telegraph messages in geometry a thousand years ago.

I nodded, pulling my arm out of his grasp and moving to the near end of the sofa. "I tried to come see you this morning," I said, perching on the edge of the cushion. "I met your boss. He doesn't like me very much."

Kyle rolled his icy blue eyes as he sat down on the other end of the sofa. "MacAulay doesn't like people. He likes results. And really expensive scotch. I'm pretty sure that's the entire list."

"Seemed partial to you, for whatever that's worth."

"He trusts me to get shit done. He is still pissed that I had an informant I didn't report to him—probably rightfully so. I'm a little tired of him micromanaging a case I've been running on my own for years now, but he's smart. Definitely brings insight that has me looking at things differently. He even had me go talk to a senator yesterday about some proposed legislation that could choke off a significant source of the family's income. MacAulay is the perfect cop: methodical down to his bones, and able to place his drive to see justice done above any emotion," he said. "I wish I could be more like him in some respects. But I'm under no illusions about personal feelings: he tolerates me because sometimes my unorthodox methods work, that's all."

"Kyle, I—"

"Nichelle, look—"

We laughed when we both started talking at the same time.

"Ladies first," he said.

I shook my head. "Federal agents who might have better things to say first."

"This is a complicated situation," he said.

"And it's bigger than a dead ex-lawyer-professor who fell down the opioid rabbit hole," I added.

He didn't move except to twitch his lips upward in a ghost of a smile.

"The Cacciones did own that motel. I'm guessing they were responsible for the drugs getting sold there through a shell company that used to be registered with the state as a distributor." My eyes shot to every corner of the room as I spoke, my voice low. He was making me paranoid. If his apartment was bugged, why wouldn't he just find and toss the microphones? "But something went sideways and they decided to divest themselves of that operation. Why did they do that? And do you know why Tucker Armstrong is dead?"

"My understanding is that he was shot in the head." He even managed to say it with a straight face. His I'm-stonewalling-you-for-your-own-good smirk followed the words.

I knew that look. It meant he wouldn't say anything else about the Cacciones. Funny, that he'd been trying to tell me about them for two years and I'd all but covered my ears and shouted "la la la," and here I was asking, and he wouldn't say.

"Landers hasn't arrested Katie DeLuca, which means he hasn't found her."

"Not that I know of, no."

"Have y'all checked the morgues?"

"No. None of us know how to do our jobs."

"I wasn't trying to insult anyone," I said. "Just making sure all the boxes are checked."

My fingers curled into a frustrated fist at my side. "Katie was asking around at the state capitol about the Cacciones being the contractor on the COC pipeline project," I said. "If they don't want people to know that, she might be in trouble herself. And setting her up for a murder they committed sounds like a damned tidy way to clean up a mess and move everyone on their way. You are good at your job. Really good. Be good enough to keep more people from dying here, okay?" I touched his shoulder. "Take care of yourself."

"Where are you going?" he asked.

"Not to sit at home on my hands and wait for you to call." I let myself out.

Kyle wasn't going to help me unravel this. The realization was sharp, but the sting short. We worked two sides of the same fence. Sometimes the fence needed barbs to remind us of that.

Waiting for Brooks to leave Joey's apartment, I'd found the original pipeline construction permit issued by New Kent County in early December for the LaGrace property. And then another for the same plot, issued to Caccione-run Delco Building and Excavation two weeks later.

The number on the website for the first contractor went straight to voicemail, but I'd saved it to try again in the morning.

Kyle needed to do his job. I needed to do mine, which was to get the story. And stories are about people. Normal people, not cops and senators and politicians.

24

Ward Olsen moved a little slower and had a couple of fading bruises on his face, but wasn't otherwise much the worse for wear as I followed him down the dark little entry hall to the living room.

"I'm sorry to drop by so late," I said.

"Don't apologize to me for caring enough to come here." He lowered himself slowly into a chair. "Find my little girl. That cop thinks she killed someone. No matter what she's done, I have always known my Katie Belle's heart, Miss Clarke. She didn't murder that man."

"The more I learn about all this, the more I think you're right, Mr. Olsen," I said. "And I would love nothing more than to find Katie and help her prove she's innocent." Mostly, looking at her father, I wanted to find Katie alive. These people had poured everything they had into saving their daughter. It made my stomach twist to think she might have gotten herself killed trying to help Tucker Armstrong save the planet. But Kyle said she wasn't in the morgue. They checked. So there was hope.

I leaned forward in the chair. "Mr. Olsen, do you remember Katie saying anything at all when she was here at Christmas about the COC pipeline?"

"She was on about how these people were going to destroy the ecological balance in the whole state with this one thing. She said they would wipe out whole species of animals. I asked her why it was any different than any other oil pipeline, and she got really worked up. Said I didn't understand how vital the wetlands were to keeping an ecological balance. She was on and on about people doing anything for money."

Bingo. Especially if Rowley was right and rules had been bent for the contract award, what was to say they weren't being flat-out ignored in the name of speed and cost reduction?

"And you didn't talk to her again after that?"

He shook his head.

"When Detective Landers was here earlier this week, you said you talked to Officer Brooks about Katie before she was arrested. Can you tell me more about that?"

He shrugged. "I was at that damned dive motel looking for her; she'd taken off and I tracked her phone there. Spotted the cop coming out of the alley and followed him into the office, thinking maybe they'd be able to tell me if she was still there because her phone had died."

"They?"

"He was with a tall guy in a dark suit. Young. They went into the back of the little room where the desk is in there, and then only the shorter guy, the one who was here the other day, came back out."

My fingers tightened around the arm of the chair until I couldn't feel them, but I kept my face and tone neutral. "And you talked to Brooks about Katie?" Deep breath. The words spilled out a touch too fast.

"I asked him had he seen her. He said yes right away, like he knew her."

"Did you happen to mention the pipeline to him?"

Ward Olsen furrowed his lined brow. "Why does that make any difference?"

I flashed a quick, practiced smile. Light. Untroubled. "I'm not sure it does, but I'm curious. Can you remember?"

He shrugged. "Sure, I told him she was hanging around with that crazy Tucker, he had her running all over creation trying to get people to listen to his nonsense."

Shit.

"And Brooks picked her up not long after that?"

In jail, Katie wouldn't have been a threat to the Cacciones.

"Yeah but then the goddamned judge let her go. Something about a first offense." Ward's face twisted.

The fact that she was young and pretty probably didn't hurt. But I didn't need to tell her father that.

I tapped my fingers on the edge of the armrest, my heel starting to bounce.

I needed to know where Katie had been going, who she'd been talking to. But the only person I knew of who could help me with that besides Katie herself was dead. Conveniently.

The screenshot.

I nearly shot out of the chair when I remembered it.

"Mr. Olsen, when I was here with Grant, you showed me a picture of Katie's location on New Year's Eve." I crossed my index and middle fingers on both hands.

"I always take one because they go away eventually if you don't. I learned that the hard way."

I cleared my throat. "Would you happen to have any others from the week between Christmas and New Year's?"

He pulled out his phone. "She left the night after Christmas and I pinged it then when she didn't reply to my texts. But I think her battery must have died."

"Why is that?" My voice cracked on the last word and his left eyebrow went up. I flashed the smile again. I'm not sure he bought it that time, but he finished scrolling through photos and handed me his phone anyway.

I pulled mine out and took a picture of his screen.

The pin was in the middle of a black field, no roads in the frame. "Near 6793 George Pass, New Kent" the type at the bottom of his screen read.

"Doesn't look like there's anything there," he said. "And that's a long way to go for a fix."

"Did Katie seem sober to you when she was here for Christmas?" I asked.

His eyes welled, his fist flying up to press against his closed lips. I leaned forward and put a light hand on his other arm.

"I'm sorry, I didn't mean to—"

He shook his head. "It's not you. It's my Katie. Yes." He cleared his throat.

"She seemed more like herself than I'd seen her in years. She had a project she was passionate about, her eyes were clear and bright, she smiled more. I thought I was going to get my family back. My life back, after those fucking pills stole it so long ago. And then the next night she—" His voice dissolved into a harsh sob. And less than a month later his daughter had disappeared without a trace and his wife was sitting in jail for assaulting a police officer.

That's a shitty twist of fate, right there.

I patted his arm. "Yes, sir. Thank you for letting me in. I hope every-thing...works out." The words felt downright inadequate leaving my lips, but I didn't have better to offer until I knew if my gut was right here.

He grabbed my hand with surprisingly strong fingers, taking his phone back and returning it to his pocket. "You bring her home. Tell her story. Stop this nightmare from happening to someone else."

I couldn't promise him anything, especially on that first request.

But I'd give it everything I had.

Round taillights. Sleek, spotless black paint. Silver double flag logo.

There was a Corvette in my driveway.

At ten o'clock at night. In the freezing fucking polar vortex cold.

The way my week was going, I wondered just for a second if I was wrong to decline Kyle's offer of an easy-to-use handgun way back when.

I let off the brake and my little red SUV rolled into the drive behind the sleek sports car. I had the exit clear if I needed it, anyway.

Engine idling, I let the headlights shine into the Vette's tiny little rear window. Where I saw an outline of the back of someone's head.

The door opened, and a leg appeared. Chestnut Prada wingtips, navy pants that probably had an Armani label on the inside, though I couldn't tell for sure from a calf. My pulse took off for the races, my hand closing over the door handle, Joey's name already on my lips.

I got my door open before I realized that the man brushing off his tailored jacket and turning toward me wasn't Joey.

It was Jordan Pierce.

Of course. I shook my head. Joey would've gone in the house.

"I thought I was going to freeze to death out here," Jordan said, stopping at the front bumper of my car. "Do you always stay out this late on a weeknight?"

"When I'm working a big story? Yes."

I reached back into the car to grab my bag and shut off the engine.

"You were still at work? But I went by there after dinner and didn't see your car." He put a hand out to take the bag.

I shut the car door and pushed the button to lock it. "Most newsworthy things don't happen in the newsroom," I said.

"Of course. Sorry. Sales and marketing is my wheelhouse."

"A thing I myself have been too concerned with this week," I said, pushing the kitchen door open and bending to scratch Darcy's ears. "I'll do my job if you do yours?"

He laughed. "Deal."

He pulled out a chair at the table. "Anything we can use to test run my online sneak preview?"

I fixed us both coffee, stirring milk and Splenda into mine before I carried it to the table and took the other chair. "I'm not sure I have enough for a story yet, but I'm getting close to something we could run. You really think that's going to work?"

"I talked with Bob at length about the paywall they put on some of your stories at the *Telegraph*, and I think I can make the same thing work here, plus create a spike in ad sales. The cover price for the content would cover our advertising expenses to direct traffic to it, and the ads come in as extra profit."

"You're going to advertise my story?" I asked.

"Sure. On social media. It's comparatively dirt cheap when you know how the algorithms work."

"And you do?"

"I do." He sipped his coffee. "So what can I do to help you get this story ready? I have to admit, I'm ready to test my new toy."

I reached for my bag and pulled my laptop free, flipping the screen open and clicking the photos of Tucker's map wall up on one side of the screen. On the other, I opened my maps program and typed in the address from Ward Olsen's December 26 phone tracking of his daughter.

I clicked the satellite image of the address and zoomed out. It was between Petersburg and New Kent, smack in the middle of nowhere.

"Are there explosive secrets lurking in your computer?" Jordan rounded the table, leaning over my shoulder so closely I could smell his expensive Hermés cologne.

"Something like that," I murmured, zooming in on the field at the address in Ward's phone, which was indeed random. Unless...

I made a copy of the photo of Tucker's map of Richmond and the surrounding area, zoomed in on the same part of New Kent County, and took the saturation level down to make the photo transparent.

Jordan put a hand on my shoulder, warm on my skin even through my sweater, and leaned down more. His breath tickled my ear. I squirmed in the chair and dropped the map overlay.

Boom.

Not only was the pin on the pipeline, there was a red star by it. The gold ones were battlefields, but I hadn't found an answer for the red. Yet.

Had Katie?

"I'll be damned," I breathed, the pleasant-smelling sexy man behind me forgotten. Not that I was thinking about him being sexy. Joey had just given me a weakness for a hot guy in a good suit.

"What are we looking at?"

I barely heard him. I ought to call Kyle. Or Aaron.

But it was three degrees outside and ten o'clock at night. Nobody was out there. If I was going to go, I should go now.

"How would you like to go for a"—I turned my head, putting my face about three millimeters from Jordan's—"ride?" I forced the last word out, his eyes locked on mine with his lids dropping in a way I couldn't allow.

Leaning back and to my left, I ducked under his chin and laughed. "Sorry about that, I didn't realize I was about to invade your personal space." *And keep out of mine* was the part I didn't say out loud.

He stood up straight, taking a step back. "No problem. A ride to where?"

I shot to my feet, making a beeline for the closet in the hall where I'd ditched my snow boots the night before. "Ever seen an oil pipeline?"

"Can't say that I've ever cared to," he called from the kitchen. "Is there a reason we need to see such a thing in the frigid darkness? I saw a chimney from outside." He paused, footsteps falling on the linoleum until he was leaning against the door jamb. "I build a good fire." The undertone was unmistakable.

I finished lacing my boots and pulled my Michelin Man parka from the hanger in the back of the closet. Not only was it my warmest article of clothing, it was my most unattractive. I had a feeling it would more than earn its keep tonight. "If you want the story you need to test your new toy, I have to run. You're welcome to come with me." Safety in numbers is a real thing. I've learned it the hard way.

If Katie DeLuca went to this place a few days before she went back to the capitol for a late meeting when Rowley said the building shouldn't have housed so much as a janitor, I was going to see what she saw.

25

The Air Force could have landed planes by the stark white light washing the construction site. I crawled past it three times before I pulled the car over, satisfied that the crew had just left the lights on by the utter absence of vehicles that wouldn't fit right in on an episode of *Bob the Builder*.

"I'm afraid I'm not wearing my slide-around-dirt-piles shoes." Jordan hadn't spoken in fifteen miles.

"Do you own slide-around-dirt-piles shoes?" I asked. The only person I'd ever seen dress like Jordan was Joey.

"I run." He sounded insulted.

"Don't climb anything in those," I said, kicking my door open. "You'll be fine."

The cold bit at every square inch of me not covered by my parka, and I've never been so thankful for still air in my life. The barest hint of a breeze would have sent me running right back to the car.

I picked my way across the frozen ground to the first backhoe, sitting at one end of a ditch housing a concrete and copper pipe about four feet in diameter. Jordan stopped behind me. "What is this for?" he asked. "I thought you were writing about dead drug addicts."

"The why-it-is-that-they're-dead part is kind of my specialty." I surveyed the site, the ditch lined on the left by mounds of rich black soil. Walking around the backhoe to the nearest pile, I stuck a finger into the side of it. Even frozen, it was soft. Almost loamy. It smelled like the woods that surely once extended to this spot before the land was deemed valuable and the trees cut back for a hundred or so yards. Was that what had Tucker Armstrong so worked up? Was this a protected area? Ward said Katie was on about destroying ecosystems...I made a mental note to check into what kind of wildlife might be endangered out here.

Closing my gloved fist around a handful of the dirt, I stuck it into my pocket. Wouldn't hurt to ask someone to put it under a microscope, either.

I threw a glance toward the woods, not keen on the idea of dragging Jordan back there with just the flashlight on my phone and a cylinder of mace. I knew way too little about predatory wildlife to risk it, and a bear or a wolf was a whole lot scarier than a human with a firearm. I'd been shot. If it came down to it, I'd take a bullet over a mauling any day. Whatever Katie DeLuca might have come here looking for had to have something to do with the construction. So why didn't Katie want them digging out here?

I turned back for the ditch, my boot sliding on the frozen soil. Arms flailing, I reached for the nearest object I could stabilize myself with—the discarded dirt pile. But the loose soil just moved under my hand, giving way until I was half-sitting in the pile, my arm buried up to my shoulder and my legs tilted up at an awkward angle. I wriggled, trying to bend my knees enough to get my feet back under me.

"Need a hand?" Jordan laughed, but he was polite enough to do it quietly.

"This dirt is a whole other level of fucking stupidly cold," I said, kicking my legs harder.

He leaned back, a grin lighting his face. "It's not polite to kick the knight in his shining armor when you're being rescued."

"I haven't needed rescuing in a while now," I said. "I'm rusty."

He leaned down, locking his eyes with mine, and closed his fingers around my free hand to pull me up. Butterflies took flight in my middle and I tried to will them still, but I couldn't look away from Jordan's dark, half-hooded eyes.

"Ready?" he breathed.

For what?

And no. Absolutely not.

But my limbs didn't seem to be obeying my brain, every muscle going tight right down to my buried fingers. Which closed around a rock when they tightened into a fist.

I swallowed hard, fighting to pull air into my lungs, and pushed myself to standing when he'd pulled hard enough to get my feet back on the ground. And my face about a breath and a half from his. For the second time in two hours.

Damn, he smelled good.

I couldn't step back without falling right back into the neat little Nichelle's-ass-sized hole in the dirt. So I concentrated on my still half-buried hand.

The rock slid free of the soil when I pulled my arm out. I turned to see what kind of stone the size of a softball was also as light as one. Round and white, I thought it actually was a softball for two heartbeats.

Until the piece of jawbone protruding from the lower half registered. I twisted my wrist. Round, vacant eye sockets returned my stare, a not-quite-full set of teeth fixed in a ghoulish grin.

My brain stuttered to a stall, everything in me wanting to drop the human skull resting in my left palm and run. But somehow my fingers closed tighter on it, the bone cold even through my leather gloves.

"What the hell?" Jordan saw it just after I did and managed to get words out when I couldn't make my anything work like I wanted. I stumbled backward three steps over the uneven ground cut by the backhoe belts.

I finally managed to let go of the thing and get some air, a scream ripping up my frozen throat as I watched it half-disappear back into the dirt.

26

"I take it that's not what you came out here looking for?" Jordan's arms were a hair tighter than necessary around my torso, and I pushed off his shoulders with both palms, standing up straight and sucking in such a deep lungful of cold air I gave myself a brain freeze—the regular kind this time.

"Not even close." I couldn't seem to pry my eyes from the skull, the face peeking out the dirt like a leftover Halloween decoration. I'd seen more fresh corpses than I cared to count, but somehow the disembodied head in my palm had dredged up some primal level of horror I hadn't even known existed. I couldn't look away, couldn't unsee it by closing my eyes, and couldn't reconcile it with what I had come out here looking for.

Katie DeLuca hadn't been missing nearly long enough to decompose to that degree.

"*Tucker said he had something that would bring it all to a halt.*" Rowley's words floated through my head so loud I could've sworn he was standing behind me.

Holy Manolos.

Dumping bodies in a construction site?

While my mother was a firm believer that's where Jimmy Hoffa had ended up, I always figured if that were the case, someone would know. It seemed so...obvious. Cliché, even.

I'm having trouble getting information into the hands of the people who can use it to effect change. I believe you're the answer to my problem, Tucker had written me.

Dead people would shut it down all right.

I opened and closed my fist until I could feel my fingers again and fumbled my phone out of my pocket.

Favorites. Kyle.

"Nicey?" He coughed over the sleep in his voice. "What's wrong?"

"I think I know why someone killed Tucker Armstrong," I said. "And it doesn't have a damned thing to do with drugs or Katie DeLuca. But the human skull I just pulled out of this pipeline construction site probably figures in."

"The who?" Kyle's phone hit the floor with a loud *thunk* and I pulled mine away from my head. I heard him mutter a string of swearwords before his voice was back. "Where the hell are you?"

"I'll send you a pin," I said. "Head southeast out of the city, and call whoever governs dead people out here on your way. I'm going to go wait in my car."

"Are you sure?"

I kept my eyes on the teeth, noting the smattering of missing ones and a chip in the right incisor. "I'm sure. It's not fresh by any stretch, though. I can't figure it."

"Jesus." He blew a slow breath into the microphone, his keys jingling in the background. "Okay. On my way."

I hit the end button and stuck the phone back into my pocket, tapping Jordan's shoulder and tipping my head back toward the SUV. "I have a friend who's a federal agent. He'll be here in a bit. Let's get out of the cold."

We'd been outside maybe a total of twelve minutes that felt more like twelve hours, and I was pretty sure I'd never be truly warm again. Inside or out.

"You okay?" I asked gently as Jordan turned wide eyes on me. Most people take a minute to process real-life horror scenes, and sarcasm is a common defense mechanism.

He shook his head. "I can't. Is that? How did you—" The jumbled words fell out in a rush and he started over after a deep breath. "What the fuck?

Who is building what out here and how did you know there was a dead body?"

"I didn't have the first clue about that or I wouldn't have dragged you out here with me." I couldn't tell him any more until I had a chance to talk with Kyle and figure out what to put in my preview story, what to leave out, and how dangerous that might be for everyone involved.

I put my hand out and Jordan took it, stepping over a ridge in the soil left by the construction equipment. "Do you do this a lot?"

"Traipse around in the middle of nowhere chasing a story? I wouldn't say a lot, but this isn't my first rodeo."

"Being a reporter is more exciting than I thought."

"For me? Yeah. And occasionally more terrifying."

I made it three more steps toward the car before I noticed the hole.

Half a dozen paces to my left and a few more toward the ditch: the edges were squared with a precision that didn't come from the large equipment dotting the perimeter of the site.

My stomach shrank in on itself and churned until I was glad it was empty.

I planted one boot heel and pivoted. Jordan's grip on my hand slipped a bit. "The car is this way."

"I just want to see what's over here."

"Nichelle. For real, there's a cop on the way. Let him go fall into the pit of doom over there trying to see what's probably some sort of auxiliary dirt source or water hold for whatever these people are building. Come on." He tugged my hand.

I shook my head, tugging back. I wasn't in immediate danger, there was nobody there. Nobody alive, anyway. And the hole had me wondering— what if the problem wasn't people being buried, but people who had long been buried? If the skull I'd pulled from the dirt pile had come out of there, I wanted to see for myself.

"Come on, Jordan. This is the kind of stuff readers will gobble right up. People love to read about the gruesome things humans can do to one another without having to get up close and personal with it. And I'm good at telling those stories in a way that makes them appropriately shivery, but not snatch-your-babies-out-of-their-beds creepy." I pulled out my phone. "I can even get my own art. The miracle of modern technology."

He frowned. "I'm serious, Nichelle. Let's just go to the car. I don't think my nerves can take any more up close and personal with gruesome things tonight." He pulled so hard on my hand that my glove slid off.

I reached for my glove and pulled it back on before I tossed him my keys. "Go on. I forget sometimes that not everybody is as curious as I am. I'll be right behind you."

"There's a saying about curiosity and a cat," he said. "Come on. Let the police do their jobs. Let's go warm up."

I glanced at my car. We could. Warm sounded damned appealing, especially the further we got from the encounter with the skull.

But whose skull was it? And why was it here? And how did Katie and Tucker know about it?

The questions piled one on top of another in my head until they were all I could see. I didn't have to go look. I wanted to. Just like I did this job because I wanted to. Answers, the truth—those are my motivators. Maybe the hole was empty. Maybe it wasn't.

The only way to know for sure was to go look. There was zero harm in it, and Kyle would be a little bit yet.

"I'll be right there." I whirled and strode across the frozen expanse of dirt before he could say anything else.

Behind me, I heard a long sigh, a mumbled "dammit, woman," and crunchy footsteps.

I stopped a good three feet back from the edge, testing my footing an inch or so at a time until I had crept close enough to see inside the pit.

A gaping maw that could have swallowed us both yawned in front of me.

"See? A hole. Dark. Creepy as fuck. Pardon my crass language. Let's go." Jordan hit the last word hard.

I pulled out my phone and clicked the flashlight on.

"Damn," I murmured. "That's pretty deep for any kind of auxiliary anything."

I inched closer, not wanting to step on ground that might slide into the hole.

Probably ten feet below the soles of my boots, loose dirt was piled in random drifts across a space twelve or so feet long and half that wide.

"What is it?" Jordan put his hands to his face, blowing warm breath over his leather gloves.

"Looks like a hole." I shined the light into the far corner, and it bounced back at my eyes.

I backed up and walked that way around the outside of the pit, my heart dropping a couple of inches with every step.

Bones weren't my area of expertise, but damned if that didn't look like the tip of another one.

Stopping straight above it, I couldn't see anything but a rounded white nub peeking out of the earth.

But when I swept the light up to return the phone to my pocket and go back to the car like I'd told Kyle I was going to, I saw something else.

Dark. Not dirt. Blue. Rounded.

I focused the light and took two steps toward the corner farthest from where Jordan was busy shrinking his neck into the collar of his overcoat and pulling his hat way down over his sideburns. "I'm torn between the guilt of abandoning you and not wanting to get frostbite," he called, his words muffled by the collar.

"I'm a big girl, go warm up the car." I called the words without really hearing them over my pounding heart.

Peeking out of the far corner of the dirt, I spied a half-beaten-to-hell Richmond Generals cap, Nate DeLuca's number in the lower right beneath the team logo.

Katie had been here.

What if she was still here?

27

It took Kyle less than an hour to set up and secure a perimeter, additional lights illuminating the area from the road to the forest such that I heard birds chirping at almost midnight.

I pulled a blanket Kyle had fetched from the back of his Explorer tighter around my shoulder, sliding my eyes to Jordan to make sure I wasn't hogging it. Kyle didn't look happy when I offered to share, and I wasn't super thrilled about encouraging Jordan's overtures, but the poor guy had seen his first human remains and half popsicled himself because I asked him to join me on this little adventure.

It was the very least I could do.

"How did you know to come out here?" Kyle asked through his scarf, walking up with another agent and the New Kent County Sheriff.

"Katie's cell phone," I said. "When I left your place, I went back to talk to her father, and he had screenshots of all the places it had pinged. She left her parents' house and came out here the day after Christmas. Her dad said she was talking about the pipeline, and I thought this might have something to do with Tucker's death, so I mapped the location and came to check it out."

I left out the part where the location was on Tucker's map. I wasn't even really sure why. It just didn't feel like a good idea to include it.

"And you? What did you see?" Kyle rounded on Jordan, whose face was practically invisible thanks to his pulled-up collar and pulled-down hat. We were sitting on the tailgate of a Sheriff's Office truck, watching forensics teams in ATF gear excavate the pit and the pile. I'd counted enough bones to make at least five people, and they weren't near done.

"The skull she pulled out of there." Jordan raised a pointing index finger. "I stayed back from the giant hole in the ground."

"But you let her go poking around it alone." Kyle said it under his breath, but I heard it anyway.

"You know better than to think he 'let' me do anything."

"Why is he here, anyway?" Kyle jerked a thumb at Jordan. "You said you're a consultant for the newspaper?"

Jordan nodded.

"He came over to talk to me about a new publishing strategy," I said. "I was already hooked into this. And I figured it was better to bring someone along than to come out alone."

"And you couldn't have called me?" Kyle sounded hurt. And probably a little pissed at the whole ten p.m. work meeting story. It sounded like bull-shit to me, too, from here, I just hadn't recognized it as such when I'd invited Jordan into my house.

Jordan's slowly swiveling head and wide eyes said "yeah, you couldn't have called him?" without a word passing his lips.

"You didn't really seem to want to let me in on what you were doing," I said, swinging my foot. "So I didn't want to let you in on what I was doing. Until I knew if I was right."

Kyle's shoulders rose and dropped with a heavy sigh. He cut glances at the other officers and grabbed my hand, pulling me off the back of the truck. I let the blanket go in time to keep from dragging Jordan to the ground.

Draping one heavy arm over my shoulders, Kyle pulled me into his side. I pressed closer, trying to find a way to get warm.

"We have to wait for an autopsy, but I'm ninety percent that the fresh remains in that pit are Katie DeLuca's. I need you to leave this the hell alone and let me do my job. There are things happening here that you don't understand and I cannot explain right now. You don't need to know.

Your readers, I promise you, don't want to know. They sleep better not knowing."

"I think I'm a better judge of that than you are."

"Nichelle. We've seen some wild shit in the past couple of years, you and me." He stopped walking. "I know you know I'm good at my job. I know you're good at yours. I'm asking you as a friend. Back the hell off. Please. You cannot be in the middle of this one."

"Is that why everyone is being so weird?" I tilted my head back to look up at him. "Did you tell Landers to freeze me out?" But that didn't explain Aaron's theory that he had a crooked cop. Even if I thought it was Brooks and not Landers, Kyle couldn't have had anything to do with that.

"Do this for me." He touched the end of his cold nose to my colder one.

"Nobody else gets who killed Tucker Armstrong and Katie DeLuca before I do. For the racks, not this online bullshit Jordan is test driving."

"You want me to keep—" He raised his free hand when I narrowed my eyes. "Okay. I will figure it out. As long as you promise me you're at home with the dog for the foreseeable future."

He hit "the dog" a little hard and started walking again.

"I'm not seeing Jordan," I said softly. "I'm not seeing anyone but Joey, even when he's not here. In case you were wondering."

"I didn't ask," he said. "But since you brought it up, I had a date last week."

"And will there be another?"

"I'm sure. Maybe not with her, but there are plenty of girls in my phone app."

I rolled my eyes. "I might miss Joey, but damn I'm glad I don't have to fool with all that."

"Rightfully so."

"I'll back out. You're going to get them? The right them?"

"I swear on my momma's chicken fried steak."

Kyle didn't mess around with his mother's cooking.

"I get it first."

He squeezed my shoulders and stopped next to my car. "Drive safely. I'll send your colleague over."

Before he made it two steps, the growing whine of a distant engine drew both our eyes to a pair of headlights speeding across the frozen dirt toward us. I put one hand on my car door as a large black sedan lurched to a stop a few feet away.

"Miller." I heard the voice and saw Kyle's shoulders tighten before MacAulay actually made it out of the car. "What in the blue hell is going on?"

I shrank back into the side of my car, wishing I could blend into the paint.

A single twitch of his right eye was the only indication that Kyle's boss noticed I was there as he crossed his arms and waited for an answer.

"I was alerted to the presence of human remains at this site and pulled in my team to protect the area and investigate the origin. Sir." Kyle stood up straight, folding his hands behind his back.

"In the middle of the night, in dangerous weather? Why not wait until daylight? Or at least work through proper channels, which I believe still include alerting your commanding officer. Especially when you're on probation."

"I didn't see the need to bother you so late until I knew more about the situation, sir," Kyle said. "And I've never been one to postpone involvement for personal comfort."

"We're not talking about comfort, we're talking about danger of exposure, especially if the wind kicks up. If there are dead people out here, chances are they would've still been here at daybreak," MacAulay said. "And while you've proven yourself in your time here, this is not your case, Miller. Really, it's the local sheriff's case until proven otherwise."

"The sheriff is right out there, sir." Kyle's voice was tense but even.

"But you have involved a federal agency in a local situation without due process, Special Agent Miller. As the ranking local officer, my ass is now on the line for anything that might go wrong here, regardless of your dragging the sheriff out of bed tonight." He waved an arm at the scene. "You're a better cop than this. What would possess you to do such a thing?"

"I had a tip and I followed it." The words had a sharp edge. "Due respect, I'm not convinced this isn't pertinent to my investigation, sir. And I take full responsibility for the bureau's involvement in it. I'm sure we'll learn which one of us is right over the next few days."

MacAulay sneered at me. "I don't have to ask if this was the source of your tip."

He really didn't like me.

"Miss Clarke was following a lead and did the responsible thing by noti-fying law enforcement, sir." The way Kyle said that made me think my failure to call reinforcements at times had been a topic of prior conver-sations.

I held MacAulay's hard gaze without blinking. "I'm sure you know better than I do that Agent Miller's integrity would prevent him from ever compromising an investigation, no matter who was asking the questions."

MacAulay spun before I finished my sentence. "Let's get this over with and get these people back inside where it's warm." He pointed Kyle to the passenger seat of his car and drove off.

I watched them until Kyle sent Jordan toward me and followed MacAulay back into the crime scene.

Kyle knew how to handle himself.

So did Joey.

I could sit this one out and wait for the story like everyone else.

It would be fine.

I almost believed it.

28

Several sets of human remains were recovered from an active Coastal Oil Company Pipeline construction site in New Kent County Thursday night, federal and local officials confirmed at the scene.

"A forensics lab will have to DNA match the remains, but there are at least six skulls," Special Agent Kyle Miller of the Bureau of Alcohol, Tobacco, and Firearms said. "The ATF is cooperating with state and local authorities to bring swift answers to the victims' families and justice to the perpetrators."

I stared at my blinking cursor, reading everything I was typing through a Caccione lens.

They watched my stories. I knew that; they'd been doing it since before I'd met Joey, and with him out from under their sizable thumb, I had no doubt they were paying more attention than ever. Was using that quote from Kyle all but saying "come and stop me" to a group of people who had killed more men this month than I had dated in my lifetime?

I read it four times. I was probably overthinking it. And I didn't have a whole lot in the way of useable quotes. In an ongoing investigation, if Kyle told me too much on the record, he'd end up taking shit not only from other reporters but from his boss. I walked a fine line with Kyle between getting the best story out first and protecting him from blowback for talking to me.

I added all the other details I could muster, from the palm-sized skull to the sheriff's involvement and a brief history of the pipeline project. At 1:37, I attached the file to an email and sent it to Bob, copying Jordan with a note to wait for Bob's changes before he put it online.

Nobody replied. Because normal people do things like sleep at almost two in the morning.

Darcy had long since turned in for the night. I tiptoed into my room and tucked her blanket around her, picking my way around the creaky old floorboards and slipping into sweatpants and a hoodie before I slid under my heavy down comforter. My house is cute. The character is charming. The seventy-eight-thousand drafty spots in the polar jet stream cold, not so much.

The numbers on my alarm clock gave off enough of a glow to light the small origami box my beach glass had arrived in.

Was he trying to tell me he was near the water? Or just that he was thinking of me because of my collection? I had flipped that question so many different ways in my head for the past five weeks, it almost didn't make sense anymore. Like when I looked at a word on my computer screen for too long and all of a sudden found myself unsure how to spell it.

A single tear escaped the corner of my left eye and rolled across my nose toward the pillow before I fell into a fitful sleep haunted by the skeletons of victims—both past and dreaded possible future.

By the time I sat up and rubbed sleep out of my eyes at 8:15, Bob had approved my story, it was live behind a ninety-nine-cent paywall on our website, and everyone in Richmond was blowing up my phone.

Bob, with the one I'm pretty sure finally woke me up: *Looks like somebody got her groove back. Always the dead people with you. Five skulls? What the hell did you stumble into?*

Jordan, ten minutes ago: *We've already made the ad costs back, Sylvia has four new accounts lined up, two with a full page for the next two months, and the numbers are climbing. By the time your whole story is ready, you could go viral.*

Aaron: *What did you need last night? Sorry. I was tied up in meetings.*

Aaron again, ten minutes later: *You found skeletal remains? Like, by yourself? Call me.*

Kyle: *I have messages from every reporter from here to New York and about a million hours of trackdown to do here. Hope you're happy with yourself. I thought the new gig was a weekly?*

Dan Kessler: *You were on the scene of the big skeleton harvest last night? Can I have five minutes?*

And the earliest one, the one I needed coffee to even begin to process.

Shelby Taylor: *Can we talk?*

I yanked my hair back into a messy ponytail and shuffled to the kitchen, Darcy on my heels. I opened the back door for her and watched her pick her way around the lingering patches of snow on the steps before I turned to the coffeemaker.

Shelby. What the actual fuck could she possibly want? Surely she didn't have the guts to be texting me for an interview.

Sipping my coffee, I read Shelby's words for the ninth time, tapping one finger on the side of the phone, Jordan's comment about the curious cat flitting through my thoughts. I would regret it. But I had to know what she wanted. With the same sort of morbid curiosity that fueled watching bad reality TV, I couldn't look away.

Meet me at Thompson's in half an hour. Send.

Like she'd been watching for it, she sent back a thumbs up.

I took the coffee with me to the bathroom to get ready, pulling on thick black wool pants and a soft gray cashmere sweater and sliding my feet into my favorite standby scarlet Manolos. They weren't the prettiest shoes I owned, but the classic lines went with everything, and the first pair I'd ever bought always made me feel a touch more confident.

I needed all the boost I could get, going to talk to Shelby. And probably Kessler. I owed him a favor.

Hair up in a quick French twist, enough makeup to take the half-dead

29

Shelby looked worse than I felt.

I stopped dead on the wide plastic mat inside the door at Thompson's, my eyes on her tiny frame curled into one of the overstuffed armchairs in the back corner, both hands locked around a mug she was nursing as she stared out the window behind her chair.

Walking to the counter, I ordered a white mocha latte and stuffed two bills into the tip jar, turning to watch Shelby as I waited for my drink. If she had noticed me, she was hiding it well.

Her hair was limp, obviously dirty, her oversized sweater and jeans not at all reminiscent of the barbie doll fashions she favored for the office. I couldn't make out a speck of makeup, and her too-wide eyes had hand to God sunken back into her head.

But the vacant eyes were the thing that worried me the most. Shelby Taylor was scheming, mean, and generally frustrating as all hell, but she was smart. She'd played a long game to get me out of the *Telegraph* newsroom and land herself in my job, and even though I'd left of my own accord —sort of—she'd won.

I don't lose often.

Something was wrong.

I took the cup the barista put on the counter and crossed the room, touching Shelby's thin shoulder as I took the seat next to hers.

"What's up?" I kept my voice soft, all my irritable intentions of telling her to go find her own damned story flying right through the glass behind us.

Shelby's hands shook as she lowered her mug, her lower lip trembling and tears welling in her eyes. "I'm in way over my head here, Nichelle. I watched you do this job for years. I thought I could do it better than you. But I don't want it anymore."

I blinked. That wasn't at all a Shelby-like thing to say. "I think you need to start at the beginning."

Her hand shot out, her fingers closing around my arm with surprising strength. "I'm serious. I just want to go home and hide under my covers and have it all go away. How do I get out of it?"

"Shelby, what the hell are you talking about? Get out of what?"

"The thing with the dead guy at the motel. I know you were there when the PD found him, and I saw your story this morning so I know you found out about the cemetery. But I've been getting creepy messages, and Charlie seems to have disappeared off the face of the earth, and if she's dead, I don't want to end up dead, too. So how do I get out? Do I have to quit? You want to come back?" She ran one pale hand through her greasy hair. "How did you do this for all this time? Why would you do this?"

Holy fucking shit.

I put my cup down next to hers, twisting my wrist to loosen her grip, my brain trying to process everything she'd just said.

Charlie. Was this the "assignment" they'd told me she was on?

Shit.

In that moment, I gave not half a damn that she might be able to scoop me. Shelby Taylor's terrified demeanor had me worried. Charlie and I kept each other on our toes for years. I liked beating her to the big stories. But I also liked her. She was a damned fine reporter, and I wouldn't be as good at my job without her.

What if she jumped into this without the background I had, and she didn't tread carefully because she was trying to beat me—and also because she hadn't nearly died chasing a headline as many times as I had? What if she really had barreled into something with a camera and gotten herself killed?

Skulls flashed, one after the other, through my head.

If the Cacciones killed a TV reporter, they wouldn't want it traced back to them. Kyle had already ordered the remains we'd found double-checked against unsolved cases involving officers. But cops weren't the only people the mafia wouldn't want credit for disposing of.

I kept my face still and calm. Grabbing Shelby's hand, I picked back through the word vomit she'd spewed at me.

"What cemetery?"

Her brow furrowed. "The one out in New Kent. For the old LaGrace Tobacco Plantation? Isn't that why you went out there?" She shook her head. "I thought I had finally gotten something that would, like, actually scoop you. I know you were trying to beat my pieces on the overdose victims, and you got lucky with the dead guy waiting for you when you got to the motel, but I was going to beat you." She reached into her bag and pulled out a short stack of slightly battered white envelopes. "I thought this woman was batshit crazy at first when the letters started coming, but then they stopped and the guy she wanted me to talk to ended up dead. I've barely slept all week, researching everything I could about the geography of the areas on that map."

I had started that, and then gotten sidetracked by Aaron and the city council and my own publisher until I'd all but forgotten the map until last night.

"The county wouldn't approve a construction permit with a cemetery on the property," I said. I might not have spent a week of sleepless nights reading about it, but I knew that much.

"There's no official record of it being there." Shelby picked a thread on her sweater. "Do you really not know this? Why did you go out there in the middle of the night and dig up dead people, then? How did you know where to look?"

Dumb luck, mostly, it looked like. I wasn't telling her that, though.

"I had a different lead." More than one way to skin a mob boss, it seemed.

My brain clicked the suddenly-raining puzzle pieces into place. Plantation.

She was saying they'd dug up an old slave cemetery building the pipeline.

And suddenly everything made so much more sense. I'd found the battlefields marked on the map with the gold stars and assumed the red ones were related to them somehow. But they weren't. When nobody gave a shit about the battlefields because the politicians who would want to preserve them were the same ones who took in hefty donations from the oil company, Tucker found something better: something people would care about.

I can't name many people who can stomach disturbing the dead in the name of making a buck.

And that was why the oil company got in bed with the mafia—they found the bones and needed a contractor who wouldn't care about plowing through them.

Holy freaking Manolos. My heel tapped on the dark tile floor.

"What do you mean creepy messages? The death threats people were posting on the paper's Facebook poll about wanting you to leave Katie DeLuca alone?"

Shelby shook her head. She touched her phone screen and handed it to me.

Gobbledygook ghosted number.

Thursday: *Let dead junkies lie, Miss Taylor.*

Friday: A photo of Shelby getting out of her car in front of her apartment.

This morning: *We have room for one more.* And a link to my story.

Jesus. I passed the phone back. "That, you need to show Aaron. Did Charlie know this? This grave plowing thing?"

"I saw her at the cemetery commission office when I went to talk to the head of African genealogy there. So I'm guessing she did."

They both figured it out before I did?

I plucked the letters from her hand and opened the top envelope. Addressed to me, but at the *Telegraph*. Shaking out the paper, I skimmed.

Katie DeLuca, thanking me for getting to the bottom of her husband's death, asking me to meet her friend Tucker. In the second one, she mentioned the pipeline. In the third, she hinted that the construction was disturbing graves.

Shelby got lucky when she intercepted letters Katie didn't know she was mailing to the wrong place.

No time to linger on that. What mattered now was that Shelby was close enough that someone was trying to scare her—and it seemed it had worked. It also meant these people weren't messing around. And now they knew I knew what they were up to. They probably also knew I was harder to scare than Shelby.

"Why do you think Charlie's in trouble?"

"Aaron White said her producers called him asking how to file a missing person's report yesterday."

He was in meetings all day.

Shit.

I stood, putting out a hand. "Come on."

She shrank back into the blue velour upholstery, shaking her head. "I'm serious. I cannot do this."

Shelby liked the glory. Knowing all the police brass, writing up rah rah stories from reports and officer interviews, going to cocktail parties with lawyers. But she didn't want to get her hands dirty chasing the truth.

I huffed out a sigh. "Can you send me the research you did on the cemeteries?"

I had the locations, the whole time, marked with red stars on Tucker Armstrong's wall.

And Shelby Taylor had to help me figure out what they meant.

It would take a while for that to stop stinging.

"You got it," she said. "Where are you going?"

"To find Charlie."

Two cops had mentioned her absence to me in the past three days. I had noticed it myself, but maybe not actually wanted to believe she might be in trouble. Her bosses calling Aaron said she was in trouble. Probably my kind of trouble.

30

I parked my car outside the Medical Examiner's office ten minutes later and checked my email. Shelby had sent me sixteen pages of notes. I didn't have time to read it all right then, but it looked like there was a time when, all across the South, slaves and sharecroppers were buried in unmarked graves, usually in an area near their quarters or in a section of field that couldn't be farmed. Like one with loose, acidic soil, probably in the woods.

I tapped a *thank you* and clicked send before I went inside and asked to see my favorite coroner. I'd texted her on my way out of Thompson's, so she knew I was coming.

"Miss Clarke, right this way," the college-age guy in the white coat behind the desk said. "Dr. Morgan is expecting you."

I followed him down a long hall, pausing when he went past all the offices. "Isn't it this way?"

"She said to bring you into the bone room," college guy said over his shoulder. "She's too busy with this ATF case to take a break this morning."

More up close and personal with the dead people.

Whatever it took. At least until I knew Charlie was okay.

He pushed through a set of double doors at the end of the hallway and pressed his badge to an electronic pad on the wall outside a windowless room.

"Dr. Morgan? Miss Clarke is here to see you."

Holding the door, he waved me inside.

Thank God the bone room didn't smell like formalin. I sat in on one and only one autopsy my first year out of college. I puked on the floor and decided that was a thing I could read the reports on.

"Thank you for working me in." I dropped my coffee cup in the wastebasket, peeking at her shoes as I crossed the square white tile floor. "Ooooh, I love that ice blue! Very chic and seasonal. Jimmy Choo?"

"Nicholas Kirkwood. I got them at Hall's consignment for a hundred bucks, barely worn." She stuck one foot out for inspection, beaming. "Thanks to my smart shopping friend."

"A girl's got to work her habits into her budget."

She grasped my right hand with both of hers. "It's good to see you, Nichelle. I worry sometimes I'm going to come in one morning and find you on my table. How's the new job? Less harrowing, I hope?"

No comment. Jacque was a good friend and she had a big heart. If she thought she was helping me get myself into trouble, she wouldn't. And I needed her help.

I gestured to the light table next to us when she let go of my hand. "It's different," I said. "Still getting used to it. Tell me about these guys."

"They're fascinating. New Kent doesn't have the capability to run forensics on skeletal remains. So here I am." She had the skulls lined up sideways on the table, a random array of other bones spread out in front of them. If I didn't think about it too hard, I could pretend she was getting a super early start on a Halloween table setting plan and resist the urge to sprint from the room.

"Agent Miller and his team are still on site, and I hear I have more coming, plus there's a much fresher body in the freezer with a fair amount of decomp activity that I'm going to get to in a bit. But the historical ones always fascinate me."

Historical. Like Shelby said. I'll be damned.

"How historical are we talking?" I asked.

Jacque picked up a skull. "I won't have dating back for more than a week if I'm lucky, but there are some unique features here." She pointed to the nasal cavity. "See the wide bridge here, topped by the sharp ascension to the orbital plane?"

I tucked my hands into my pockets. "The forehead?"

She laughed. "Sorry. Clinical speak. Lab. Yes, the forehead. So, that's African descent."

That tracked with what Shelby said.

"Are they all African-American, then?"

She shook her head. "These people were from Western Africa." She pointed to a book open on the table behind her. "I'm guessing they were brought here and sold as slaves. The features of the skulls are too perfect to have been diluted with European DNA. These were first-generation African immigrants. I can't be sure of anything without the dating confirmation, but if they weren't slaves, then there was a later colony out there with a strange burial ritual."

"And they were buried?" I asked.

She pointed to a scrap of linen so threadbare I had missed it altogether.

"I pulled that off a phalange from one of the subjects. They were wrapped in cloth and placed in graves. Miller said he pulled these all out of a single pit, but I'm pretty sure from what I've seen here that's not how they started out." She picked up a long bone. "This tibia has scarring—recent, fresh scarring, from some kind of metal." She pulled a magnifying glass out of her pocket. "See?"

I leaned over and peered at two parallel gashes in the bone, lined with flecks of yellow and silver.

"There was a backhoe at the site," I said.

"That could do this." She put the bone down and leaned on the table. "So these people were buried by those who loved them, and someone dug them up with large equipment and dumped them in a mass grave?"

"It sure seems that way." I blew out a slow breath.

"Jesus. What is the matter with people?"

"If you figure that out, let me know," I said. "Thanks, Jacque. Keep me posted? And when you get a positive ID on the young woman, can you let me know?"

"I'm going to start on her in a few," she said. "You okay, friend?"

"I just want to know what's going on here."

"Not to put too fine a point on it, but if whoever dug up these people is leaving fresh dead bodies, maybe you don't."

I stepped toward the door. "Anything unusual that jumps out at you, I'd appreciate a call."

"Anything for my favorite shoe guru." She waved as I let myself out.

A slave cemetery. It would sell a shit ton of papers. And Shelby was too terrified to want to write about it anymore, so I didn't have to put it on the web first.

But I owed Kyle a warning that when it got out, his scene was going to explode.

Kyle picked up the third time I rang his cell phone. "Little busy here."

"Listen, y'all need to work fast because when people find out what you're into, you're going to have a real mess on your hands." I didn't bother with pleasantries he didn't have time for. "I just left the coroner's office. Those skulls we found last night are all of African descent, no apparent mixture with Caucasian DNA. She can't have the dating back conclusively for a week, but seems pretty confident COC was bulldozing an old slave cemetery to lay their precious pipeline, and I think there might be a couple more of them on the route. Do you know anyone at the state cemetery commission?"

I paused for a breath.

"I do now." Kyle's words came through gritted teeth, and I noticed a buzzing in the background.

"Do you not have a signal out there?"

"What I have is a fucking circus. The state cemetery commissioner and about five dozen of her closest social media followers waving signs and screaming and slowing down the excavation work. Like we haven't worked a body recovery before."

"Kyle, this is different. I know you want to get the bad guys. I do, too, but the bodies out there aren't there because they were murdered and tossed in a hole. They're there because they were victims of a horrifying system of subjugation that ended with their graves not being properly marked or recorded, and now like two hundred years later they're victims of some-body's greedy, corner-cutting bullshit. Don't be too hard on the people who want to prevent any more of them from having their remains disturbed."

He was quiet for a minute and then blew out a long breath. "Yeah."

"I'm sure there's a protocol for relocating the cemetery," I said.

"There is. We did it when I was at the DPD, they were building the Bush turnpike in Dallas and dug up a family cemetery nobody knew was there. This is just all fucked up because the construction people already moved so many of the skeletons, and they don't know what goes where or who the bodies belonged to. But you're right. This is their thing."

I paused.

It was their thing. As soon as someone with authority to investigate and move the existing graves showed up, the police should have shut the construction down and left it to the cemetery folks.

Kyle knew that. His tone said we were on the same page.

"Kyle." I tried to keep my voice even. "Why are you still there?"

The silence roared it was so loud.

"Kyle!" I didn't mean to yell, but I was more terrified than Shelby had been of what he might be about to say.

"Nicey, I..."

Oh, my God.

"No." I whispered it.

"MacAulay's coverage unit lost Joey day before yesterday. My print run on Katie DeLuca's body came back about three hours ago. We're just making sure she's the only recent victim they hid out here." He coughed. "I'm sorry, honey. I didn't want to tell you anything until I knew for sure."

I hung up and threw the car in reverse.

To hell with promises.

31

I flew off the elevator into my office so fast I almost mowed over Jordan.

"There's my star reporter!" He grinned as he jumped out of the way. "In hot pursuit of the next story?"

He furrowed his brow and caught my eye. "Hey. Are you okay?"

I just shook my head and made a beeline for the photographer's desk. I needed to see those maps in better resolution and up closer. If Kyle was searching one burial ground, I'd go search another one. I just had to find it.

"Hey, kiddo, what's going..." Larry let the words trail off. It had taken Bob about six minutes and half a cup of coffee to get the *Telegraph's* old-school shutterbug photo editor to come with us when we jumped ship. Larry was a wizard with photoshop and enhancements, and I needed him to work his magic on some pictures for me.

"Trying to save the world. You know. It's Friday," I said, fishing my phone out of my purse and trying not to let him see how freaked out I was.

"How can I help with the superhero gig today? I heard you might have saved this place from falling down around our ears already."

I really might if I could land this story without anyone else dying. But right then I wasn't sure my superpowers were up to that task.

I touched the screen three times and landed on the first map photo, handing my phone to Larry. "Can you enhance that enough for me to make out any of the smaller type?" I asked.

"Sure thing, sugar." He dropped his glasses over his eyes and squinted at the screen, touching it to airdrop the photos to his computer. "I'll do my best."

"Hey, Nicey, what was in that cool box on your desk?" Sylvia's voice came from behind me.

"Box?"

She nodded. "We thought maybe Connolly sent you something. Like some shoes or something. For the ad pickups. You did have to see skeletons to get the story."

"So did I, and I didn't get any shoes," Jordan said.

"They'd hurt your feet." I patted his shoulder, rising on tiptoe to look toward my desk.

"Go on. I'll holler when I have something for you," Larry said.

I glanced at Sylvia. "You haven't talked to Charlie Lewis lately, have you?" I kept my tone light. Conversational. They used to work together, but I had no idea how well they knew each other.

"No." She ran a hand through her chin-length hair. "People on my side of the ad wall didn't really know Miss Lewis too well."

My eyes locked on the intricate origami box of thick paper on my blotter, I couldn't breathe or move enough to reply to her.

No label.

But it was a larger version of the one I'd fallen asleep staring at every night for weeks.

Was he okay?

I sprinted for the box, trying not to tear it but not a hundred percent sure I'd succeeded as I pulled at the top.

Yellow. Black.

Not leather.

Feathers.

And that smell. Loamy and dank floating under the overwhelming stench of rotting meat.

"What the hell?" Parker stepped up next to me and caught the box as I let it go, tears blurring my vision.

A canary.

The box held a dead canary with thick black stitches sewn over its eyes, its beak cut off.

"Jesus!" Parker slammed the flaps back down. I spun away, a small sob escaping my throat, and felt Parker's big arms come up around me. "Pierce. Take this, man. Get rid of it."

"Sure, of course."

Parker's hands landed on my back, rubbing slow circles as I fell apart in the middle of my office.

"Is she okay?" Jordan sounded glad I wasn't interested in him for the first time in days. It was so absurd I almost laughed.

Parker's chin, resting on top of my head, moved as he shook his. "We're not going to let anyone hurt you, Nicey."

"Wait!" I jerked my head up and sent Parker's teeth slamming together. "Don't get rid of the box. Please. Sorry, Grant."

He rubbed his chin as Jordan blinked at me. "Why the hell would you want to keep this?"

"The box is a message. The bird is a message. I need to make sure I'm not missing anything. People's lives might depend on it."

For the first time in an hour, my heart lifted with a tiny bit with hope. Why would they send me a dead canary—a symbol of an informant so classically tied to the mafia it was in every old movie about Al Capone—if they had already killed him?

What they wanted was to keep right on doing what they were doing, right? That wasn't exactly my call, but if they wanted to think I had sway there and I could play it to get Joey back still breathing, I was in.

No more tears.

I wiped at my face and squared my shoulders, putting my hand out.

Jordan shoved the box into it and pulled out a silk handkerchief to wipe his fingers.

"How can we help?" Parker asked.

Sylvia and Jordan looked away, mumbling about meetings and work.

Parker dragged me into Bob's office and shut the door. "What the hell is going on here? Mel says Shelby is losing her shit, talking about danger and you and how she didn't know what she was getting into, because she's suddenly decided Mel is her BFF. Early this morning Mel got a word-salad text we thought meant Shelby had been drinking, but I'm pretty sure there was something in there about Charlie Lewis going missing chasing a story, and now people are sending you dead pet songbirds. I want to help, Clarke."

Bob spun his chair to face us. "Dead birds? What?" He fixed me with a hard stare. "Does this have anything to do with what we were talking about yesterday?"

I nodded.

"I said be careful."

"I'm trying. I scared the hell out of poor Jordan with real skeletons and one dead body last..." I stopped. Shit.

"What?" they said in harmony.

I looked up at Parker. "I'm so sorry, honey."

It took him a minute, and then his eyes popped wide. "Damn."

"She was trying to do something she really believed in, and I don't think she was using," I said. "I mean, there's no official word yet, but I saw the hat."

"She's probably happier being with Nate again." Parker's voice was hoarse. "She was troubled, but he was so in love with her. Have they told her parents?"

"As far as I know, her mother is still in jail. Kyle will send people to see her dad."

"And the people who killed her, that's who you're after?"

Well. "That's who Kyle is after. I'm looking for victims I'm hoping aren't dead. Yet."

"One of them wouldn't happen to be your friend you don't like to talk about?" Bob asked.

I just nodded, not trusting myself to speak.

"Oh no." Parker shook his head. "Shit, Clarke, I assumed you got dumped."

"I let you. It's complicated."

"Not letting people get killed seems pretty straightforward," Parker said.

"What's in the box, children?" Bob asked.

Parker took it from me and handed it to Bob. "It's rotting," he said. "Careful."

Bob opened it and recoiled from the smell. "Jesus." He peered into the box. "It is a canary. Was your—? Oh." He pinched his lips together.

"Why is the box a clue?" Parker asked.

"Joey sent me a gift in one just like it a few weeks ago," I said. "It's unique. Handmade. They probably got it from his place, which means they got him, too. And they want me to know it beyond a doubt."

"And the canary—" Bob stopped when Larry opened the door.

"I got this as close as I could, and wrote down the only street names I could make..." He glanced around the room. "Who died?"

"Tweety there." Parker pointed to the box.

Larry leaned over, his nose not so much as twitching at the smell. Years of long exposure to developing solutions will do that to a person. "Tweety was a canary. That's not a canary."

"Yes it is. Little. Yellow." I stepped closer. Larry often spent his weekends in remote areas of the state, snapping away with his Nikon looking for the perfect bird shot.

He shook his head. "Nope. That's a Prothonotary Warbler. They're pretty rare." He leaned close to the box. "Jesus who would do something like that to such a beautiful creature? Their song is really pretty."

"You're sure?"

"I'm sure. I have a picture of one of these babies I took last summer." He pulled out his phone.

"I believe you," I stammered. "Please show me later. Larry, where do these birds live?"

"Out in the swamp," he said. "They're native to an area that covers the Great Dismal Swamp and the surrounding area, out near Suffolk."

I yanked my keys from my bag. "I'll call Kyle," I reassured Bob. "But I have to go, they'll shut the gates to the swamp before dark this time of the year."

"Five o'clock," Larry confirmed. "So do you need this map?"

"Can you send the enhanced image to my phone?"

"Sure, hon."

I put one hand on the doorknob. "Thanks, guys."

"Be careful," they said in unison.

"Always." It wasn't terribly true, but it made everyone feel better for me to say it.

I would do my level best to mean it today.

32

I didn't get my phone open to call Kyle before it started buzzing.

Jacque.

I hit the talk and speaker buttons and set it upside down in the cupholder. "Hey, girl, what did you find?"

"The ATF identified this victim by fingerprint match as Katherine Elizabeth Olsen DeLuca, twenty-eight, of Richmond," she said. "Is that who you thought she was? Her husband was the pitcher who died out on the river a couple of years back, right?"

"Yeah. To both." I sighed. "Anything else interesting?"

"Well, other than the fact that she wasn't murdered, not much to speak of," she said. "When you find a body in a makeshift mass grave, it's certainly normal to expect foul play, but I didn't find evidence of any."

I almost ran a red light trying to fold my brain around that.

"I'm sorry?"

"Yeah, that's what your friend at the ATF said, too." She snorted. "You two are so much alike I'm surprised you're not either related or married."

"So then why was she dead?" She hadn't had time to get lab work back if they could get blood to test—Katie had been in an open hole outdoors in the brutal cold.

"Animal attack," she said. "Most of her face was gone, and the claw and gnawing marks on the bone underneath the tissue suggests a bear."

"It's January," I said. "What on earth?"

"Just telling you what I see. How long since she was last seen?"

"Christmas. She was at her parents' house."

"Huh. Well. Insomniac bear. I'm not a wildlife expert, but if this was a wolf, it was a fucking hulking big one. I can test the gouges for saliva and DNA, but it will take a couple of weeks to get all that."

"Let me see what I can make out first," I said, my thoughts racing about an hour down the road. "I wonder if they have bears in New Kent County."

"Again, not my wheelhouse, but she wasn't killed there."

"What?"

"Yeah, there was peat-riddled soil embedded in some of these wounds, and all in her hair and on her clothes," Jacque said. "The only place I know of that they have soil like that in Virginia is—"

"The swamp," I cut her off.

Fuck. Katie DeLuca wasn't a bad detective. I'd noted the black magic marker star over the swampland what felt like a small lifetime ago now. And she'd gone looking for remains in the marshy wilderness and gotten herself eaten by a bear.

"Exactly." Jacque sounded surprised. "You good, chère?"

"I'm good. I just hope some other people I don't want to see hurt are good, too. Do you have an approximate date or time of death?"

"It's tricky because the weather has been so weird and she was clearly outside, even before she was moved, but I'm going to guess two weeks."

"That's three days after Christmas," I said.

"I suppose it is," Jacque said. "Sad."

"No...Could she have been alive on New Year's Eve?" I asked.

"I guess it's possible for a three-day error, but I wouldn't call it likely. I've been at this a while, I'm pretty confident in my calculations."

Holy Manolos.

Katie wasn't at Capitol Square that night.

Her phone was.

I clicked off that call and dialed Kyle again.

No answer. I rang it twice more and finally got a text from him. *I know,*

Katie was attacked by an animal in the swamp. We are spread all over hell looking over this map you sent me and I have protestors fucking following me around like it's their mission to make my life miserable besides. Go home. Lock your doors. Call you as soon as I can.

I touched the speech to text and found a phone number for Ward Olsen. He picked up on the third ring. "I don't want any, I know who I'm voting for, and my car is fifteen years old," he said.

"Mr. Olsen, it's Nichelle Clarke from the paper." I spit the words in a hurry. "Don't hang up."

"Oh. Hello there, young lady," he said. I could tell from his voice that Kyle hadn't gotten time to send anyone to break the news to him. And damned if I was doing it over the phone.

"I have a weird question for you, sir, if you wouldn't mind humoring me," I said. "Can you check and see where Katie's phone is now?"

"I haven't gotten a signal from it in more than a week," he said.

I had a theory about that. If whoever dumped her body took it off her to make sure she didn't have anything incriminating on it, they might have put it in their glove box and forgotten about it. They were at the capitol in the middle of the night on a holiday, and the phone was in the car outside.

But if my story had caused a panic this morning and they were doing cleanup, they'd either tossed the thing or plugged it in to try to see what might be on it. Damage control.

I was crossing my fingers for the latter as he said, "Okay, sure, if you say so."

"See, it just says locati—" He stopped short of finishing the last word. "I'll be damned."

"Where is the phone, Mr. Olsen?" I asked.

"In Norfolk, near the bay," he said. "Is my Katie out there?"

"Her phone is," I said. "I think someone stole it. Thank you so much for your help, sir."

I clicked off the call, my foot pressing the gas pedal way harder than the law allowed. Swinging into light traffic on Highway 460, I clicked the radio on as a text buzzed.

I waited until I hit a red light and raised the phone.

Gibberish number I didn't recognize. Whoever sent it was using a ghosting program. My gut twisted back into itself as I touched the message.

And dropped my phone.

The light changed. I didn't move, my eyes on the photo. Joey was sitting slumped in a ladder back wooden chair, his arms tied behind his back, his face a bloody, swollen mess. A black laptop rested across his knees, my story from this morning on the screen.

He wasn't dead.

Relieved tears welled in my eyes.

Another message buzzed in.

Let's make a deal, Miss Clarke. No cops. I will be in touch.

33

The gray clouds split with fading pink-indigo streaks as I turned into the parking lot at the ranger station near the entrance to the Great Dismal Swamp National Wildlife Refuge. Joey had to be there. The bird, the soil in Katie's bear mauling wounds, the pipeline...the floor in the picture on my phone was dirt, the wall behind him bare wood with light filtering through small cracks. My entire shoe collection said he wasn't in a publicly accessible area. But I couldn't search more than a hundred thousand acres of swampland by myself.

It was getting dark. It was still cold. And Jacque's words about Katie wouldn't stop ringing in my ears—there might be bears.

It would take every reporting skill and ounce of charm I had ever laid claim to if I wanted to talk a ranger into helping me without following me, but I had to give it a shot. I didn't have any other options.

I parked the car and pulled up the photo, zooming in and keeping my eyes away from Joey's battered face. I couldn't see a roof, but there was no snow on the floor, so I guessed there was one.

So what I needed was a building off the beaten path here. What were the odds of happening across that?

I crossed the little wooden bridge to the ranger station and pulled the door open, fixing my best, most practiced smile on my face and training my eyes on the away-facing broad shoulders behind the desk.

My eyes lit on the ponytail a split second before the ranger stood and crossed the room with a laugh. "Hey there. You're the first human I've seen all day. What can I do for you?" Her eyes went to my clothes. "You looking for the gift shop?"

A woman. I hadn't even considered that possibility, which was rather disappointingly sexist of me. But five words and ten seconds into meeting her, charm wasn't going to work for me here. She was nice, but no-nonsense. A lot like my mom.

Her brass nameplate said Souders.

"Hi, Officer Souders," I said. "I'm not looking for a gift. I'm actually looking for a friend." I crossed my fingers inside my pocket and prayed my reading people superpower was in top form today. My mother loved to help people. It runs in the family.

Ranger Souders leaned on the counter, and I tipped my head back to look her in the eye. Hers were a pretty amber-and-green-flecked hazel. And damn, she was tall—I touch six one in my shoes, and I bet she had three inches on me.

"I'm afraid there hasn't been anyone in here today but you," she said.

"I think he might have gotten here before today. Or maybe not through the ranger station. And I think he might be in trouble," I said. "Is there dangerous wildlife out here?"

I had to tread easy here. If I said Joey was being held hostage somewhere in her swamp, she might call the sheriff. And then not only was I going to be longer about getting to him, I'd be in violation of the no-cops edict in my texts.

"We clear the park at nightfall. Every night," she said. "And the only traffic I've seen all week was a work crew cleaning up from the fire in December. No hikers. I'm afraid I don't know what you're talking about, honey."

Words fell out of my mouth as fast as they came into my head, and all I could do was hang on and hope they made sense and she bought them. "My friend is a bit of a hiking daredevil. It was so cold he was convinced the swamp would be frozen." I talked fast. "He was looking for a certain kind of yellow bird. Something warbler? And he was going to slip off the trail and go out to find one, he said. But he also said he'd be home yesterday and he never made it. I finally got a ping on his phone and it says he's here."

I batted my lashes and widened my eyes a bit. *Believe me*, the eyes added.

She shot straight up and reached behind her for her keys and a large cardboard tube.

"Jesus, it's freezing out there now, but it was so warm in the early part of the winter not all the bears are hibernating this year," she said.

Poor Katie.

I scrunched my face to the appropriate level of worry. "He's pretty handy on his own, and I'm guessing if there's any sort of structure out in the swamp, he'd go in there to get out of the wind." Hell, I even almost believed me. If I hadn't been terrified I would get there to find Joey dead, I'd have worried about how good I seemed to be getting at lying.

She spread a map of the entire park on the counter. "He didn't tell you what he wanted to see, other than the bird?"

I shook my head. "I tried to tell him a bird wouldn't be out here in January anyway."

"Those stay, when the winter is warm, which it really was until last week." She looked up. "He came this week? In the cold?"

"He's always dreamed of hiking in Antarctica," I lied.

"I suppose this would be a cheaper way to get a similar experience," she said, pointing to an area of the map in front of her and making me wish desperately that I'd paid more attention in any geography class I'd ever taken. "Here, there's an old shiner shack, from back a hundred years ago when the moonshiners hid in the swamp from the revenuers—that's what the folks out here called the federal agents. It's not the nicest place you'll ever see, but it would probably still be sturdy enough to protect a body from the wind. I sure hope he bundled up, though."

Me too. He'd been wearing a pair of black pants and a white, blood-spattered button down in that photo.

"You're an angel." I flashed the smile again. *Trust me.* "How do I get out there?"

She scowled. "I can't send you off the trails at near dark on your own," she said. "I'll take you back and we'll check it out."

I caught a breath so sharp I coughed. "I can handle it, really. We hike together all the time. I don't want to put you out."

She shook her head, her mouth in the same determined line my mother got when arguing with her was about to get totally fucking useless.

Shit.

She hurried to the closet. "Let me get my coat."

I played interview Ranger Souders as the truck rolled out over the bumpy frozen swampland.

"Please call me Penny," she said. "My granddaddy was 'Officer Souders.' He was a policeman for forty years, and he was a gruff old fart. I like to think I'm a bit more personable."

She was. And I might be about to get her shot. I couldn't have that. My brain ran through every scenario I could muster, including leaping from the moving truck—we weren't going that fast, but my sense of direction sucks in direct proportion to how much my fashion sense rocks. I'd end up eaten by Katie's bear for sure.

"What do we do if we see a bear?"

Penny patted a black case on the console between our seats. "Tranquilizer gun," she said. "We don't put the wildlife down for doing what comes naturally to them, but we'd be able to get away in the time this would keep him down."

"It won't hurt him?"

She shook her head. "There's not even enough in there to hurt one of us. But it'll knock him out for a good half hour."

Thank you, God.

"Did you say there was a fire last month?" I asked. "Was it in this part of the swamp?"

She shook her head. "No, they ought to be back south nearer to Lake Drummond," she said. "But I didn't see them come back in after that first day. I assumed they got what they wanted."

"Are there any commercial projects allowed to cut through the swamp?" I asked. Not according to Tucker's map, but I didn't want to assume anything. I was still trying to piece together why Katie came here.

"Like what?" she asked, rounding a lightning-scorched tree and turning...north? I thought.

"Like, I don't know, oil pipelines?"

She nodded. "There's one that runs through the south corner, but the government denied the application last year for the COC pipeline to cut through here. They said it was concern for disturbing the ecosystem." She rolled her eyes.

"It's not?" I asked.

"Of course it is. But no politician gives a bald eagle's toenail about the ecosystem when there's money to be had," she said. "There's oil under this part of the swamp. But the government owns the mineral rights and there's all kinds of politicking around what to do or not do with them."

Bingo.

What if someone could extract the oil without the government knowing? Miles of open land nobody was allowed on by law, unless there was a natural disaster.

That's not just a construction contract and possible jail time for grave robbing. That's a whole fucking lot of money. The kind of money that makes killing people a cost of doing business.

It had to be the secret they wanted to make me a deal about.

I sat forward in the seat when I saw the shack take shape in the distance, my fingers inching toward the tranquilizer gun.

"Here we are," she said. "Looks like the old girl is still standing."

She saw the car the same time I did. "What the—" She slammed the brakes, swiveling in the seat to face me. "What's going on here?"

I flipped the box open, raised the tranquilizer pistol, and fired, shoving the truck into park before her foot came off the brake and reaching over to cut the engine. She looked shocked for half a second before her eyes fell shut and her head slumped forward. I reached to her shoulder and pulled the dart free when I was sure she was out, pulling her handcuffs from her belt and cuffing her to the wheel before I took her keys. "I'm so sorry, Penny. I'll be back, I hope. You stay here."

I hopped out of the pickup and double-timed it to the shack, my shoes miraculously only sliding twice on the icy ground. Not what I would've picked for traipsing around the frozen tundra here, but I hadn't intended to leave downtown Richmond when I got dressed. I took a lap of the shack's exterior in the rapidly-fading sunshine. The car, a black Ford sedan, was empty, the hood cold. I held the tranquilizer gun like a security blanket. It was empty, but they didn't need to know that.

I didn't see a soul.

I stopped in front of the door, settling my breath and standing up straight.

Here goes nothing.

34

Joey was still in his shirt and pants, but the chair was tipped over and he was tied to it, lying on his side on the dirt floor. From the doorway, I couldn't tell if he was breathing, but thanks to the shoebox size of the room, I could tell he was alone. I stuffed the useless weapon in the waistband of my pants and ran to him, falling to my knees and putting my cold hands gently on his face. "Baby?"

His eye twitched, a groan escaping his throat.

Tears welled and spilled faster than I could realize they were coming. I bent my head and pressed my lips to the side of his face, landing just above his ear. I didn't care. I was there. He was there. He was breathing. Penny had a truck outside and we were goddamn getting out of there right now.

I sucked in a deep breath, the real thing so much better than the scent clinging to his suits. God, I had missed him more than I had even dared to admit to myself.

But I had to hold it together long enough to save the day.

Focus, Nichelle. We'd have time for cuddling when we were back safe on my couch.

I raised my lips above his ear. "Joey, I know you're hurt, but we're going. Right now. If I get you up, can you walk if you lean on me? Wake up, Joey. We have to get out of here."

I didn't know where the car's occupants had gone—likely to check their oil well, from what Penny had said, but I knew our clock was ticking.

"Princess. No. Stay away," he mumbled, his eyes still closed. "Home. With Miller. I love you."

"I'm not anywhere with Kyle. I'm here with you. Where I belong. Please wake up." My voice cracked. "We have to go."

Bastards. They'd pumped him full of some kind of drug.

"Love you so," he mumbled, his eyes fluttering before they fell shut again.

I went to work on the ropes, every knot taking me a hundred years and two or three fingernails to work loose. When the last one around his waist came free and his whole body slumped to the floor, he stirred again. "I didn't tell them anything about the fucking wells," he muttered. "I didn't even know about the whole operation."

"Joey?" I tried touching his face again, but was afraid I'd hurt him if I pressed too hard.

Nothing.

"Kettlebell class, don't fail me now," I said, standing and rolling him to his back, hooking my arms under his before I straightened my knees and stood up, lifting him with me. His head thumped into the center of my chest and lolled back, his eyes open just a sliver, showing red-rimmed white. I took a couple of steps back toward the door, pulling him with me easier than I would have expected. If I'd had a free arm, I would've been tempted to flex it.

We were going.

Awkward as it was, I got the hang of walking backward and tugging Joey along, and made it to the door in less than a minute. I pushed it open and stepped out into the fading, cloud-filtered sunlight, wincing as his heels scraped on the edge of the bottom doorframe. "Sorry, baby," I whispered.

"He's been through worse." The voice behind me stopped me cold.

I turned, my arms still around Joey and my jaw somewhere around my knees.

"You—you bastard," I stammered. "Kyle looks up to you."

Special Agent in Charge MacAulay shrugged. "But not as much as he likes you, I'm afraid." He drew a gun. A real one, with ammunition inside. "Put him down. And step this way."

I laid Joey carefully on the cold, damp ground before I stepped forward. "Now what? You said let's make a deal. I'm listening."

MacAulay threw his head back and laughed.

"Silly woman. The deal is that you two will get fed to the bears, and my associates get to keep their wells and their business without any more inter- ference." He tossed a disdainful glance at Joey. "He was weaker than I thought. I never would have sent him to talk to you if I'd known this would be the end of it. He's very good, Joe."

"You...you sent?" I shook my head. "No, Mario did."

"Sure. Because I told him to. But then Miller got too close and I couldn't have my role in either organization compromised, so Mario had to be disposed of. And he was. But you opened a door for Joe to want to switch teams. He wanted to marry you, you know. Bought a ring and everything. I heard him talking to Miller about it not long after the president's botched visit last fall."

"He wouldn't have come to your office." I stopped short.

Kyle's apartment was bugged. And Kyle knew it.

Kyle was allowing it.

But Kyle wasn't here, and I was staring down a gun with no help, no weapons, and no cell signal.

I needed a miracle.

"I have to give you that you taught me something here. I wanted to see if the two worlds I live in could ever find a way to be one, if we could bend laws without breaking them. Joe was all for it. No killing people, no steal- ing. Loopholes. Working around the edges of the law."

Dear God. Joey had said that to me, like the second time I ever spoke to him. I blinked. MacAulay was still talking.

"But then you came along," he said. "And taught me that the answer is no. They can work parallel, but they can never meet."

"I mean, the mafia and federal law enforcement are sort of opposite ends of the spectrum of right and wrong." I wasn't at all sure why he was still talking to me, but I'd go with it. I didn't see a way out of this, really. I wasn't taking a trained federal agent in hand-to-hand, I didn't have a weapon of any sort, Joey was too heavy for me to run with, and I wouldn't leave him there to die.

My brain fought through a fog of trying to reconcile too much information too quickly. All this time—since before Kyle came to Richmond, since before I met Joey...the actual head of the Caccione crime family was fucking ATF command staff?

I wouldn't have picked that as a possibility in a thousand years, but from this side of the revelation, it was the one thing that made every single thing that had been bonkers about my life in the past two years make perfect sense.

"They're two sides of the same coin," MacAulay said. "Nothing but a sliver of ideas between them. Except."

"Me. I know," I said. I reached behind me and whipped the dart pistol up quickly, leveling it at him and trying to look a whole lot braver than I felt.

"Joey and I are leaving," I said. "Leave him alone. Leave Kyle alone. Steal all the oil you want, but stay away from us."

He walked toward me, his gun still straight out in front of him. "You won't shoot me," he said. "You don't have it in you."

Bullshit I didn't. I squeezed the trigger, praying for a reserve dart.

The gun clicked.

Nothing happened.

MacAulay pulled the weapon from my hands and tossed it aside. "Goodbye, Miss Clarke."

He pressed the cold muzzle of the gun against my chest, and a roar split the still, silent evening.

35

I closed my eyes and waited for the pain, one I knew because I'd been shot before. It didn't come, and the roar got louder instead of fading.

I opened my eyes and yelped. A white police cruiser sped across the swamp, flinging slushy mud from every tire before skidding to a stop ten feet from where I stood. Landers. Aaron.

Thank you, God.

I took two steps that way before the door opened and Griffin Brooks stood, his weapon raised.

Pointed at me.

"Get your hands where I can see them," he barked.

I threw them up, shaking my head, my eyes darting to MacAulay. He leaned on the hood of his vehicle, nodding.

Shit.

Brooks was indeed Aaron's bad apple. And I'd been too desperate to be right about him to admit it when I could've told someone.

So now the boss didn't have to shoot me? Is that what this was?

"I can't believe I trusted you," I spat.

"You trusted me? I liked you," Brooks said. "And all this time you were in with the fucking mafia? That's your 'I'm seeing someone?' Really?"

Wait. What?

"You have this all wrong," I said.

"Sure I do." He rolled his eyes. "I just watched you point a gun at an ATF commander."

"You can shoot her, son," MacAulay said. "She's dangerous, she might have another weapon."

"He's only saying that so he won't have to sit through the investigation into my death because he doesn't want to be investigated," I said. "Brooks. This isn't your mission. You're not helping by killing me, I swear."

The other door on the front of the cruiser opened, and Jordan Pierce unfolded himself from the passenger seat. "What the hell are you doing, man? I told you we needed to come save her, not point guns at her."

Brooks pretended Jordan hadn't spoken. Jordan's wide eyes went from Joey to MacAulay to me and back around again. "Nichelle? What the hell is happening?"

"Did you know the mafia was supplying most of the drugs being sold at the Hideaway?" Brooks asked. "That it's their fault Tucker and Katie are dead? Of course you know. You just don't care."

"Believe me, I do care." My voice was two octaves too high and way too shrill. "You've got this whole situation all wrong, you have to listen."

"The mafia? Like in *The Godfather*?" Jordan raised his hands and ducked behind the car door.

"Jordan, you know me," I said. "I'm not a criminal. This whole situation is screwed up, but please, y'all have to believe me."

Brooks and MacAulay exchanged a look. Brooks's finger twitched on the trigger guard.

Oh shit.

They were playing me, because they had a witness. Jordan. He'd testify that Brooks saw me try to shoot MacAulay and then he shot me, somehow Joey would wind up dead, and the whole thing would get swept under a neat little rug, the Caccione operation safe and more profitable than anyone ever thought possible.

Unless I could get Jordan on my side.

"You are in this with them, aren't you?" I kept my eyes on Brooks. "Aaron said there was a crooked cop in this, and it's not Landers, it's you," I breathed. "That's why you were at Joey's apartment. Jesus, Brooks. Did you shoot Tucker Armstrong yourself?"

MacAulay leaned back and folded his arms across his chest. "Joe did always go for the smart ones," he said.

Damn. And Aaron might not know for months, or even years. I couldn't believe I got so thoroughly played. But on balance, it wasn't as bad as the about-to-be-bear-food aspect of the day, so it was hard to care too much.

Brooks's eyes narrowed to slits too tiny for me to see the color in the encroaching twilight.

He moved, a small flash of fire and an actual shot ripping through the still air.

I flinched.

MacAulay crumpled to the hood of the Ford before he slid off, almost in slow motion, into a dark heap on the ground.

Before I could make my eyes move back to Brooks, more gunfire popped from the far side of the shack, bullets whizzing as another man rounded the corner in the deepening pitch-black evening and dove behind the car, rising on his knees to peek over the hood and return fire.

Brooks ducked back into his car. Jordan disappeared.

And I dove for Joey, lying across him and covering my skull like my fingers were going to stop a .45, trying to put together what the fuck had actually just happened.

"Nichelle." That was Brooks, calling from behind his car door after the gunfire stopped. "Are you hit?"

"You were just going to shoot me," I said, not raising my head. "Making sure you got the job done?"

"I was not ever going to shoot you." He sounded annoyed. "I had to make MacAulay think I was for a minute until I could be absolutely sure he was our double agent."

"I. What?"

The gunshots still ringing in my ears, I wasn't a thousand-percent sure I'd heard him right.

Something hit my back, and I screamed.

"It's me," Brooks said. "I thought MacAulay was alone. I didn't expect anyone else to return fire. I'm sorry."

I pushed myself off the ground and sat up. Joey's head tossed from side to side.

"He needs a doctor," I said, looking around. MacAulay had one hole in his chest and one in his forehead, and the other dark suit guy was down just the other side of the car.

"Jordan?" It came out more than a little panicked, and was met with a groan from behind the passenger side door of the patrol unit.

"That dude doesn't take no for an answer," Brooks said. "I went to your office looking for you because Detective White said he had a weird message from your boss, and they told me you came out here because you got a dead bird in the mail. And this guy, he freaks out and says he didn't know you were going to chase actual criminals and he has to save you, and he just kept talking while he was getting into my car. And now he got himself shot. Which I'm going to have to write the report for."

"He's a good salesman. Very charming and big on the bravado," I said, pushing to my feet and striding to the door to look down at Jordan. "Are you okay?"

The wound was in his shoulder. I walked around the car door and knelt to look. "It went through. That's going to hurt and you'll need a sling, but you'll be fine."

Listening to the words coming out of my mouth, I shook my head. When did gunshot wounds become a minor first aid situation for me?

Jordan grabbed my fingers. "Was that guy really the Godfather?"

I patted his knuckles with my free hand. "Something like that."

I let him go and went back to Brooks. "We have to get them into one of these cars and get the hell out of here," I said, shivering.

Brooks pulled his head from under the hood of his squad car.

"They shot the radiator and the battery," he said. "This one's not going anywhere."

Dammit.

I whirled, my eyes counting five bullet holes in the front of the Ford. "I'm sure they hit some vital organ in that one too."

Oh.

"Penny!" I yelped.

"What?" Brooks slammed the hood of the squad car.

"The ranger who brought me back here," I said. "Her truck is just back there, and it runs fine. She had tranquilizer darts for the bears, too."

And I didn't feel even a little bad for knocking her out now, what with the hail of bullets and all.

I glanced at Joey and then at Jordan. "You stay here with them, you have the gun," I said. "I'll go bring the truck back."

Brooks nodded. "I'd bet on you against a bear, if it came down to it."

"Let's not find out," I said.

My heels sank into the tire-softened muck covering the ground as I hustled back through darkness that wasn't fazed by the wimpy flashlight on my phone. Damn, I thought she'd been closer to the hut. I stopped after ten minutes and turned a circle, shining the light. I was lost. Son of a bitch.

Retracing my steps through the mud, I let my brain wind through the events of the day.

Kyle's boss was the actual Don of the Caccione crime family. And now he was dead. I hadn't gotten a look at the other guy's face. But how the hell had Brooks and Jordan found us, in this specific spot, off the marked trails? And why would Jordan have come with a police officer going to a crime scene, when clearly he hadn't enjoyed his excursion with me the night before?

I'd gone into the newsroom at full speed that morning and almost mowed right over Jordan.

I'd finished talking to Larry and there was a box on my desk. A paper box, with super smelly contents nobody had complained about before I arrived. And no address label. And I'd been so focused on what it meant that I hadn't stopped to wonder how in the blue hell it got there.

Last night, Jordan had begged and pleaded and claimed frostbite and pulled my glove right off trying to keep me away from that pit. He'd kept his face hidden from Kyle between his collar and hat.

All week, he'd been making advances, trying to get me to tell him where my boyfriend was, and insisting that I drop the Hideaway Motel story.

And I didn't connect the dots until I'd left him alone in the dark with several firearms, the man I loved, and a cop I was growing more fond of by the day.

Son of a bitch.

I took off. Well. I tried to, but the heels and the frozen, marshy terrain were not a good mix. I stumbled and hit my knees and struggled back to my feet, shining the light on my favorite shoes. My red Manolo slingbacks. I had repaired the heel on the right one twice. I'd worn these shoes into dangerous situations and not died.

I whipped the right one off and planted my foot on the cold, wet ground.

Ew. It was like walking on jello. Mostly frozen jello. But I could run on jello in bare feet. I raised the light and peered into the darkness, catching the red of one taillight on Penny's truck about sixty yards to my right.

It took about thirty seconds and two frozen feet, but I got there. I pulled the door open. She was still out. I patted her face and shouted. No dice.

Sticking my hand into my pocket for the keys, I figured I'd shove her over and drive the truck to the hut myself.

Except her keys weren't there.

Deep breath. Joey and Brooks might not have time for me to hunt for them, depending on what Jordan's end game here was.

The flashlight bounced off the case for the tranquilizer gun, and I flipped the lid and grabbed the other two darts. I wanted to click the headlights on, but I was afraid that might attract a bear, and Penny wasn't in a position to defend herself, plus, I had her weapon. My feet had gone numb somewhere between trying to wake Penny and finding the darts, and I had trouble hurrying back to the hut, but I found the tire tracks from the squad car and followed them well enough. When I got close enough to hear Joey, I clicked the light off.

He was awake.

And he sounded pissed.

"I half-raised you." His voice carried, a little weary but not weak, through the still air. "I brought you on and saw you were well taken care of, and this is the thing you do? Put a knife in my back the second you see an opening? So help me God, if anything happens to Nichelle..."

Jordan laughed. "She's a peach, that one, big brother. Loyal as her yippy little dog, too. There aren't many women who can resist my charms. She must be something else in the sack—I can't believe they offered you a boss position when Mario died and you were stupid enough to pass it up. I, on the other hand, am not stupid."

I didn't know a person's blood could actually boil with rage until the feeling started to return to my feet.

He was Joey's brother?

A brother I had never heard so much as a peep about?

A brother who was helping hold him hostage and torture him? So much for family, no matter what sense of the word you were using.

My legs moved without me really telling them to, circling the site until I was close enough to smell the gasoline dripping from a bullet hole in the tank of the police cruiser.

"She's not as fast as she is pretty, though, is she?" Jordan's words were loud. Close.

I stopped short. He was right in front of me. Closing my eyes, I counted to ten. When I opened them, I could just make out his head and shoulders. Close enough to touch. "Maybe we should just dispense with you and I'll go find her myself."

I raised the fist with the darts and sank them both into his neck, pressing hard so the delivery mechanism would engage.

He folded like an origami box top, landing on my frozen left foot.

Wriggling it out from under him, I clicked the light back on.

Brooks's gun was on the ground next to Jordan's hand. Brooks was lying behind Joey, a wound in his side, his eyes open and his breaths even.

Joey was sitting up, shivering and still bloody, but awake and talking.

"My stubborn princess," he said.

"God, I missed you." I ran the last few steps and he grunted when I fell on him, but his arms went around me and tightened like he might never let go.

I was okay with that.

36

Kyle and his team served a hundred and thirty-seven warrants for everything from RICO violations to murder on Monday morning.

It was the biggest takedown of a single organized crime family in American history. And I got to write about the whole thing because at least for now, everyone my story would piss off was going to jail.

I brandished Tuesday's paper, my exclusive interview with Kyle and first-person account of how the week's events played out keeping our racks empty all over town. Larry had great art of the oil wells in the swamp being capped for the cover, and action shots of Kyle and five other agents marching into Coastal Oil headquarters with warrants on the inside.

"Connolly said our ads are up enough that next week we're back to sixty-four pages," I crowed, tossing the paper on the coffee table and snuggling my head into the soft spot between Joey's collarbone and his heart that seemed tailor-made for it.

"What are you going to write about now?" He planted a soft kiss on the top of my head with still-bruised lips.

"Parker's up with the baseball preview for the cover, so I'm probably doing a follow on this. I think people will talk about this story for more than a week, even in the age of cable news and tweet cycles. Charlie was pretty pissed that Kyle wouldn't talk to her until tonight, but a deal is a deal."

Charlie had chased the Caccione story into trouble all right, but not the kidnapped-reporter sort. Trying to go into the swamp under the guise of a work permit for the fire, she got her car stuck in the melting-snow mud off road, and then the tires froze in the ground when the polar vortex dipped into town. She didn't starve or venture out into bear country because she kept water and protein bars in the car—some days long jury deliberations mean that's all we get to eat—but she was damned glad to be home and pretty pissed that the biggest part of her story wouldn't air until after I got it in the racks when I didn't even work at the *Telegraph* anymore.

Shelby was glad Charlie was okay, and considering a move back to the copy desk, according to Mel. She hadn't asked for the transfer yet, but since she'd broken up with Rick Andrews when she caught him with another woman on their Christmas ski trip, she was weighing leaving the *Telegraph* altogether.

I would believe that when I saw it for myself.

Amy, Tuck's neighbor from the Hideaway, was in a managed care facility with state insurance under the Medicaid expansion law thanks to a couple of phone calls from Senator Rowley. I'd taken her a paper and some flowers the day before. We chatted for an hour and she didn't cough once.

I well and truly had my mojo back. Brooks was a good man, and I could trust my instincts again. It turned out he was working with the FBI, not the mafia—they needed someone inside the Hideaway because they, too, were hunting the big Caccione boss. And MacAulay knew it, of course. Given all the media—and subsequent political—attention to the opioid crisis in the past eighteen months, the drug dealing business had gotten too hot for MacAulay after Mario died, so he'd sold the properties and was moving to divest Decmar and erase the Caccione ties to opioid distribution. The COC executives who'd gone to the Caccione underbosses looking for someone who wouldn't balk at plowing up graves had great timing, because MacAulay saw a much more profitable—and less legally visible—line of operations working with the oil company. The COC leadership team hadn't known about the unmarked cemeteries when they planned the pipeline's route, but they didn't want to pay to have them moved once the original contractor discovered the first one.

Landers was kind of right: the first two shooting victims were dealers killed by a non-mafia distribution ring looking to expand into Caccione territory—an amateurish attempt to start a drug war they would've lost if MacAulay had cared.

The OD victims owed their dealers money and were a convenient mask for Tucker and Katie to overdose, too, when they started telling people what they knew about the pipeline—a good plan, except Tuck and Katie got clean thanks to Brooks and forced MacAulay to a backup scenario that had just enough cracks for people to start chipping away at the story.

Since my article ran, four different foundations had stepped in to assure that the grave sites were being carefully excavated, the remains relocated to tombs with proper markers. The pipeline was tied up in so many layers of litigation it would be years before COC moved another speck of dust at any site.

And none of it would've happened without Tucker and Katie. Once he'd recovered the documents MacAulay had stolen from Tucker's motel room, Kyle and his team had figured out that Nate DeLuca's widow and her old teacher had spent months piecing together spotty old records and pinpointing locations for both unmarked slave cemeteries and battlefields where soldiers from both sides of the Mason-Dixon had been hastily buried before their regiments moved on. Tuck knew about the oil under the swamp because he'd offered an expert opinion when Congress debated extracting it years ago. They'd solved the whole thing, but by the time Katie went to the LaGrace property to see for herself, COC knew what was there and the Cacciones were already involved.

As Jordan told it once he came to, Katie had recognized the name on one of the Delco trucks at the construction site from stories Tucker had told her about the Caccione family and their various businesses. Tuck told her it was too dangerous to go poking around the swamp, but after their fight she went anyway, convinced the Cacciones wanted the oil under that land, which was worth millions more than the construction kickbacks from COC —and she found the wells. But a bear found her before she could tell anyone. Bad luck really did seem to follow her. MacAulay's lackeys had walked up on the attack on their way to check their wells, but not in time to save Katie, even if they'd wanted to. They saw her death as a windfall: they'd swiped the gun in her coat pocket (she wasn't naive enough to go hunting the mob unarmed, it seemed) before they took her to the pit where I found her. They figured she'd decompose and blend in with the rest of the old bones there, and the gun was a tidy little last piece to make Tucker's murder look like a simple lovers' spat.

Jordan found the bird when he went to try to beat information out of Joey at the shack, and put it on my desk to try to scare me away. Kyle said he'd laughed right in his face at that—Jordan didn't understand how much I loved his brother, it seemed. Joey still didn't say much about their relationship. All I got was that Jordan had always been jealous of his big brother, no matter how hard Joey tried to take care of him. Joey was the one who had encouraged Jordan to study how the news media worked and might be beneficial to Caccione operations, so Jordan really was the best consultant money could buy—Connally just didn't know he was buying an expert with mafia ties who had been sent to kill his chief investigative reporter. Jordan would have plenty of time to think about regrets, sitting in a cell at Cold Springs for the next twenty to forty, since he'd killed Tucker Armstrong on MacAulay's orders a few hours after he'd arrived in Richmond.

Joey, on the other hand, was back where he belonged. I'd spent the parts of the last several days when I wasn't at my computer either on the couch or in the bed with him, still touching his face every few seconds to remind myself he was really there.

After the president's disastrous visit to Richmond, when someone in the ATF who wasn't Kyle had leaked sensitive information about her location to the folks who wanted her dead, Kyle and Joey had decided to wage all-out war on the Cacciones. For Joey, it was a burn-it-all-down shortcut to the life he'd decided he wanted.

For Kyle, it was the finish line on nearly five years of all-consuming work.

He was the new Special Agent in Charge, the youngest in the history of the ATF, and Joey was taking some time off from the trucking company that had lost half of its executives and accounts to Kyle's warrants, but he was intent on rebuilding it. He and Kyle both said someone would step up and try to reboot the Caccione operations—there was too much money at stake for that dog to lie sleeping forever. But anyone who had ties to Joey was either dead or in prison.

As far as any of us could tell, he was free.

I was just about as happy as I could ever recall being. My topsy-turvy world was right again—I'd even torn myself away for a belated girls' night Saturday, though Jenna was sweet enough to start yawning and beg off at 9:30.

"You don't want to live on the river, do you?" Joey murmured, moving his lips close to my ear and clicking the Netflix button on the TV remote.

"I like it here." I tipped my head back. "Do you?"

"Is that an invitation?"

I nodded. Knowing what it was like to live without him made me not ever want to do it again.

"I'm glad, because I put the condo on the market this morning." He still couldn't smile too wide without his lip bleeding, but he winked. "Home is where you are. This is the only view I care about." He brushed my hair off my cheek with two fingers.

I stretched up to brush my lips against his.

"Same here."

And now that we had this new path stretching in front of us, it seemed like the possibilities were truly limitless.

DANGEROUS INTENT: Nichelle Clarke #9

Missing teenagers and execution-style murders vie for crime reporter Nichelle Clarke's attention as she chases the stories into a web of intrigue and danger, determined to discover the truth at any cost.

Nichelle Clarke owes her boss a big headline. She gets her lucky break when a member of a notorious hate group is found with a bullet in his head, his body dumped in the woods. But then a boy from a local LGBTQ support group goes missing, and Nichelle can't turn away from an old friend's plea for help finding him.

Police across the state are reluctant to expend dwindling resources on runaways and murdered bigots, leaving Nichelle to take the investigations into her own hands. The number of missing teenagers climbs. Meanwhile, more dead bodies point to a ruthless serial killer with prejudice in his sights. As clues and dead ends pile up in nearly equal numbers and other reporters pick up the trail, the situation quickly spirals out of Nichelle's control.

The killer is a master at covering their tracks, and they won't stop until they've passed deadly judgment on every last bigot in the state.

Nichelle will fight her way through communities swallowed by fear to save lives...unless she loses her own in the process.

Get your copy today at
severnriverbooks.com/series/nichelle-clarke-crime-thriller

ACKNOWLEDGMENTS

This book marks a milestone for me: my tenth published novel. I am incredibly thankful to the fabulous readers who have given me a wonderful career doing something I never dreamed possible just ten years ago, and I hope this is your favorite Nichelle story yet. Also grateful as always to my fantastic agent, John Talbot, and to Andrew Watts, Jason Kasper, Amber Hudock, and the rest of the amazing team at Severn River Publishing for helping my books reach readers and being such fun to work with. Special thanks to Penny Lazauskas for helping me get the details of the Great Dismal Swamp right, and to Theresa Earles and the Suffolk Tourism team for inspiring a love of your community in everyone who visits. My thanks also to the book advocates and bloggers who help readers find my stories, and to all of you who read them so faithfully—I appreciate every note and message y'all send more than I can say. My amazing husband, Justin and my littles, who roll with the takeout dinners and wrinkled laundry when mom has a deadline or a pressing idea—I love you right up to the moon, and back.

As always, any mistakes are mine alone.

ABOUT THE AUTHOR

LynDee Walker is the national bestselling author of two crime fiction series featuring strong heroines and "twisty, absorbing" mysteries. Her first Nichelle Clarke crime thriller, FRONT PAGE FATALITY, was nominated for the Agatha Award for best first novel and is an Amazon Charts Bestseller. In 2018, she introduced readers to Texas Ranger Faith McClellan in FEAR NO TRUTH. Reviews have praised her work as "well-crafted, compelling, and fast-paced," and "an edge-of-your-seat ride" with "a spider web of twists and turns that will keep you reading until the end."

Before she started writing fiction, LynDee was an award-winning journalist who covered everything from ribbon cuttings to high level police corruption, and worked closely with the various law enforcement agencies that she reported on. Her work has appeared in newspapers and magazines across the U.S.

Aside from books, LynDee loves her family, her readers, travel, and coffee. She lives in Richmond, Virginia, where she is working on her next novel when she's not juggling laundry and children's sports schedules.

Sign up for LynDee Walker's reader list at
severnriverbooks.com/authors/lyndee-walker
lyndee@severnriverbooks.com